Dead of Night

Other Books by Brandilyn Collins

HIDDEN FACES SERIES

BOOK THREE

Dead of Night

BRANDILYN COLLINS

GRAND RAPIDS, MICHIGAN 49530 USA

ZONDERVAN™

Dead of Night
Copyright © 2005 by Brandilyn Collins

Requests for information should be addressed to:
Zondervan, *Grand Rapids, Michigan 49530*

Library of Congress Cataloging-in-Publication Data

Collins, Brandilyn.
    Dead of night / Brandilyn Collins.
        p. cm. — (The hidden faces series ; bk. 3)
    ISBN-10: 0-310-25105-2 (softcover)
    ISBN-13: 978-0-310-2510-7
    1. Police artists—Fiction. 2. Women artists—Fiction. I. Title.
PS3553.O4747815D43   2004
813'.6—dc22
                                                    2005002767

Published in association with Browne & Miller Literary Associates LLC, 410 South Michigan Ave., Suite 460, Chicago, IL 60605.

Interior design by Beth Shagene

Printed in the United States of America

---

05 06 07 08 09 10 11 12 /❖ DCI/ 10 9 8 7 6 5 4 3 2 1

*For my dear friend
and marketing assistant,
Gayle DeSalles.
Proverbs 31:26*

A Note to My Readers

I did not set out to write this book. I'm not that courageous. But God seemed to have His own plans.

Dead of Night presents evil for what it is—wretched, disturbing, and founded on Satan's lies. Today we live in a very evil world. *But,* thanks be to God, the truth doesn't stop there. The truth ends—and begins—with God's ultimate grace and power. Those of us living in this world have a choice. We can accept God's power to help us live, or we can reject it and go out on our own—soldiers in battle without weaponry.

In writing this story, I was greatly helped by a few key people. I'd like to tell you who they are.

My hearty appreciation to the "usual suspects"—my terrific Zondervan crew, including editor Karen Ball, and marketing guru supreme Sue Brower. Also freelance editor Dave Lambert. And I can't forget Niwana Briggs, my forever eagle-eye first reader. And Sally Ball, for all her help in describing the town and surrounding areas of Redding.

Thanks also to Paul E. Sheppard, pastor of Abundant Life Christian Fellowship in Mountain View, California, for allowing me to quote one of his sermons. For more information on Pastor Paul, his life-changing sermons, and his radio ministry, Enduring Truth, please visit *www.pastorpaul.net*.

Finally, thanks to the folks living in and around Redding, California, where this series is set. Redding denizens will recognize major geographic landmarks and streets, but will also see that I've created certain places, including Tully Road and Annie's sky park neighborhood of Grove Landing. For this entire series, I've also taken the audacious liberty of giving the Shasta County Sheriff's Department its own, fictionalized building in Redding. *The Record Searchlight*, Redding's local newspaper, does exist, but the reporters in my book do not.

It's always a trick—figuring out when to leave reality and jump into the chasm of fiction. But you *did* come for a story. I hope I've adequately prepared you for this one. So now if you dare—climb in, strap on your seatbelt, and don't forget to *b r e a t h e . . .*

Brandilyn Collins

*For our struggle is not against flesh and blood,
but against the rulers, against the authorities,
against the powers of this dark world
and against the spiritual forces of evil
in the heavenly realms.*

—Ephesians 6:12

Prologue

Not so pretty in death, are you.

Head twisted, back arched. Contorted mouth, eyes wide in shock, limbs all locked tight.

Now your outside looks like your inside—a black soul, an immoral soul, a horrified and horrifying soul, bound for the black pits, the depths of darkness, for eternity, ever and ever on.

Skin still warm, clothes all askew, bleached blonde hair tangled around your devious head, fragile wisps caught on your evil tongue. Dead, dead, dead and gone, and who will miss you now?

Sit back and look at you, deserving the work of my hands. Look you up and down, your shoes kicked off in the convulsions, wrists bent, fingers curled like the limbs of an arthritic tree, one knee drawn up toward your chest.

How hard they fall, the proud and vain and shallow.

But . . .

Sweep aside the coarse, white-yellow hair. There it is. Pretty earring. Pretty, pretty bauble, so shiny, with a big blue stone and little white stones around it, playing with the spectrum like shimmery fairies. Put my finger behind your earlobe, move it this way and that, watch the dancing colors catch the light. My earring now, only mine, to keep and smile at and watch it shine.

How to take it? It is connected to your ear, right through it. Silly, arrogant woman, piercing holes in your body in the name of beauty. Like *her*. She was self-absorbed and flirtatious, making eyes at the men, swaying hips and pouting lips, and meanwhile the child saw and was unseen, and no one else knew, and no one else cared, and who would tend the child?

Pull. Tug. Rip at the earring, and still it will not come. It latches to your ear like a leech. You defy me, even in death, you shout to me in your silence that you will not be dejeweled, not be robbed of the sparkly outward display of your wretched and gaudy heart.

Hurry away, my footsteps scuffing the kitchen floor to grab what I need. I grip the handle, one finger testing the blade. I will take the prize from you, and your yawning mouth will scream in silence, but no one else knows, and no one else cares, and who will tend to you?

There.

The earring is mine.

Hold it close to my eyes. Feel the hardness of the stone with my finger, tip it, turn it, watch the light play, the fading light of the setting sun. Darkness creeps toward the earth like it has crept over you, and to the ground you will go, ashes to ashes and dust to dust, to be remembered no more, to wither and rot.

In the dead of night you will be taken. As the dead of night, so shall you ever be.

Tuesday, June 21

Chapter 1

The moment before it began, I stood in my bedroom, folding clothes.

In the last year I've developed a kind of sixth sense—a lingering smudge from my brushes with death. A sense that jerks my head up and sets my eyes roving, my ears attentive to the slightest sound. Nerves tingle at the back of my neck, then pinprickle down my arms and spine. The sensations surge through my body almost before I consciously register what caused them. Sometimes they are right; sometimes they are overreactions to mere surprise.

Experience has taught me to err on the side of caution. And with five local murders in as many months, I was already on edge.

Something . . . something downstairs . . .

My arms stopped to hover over my bed, a half-folded shirt dangling from both hands.

"Hey!"

The male voice echoed up from our great room one floor below—a voice I didn't recognize. It mixed surliness with a throaty growl, like stirred gravel.

I didn't hear the doorbell.

"Hey!" The voice again, impatient.

My thoughts flashed to Kelly, my fourteen-year-old. She'd fallen asleep down there, on one of the oversize couches near the fireplace. My daughter in a vulnerable position . . . some man I didn't know standing over her?

Kelly gasped—loudly enough for me to hear. With the expansive wooden floor and the wood wainscoting of our great room, sounds echo. The fear in that gasp jolted me into action. Almost before I knew what I was doing, I'd run for my purse on the nightstand. My fingers fumbled, looking, searching. Within seconds I felt the smooth, frightening comfort of my gun.

I yanked it out.

No time to think. Pure instinct took over. Hadn't Chetterling told me it would? I wrapped my hands around the gun, trigger finger ready, and sneak-sprinted down the hall. Below me, the great room jerked into view through banister railings. I skidded to a halt at the landing and nearly dropped the gun. My terrified eyes fixed on an unknown man in profile to me, hulking over Kelly. He was in his early twenties. Big—maybe six two?—with vein-laden, bulging biceps. The wide nose and lips of an African American, but with dusty-colored skin. Light brown hair in thick dreadlocks. Kelly had raised up on one elbow, mouth open, her expression a freeze-frame of shock.

My legs assumed the stance Chetterling had taught me. Feet apart and planted firmly. My arms stretched before me over the banister, gun pointed at the man's head.

"Stop!"

He jerked toward me, eyes widening. Both arms raised shoulder height, large fingers spread. "Hello. Wait one minute. I was just looking for Stephen."

His cultured tone so surprised me that I almost lowered the gun. From the looks of him, I'd expected more of an urban hip-hop. *Annie, keep it together; he's right near Kelly!* I stared at him, breath shuddering. How could this be happening? I'd drawn a *gun* on someone. Someone who stood *right next* to my daughter. "Back away from her."

He retreated one step.

What if this was the man who'd killed those five women? "More."

"Would you mind putting the gun away?" He shuffled back two more steps, but he couldn't go far. Another three feet and he'd hit the armchair facing the fireplace. To his left sat a big glass-topped coffee table, to his right the sofa where Kelly lay.

Any second he could lunge for her, pull her in front of him as a shield. What would I do? *Chetterling, we never practiced anything like this!*

"Look." Sulkiness and an arrogant irritation now coated his voice. "I was just going to ask her about Stephen; you don't have to threaten my life."

My insides shook, but my hands did not waver. When I spoke, my voice carried the cynical disgust of a policeman on patrol. "I don't recall anyone letting you in the house."

"The door was unlocked."

Unlocked. Still, that was hardly an invitation. My jaw clenched. "You in the habit of just walking into people's homes?"

He shrugged.

Anger tromped up my spine. How *dare* he act so nonchalant? "Well, let me tell you something—you picked the *wrong* house to walk in to."

"So I noticed." A smirk etched his lips. "Is Stephen here?"

Kelly still had not moved. He could be upon her in a heartbeat.

God, help me! How do I get her to safety?

"Kelly." I kept my eyes on the man. "Get up *now*. Run into my office and lock the door."

My daughter blinked, as if trying to rouse herself from a bad dream. Then she scrambled to her feet. I watched my target, the two-inch barrel Chief Special aimed at his head. A double action revolver, the gun didn't need to be cocked to fire. My finger remained poised to pull the trigger if he gave me reason.

In my peripheral, I saw Kelly back away from the man, then turn and run toward the office. She disappeared beneath the landing where I stood, her bare feet slapping against the hardwood floor. My office door banged shut. The lock clicked.

Relief flooded my chest. At least my daughter was safe. I knew she would call 911. With experiences like we've had, you don't fool around.

"All right." I forced strength into my words. "Now. Who are you?"

He flicked an impatient look at the ceiling. "Are you going to put that gun down or not?"

"I asked you a question."

Cold eyes glared at me. "Blake."

Who knew if he was telling the truth? "Blake who?"

"Smith, all right? S-m-i-t-h."

Yeah, sure. His cockiness rattled me. This was not a man who'd bow an inch for authority. I could feel sweat beading on my forehead. My only hope was that he couldn't see it. "What do you want with my son?"

His arms lowered until both hands were in front of his chest, fingers still spread. "I simply need to talk to him."

"About what?"

"Business."

Business? "Really. And what kind of business would that be?"

He stuck his tongue under his top teeth, then pulled it away with a sucking sound. "You're his mother, correct? The famous forensic artist."

The way he said those words. His insolence might as well have been a backhanded slap. If we were close enough, I'd bet anything he would jump at me, swipe the gun from my hands. My palms grew clammy. I tightened my grip on the weapon.

Blake eyed me with belligerence, then slowly lowered his left hand. He pointed his right index finger at me. "You will give Stephen a message for me."

Anger ballooned my lungs, pinned them against my chest. Now he was telling *me* what do? When he'd walked into *my* home? Stood over my sleeping, innocent daughter? My fingers began to tremble. "Get out of my house!"

"All right, all right, I'm going."

He turned his back on me, as if I posed not the slightest threat, and ambled around the far side of the coffee table like some languid lion aroused from sleep. I almost expected him to yawn. Then he took his time moving around the couch. Only then did he face me once more.

"You tell your son that Blake is looking for him, you hear? He'll know why. And you tell him this." His eyes narrowed, sharpening blades that would cut steel. "He *won't* be able to hide from me."

With a sneer, he turned and stalked away, the satiated predator from a death-spared deer.

I did not move, gun still pointed. He strode onto the porch and slammed the door.

My legs wobbled as I made my way down our wide curving staircase of polished wood. *Dear God, what now?* All the terrible murders around Redding, now this. Vaguely, I heard a car door slam outside, the squeal of tires. Fear for Stephen gripped me. What had he done this time? My seventeen-year-old son had been nothing but trouble for a couple years, this last twelve months in particular. A year ago he'd faced his first court appearance for drug possession, receiving six months' probation—which he hadn't obeyed. After that came rounds of weekend work detail, then time in juvenile hall. Lately I'd begun to suspect he was selling drugs. Where else had he gotten the new clothes, the constant stream of new CDs? His "a-friend-gave-it-to-me" explanations had long since worn thin.

I hit the bottom of the steps and ran across the long great room. Gun still in hand, I locked and bolted the front door, then peeked through our tall windows to check outside. No sign of Blake. No unknown car. For a moment I leaned against the glass, forehead on my arm, and tried to steady my breathing.

Only then did a thought cross my mind, irreverent in its timing. My sister would be so proud of me. Gun-toting Jenna's insistence that I learn to shoot had finally paid off.

Far behind me, the lock on my office door clicked.

"Mom?" Kelly's voice pinched with fear.

I veered from the window. "Yes, honey, it's okay. He's gone." The forced lightness in my tone sank like lead.

Kelly sidled from around the hall corner, hiccuping a sob. She ran toward me, hands outstretched, not even noticing that I still held a loaded gun. What to do with it? I barely had time to lay it on the windowsill before she flew against my chest and burst into tears. "Oh, Kelly, I'm so sorry." Wrapping my arms around her, I rocked her as if she were a little girl. "It's okay, now, everything's all right. He didn't really want to hurt you. He was just trying to wake you up to ask about Stephen."

Her body shook. "At first I thought . . ."

Of course she had. "I know, I know." Even though the murders had occurred on the other side of Redding, anyone in Kelly's position would have feared the same thing. All denials had ceased after the third body was found in March. A serial killer roamed the area. A killer with remarkable cunning and a chilling manner of murdering his victims.

"But who is he?" Kelly's voice hitched. "I've never seen him before, and I know a lot of Stephen's friends."

I closed my eyes. If only I could close my mind to the questions. Kelly had just finished her freshman year of high school, and Stephen, his junior year. For the first time since we'd moved to Grove Landing, they attended the same school, which had afforded Kelly an all-too-vivid knowledge of the kids Stephen hung out with. But even the worst of them couldn't measure down to this Blake Smith.

If that was his real name.

"He looked older than a high schooler to me." I rubbed Kelly's back. "That's probably why you haven't seen him."

But why was Stephen hanging around with someone like that? Someone so threatening? Only one answer came to mind: drugs.

A shiver rolled across my shoulders.

"Kelly." I kept my tone as gentle as possible. "You didn't lock the door when you came in from Erin's. I know it's hard to remember in the summer, when you two are running back and forth so much, but you really *do* need to."

"I know. I'm sorry. Believe me, I won't forget again."

I patted her back.

She pulled away to look at me, her eyes red. "I called 911. You'd better call them back—I hung up when I saw the guy drive away."

"Yeah, okay." I loosened a strand of brown hair from her cheek, struck for the millionth time by her beauty. When had my daughter grown as tall as I was? "You sure were brave, Kelly. That must have been really scary."

She blew out air and stepped away, summoning the fortitude of her fourteen years. "Yeah, scary all right. I've never seen you pull a gun on somebody."

"I meant the *man*, Kelly."

"Oh."

We managed to smile at each other.

Speaking of the gun, I needed to put it away. But first I had to call the Shasta County Sheriff's Department. If Detective Ralph Chetterling had heard that 911 call, he'd no doubt be speeding here like a freight train. So would anyone else from the department, for that matter. With a massive hunt for a predatory killer under way, every member of local law enforcement had the jitters.

"Kelly, I need to make that call." I turned to pick up my weapon, and she flinched from it. Kelly felt the same way I did about guns—she was scared to death of them.

I headed into the kitchen for the phone, my artist's mind conjuring Blake Smith's features. The wide nose, the deep-set eyes. Thick, almost straight eyebrows. As soon as I got the chance, I would draw that face from memory. Give it to Chetterling, have him show it around the department. Maybe some deputy would know this guy. Although I wasn't sure which would be worse—if a member of law enforcement did know Blake . . . or didn't.

What had Stephen done?

I laid the gun down on the kitchen counter and picked up the phone to dial 911, my mother's heart quailing. If only I could stop the wreckage of my son's life. My call was answered on the first ring. "Hi, it's Annie Kingston."

"Annie! Are you all right, what's going on? We've got a car on the way."

"Thanks. The immediate danger is over. No need for any deputies to hurry now, but I'd still like someone to come so I can make a report." I explained what had happened and described Blake. "The deputy coming here should keep an eye out for this guy. Unfortunately I didn't see what kind of car he was driving."

"Okay, we've got it. The unit will be there in about five minutes. Stay safe, Annie."

Yeah. Stay safe.

Back upstairs, as I placed my gun into my purse, a dark precognition swooped over me. I had driven Blake Smith out of my house, but not out of our lives. Stephen was in real trouble this time.

Not with law enforcement, but with the criminals themselves.

Chapter 2

An hour after the deputy left, Chetterling called. "Annie, I heard you had some trouble out at your house. Just checking up on you." As if the man didn't have anything better to do. He was lead detective on the serial killer case.

"Ralph, thanks. We're okay. Calmed down now. It was scary to see this huge, belligerent guy in my house, standing over Kelly. But after it was over I realized he'd never intended to hurt us. He *did* want to make the point that he's looking for Stephen. That's what scares me now. I don't know what my son's gotten himself into this time. The guy said his name's Blake Smith. Ever heard of him?"

"Blake Smith." Chetterling paused. "No, don't think so."

"Neither had your deputy. Anyway, I've made a sketch of him and want to show it to you. But I know you're awful busy with—"

"Annie, I'm never too busy when you need something. You should know that by now."

"I do." I floundered for my next words. Sometimes I couldn't figure how to read this man. A year ago he'd even sent me roses—but of course, that was just because of the case we'd worked on.

I heard muffled sound as Chetterling covered his phone mouthpiece and told someone to give him a minute. "Sorry about that," he said to me. "Look, anything I can do to help with this, you just tell me. You may be right that this guy wasn't out to harm you this time. But if Stephen's continuing with this drug business, he may have gotten mixed up with some mighty unsavory characters. You never know what they'll do."

"Yeah, I hear you." *Oh, God, please protect us. Particularly Stephen.*

"Where is your son right now? With you?"

"He's at his new job at the video store. I called to make sure he's okay. But it wasn't the time to ask any questions, especially with his manager around, who doesn't like personal phone calls. I did tell Stephen to come straight home after work because I have something important to tell him. Maybe his curiosity will make him listen."

"Okay, good." More muffled noise. Chetterling sighed. "I've got a meeting to get to, and they're buggin' me. You want to fax me your sketch? I'll look at it as soon as I can."

"Okay, Ralph, I will. Thank you again for calling. So much."

I hung up the phone and faxed my drawing to Chetterling's attention. Then headed to the TV room to check on Kelly. She was watching some cable reality show, boredom flattening her expression. Erin and her dad were out somewhere. Nothing looks more morose than a teenager sans best friend.

"Kelly, I need to do that weeding in the backyard. Come help me, would you?"

She made a face. "It's so hot out there."

"Not as hot as in the middle of the day. Besides, it's right near the trees, in the shade."

"Oh, Mom, do I *have* to?"

Truth was, I didn't want to leave her alone in the house. "Yes."

Kelly grumbled but did as she was told.

Five minutes later we were hunkered down at the corner of our large backyard, forest stretching before us. Our house sits at the end of Barrister Court, the woods wrapping behind all the homes on our street and around our property right up to the cul de sac. The air hung with the earthy scents of dirt, leaves, and bark. I pulled some weeds, sending up a little cloud of pollen, and sneezed.

"Bless you." Kelly waved a hand in front of her face.

"Thanks."

Within minutes I was sweating. I told myself that was a good thing, even as my neck itched under my T-shirt collar. Maybe I needed to work more outside every day so I could lose those ten pounds. Then my figure would be perfect. Sort of.

"You must have stayed up late at Erin's last night." I threw a handful of weeds into a plastic bag. "Not very typical to see you fall asleep in the daytime."

"Yeah. We watched movies until after three. And then for some reason we woke up early and never went back to sleep."

The energy of the young. "No wonder you were tired."

For a few minutes we worked in companionable silence.

Kelly affected a sigh. "Do you know one year ago we were in Hawaii? That was like *so* much fun."

"Yes, it was."

"I wish we could go again this year."

Me too. But with Stephen's summer job, we couldn't. If he'd proven trustworthy, maybe I'd be willing to leave him home alone. But you don't turn your back on a kid who's sunk into the mire of drugs. Kids like that steal, cheat, lie to your face with flawless manipulation. And their friends are all cut from the same cloth. One week of Stephen alone in our home, and I knew we wouldn't have a house left standing.

"I know, Kelly. I'm really sorry we can't."

It wasn't fair that Kelly had to bear the brunt of her brother's foolishness. Some of her friends from church weren't even allowed to come over anymore because of Stephen. An older brother who bounced in and out of juvenile hall did not exactly make mothers comfortable with our home environment.

We shuffled on our knees, down the lawn. I was beginning to wish I'd brought out a water bottle. But maybe we wouldn't work too much longer. I checked my watch. After six. Stephen would be home from his job soon.

Oh, joy.

I'd get to interrogate him for the millionth time. Try to decipher any hint of the truth in his answers. Would he even admit to knowing a Blake Smith?

I sat back on my haunches, wiping sweat from my forehead. We'd moved into a small patch of sun, and the heat assaulted us. Bumblebees drifted by now and then. I ignored them, but Kelly cringed whenever one ventured too close. A few minutes later, we worked in shade again, lingering vestiges of the sun glowing red against my eyelids when I blinked.

Kelly tossed her thick ponytail. "When's Aunt Jenna flying back, Mom?"

"By tomorrow evening. She needs to stay with Stephen while you and I go out to dinner with Dave and Erin."

"Oh, yeah, great. And guess what, she said maybe she could fly me and Erin down to Disneyland when she finishes."

"I know, Kelly, that would be wonderful. You'll have a good time."

"Yeah. Aunt Jenna'll probably scream louder than us on some of those rides." Kelly laughed, then scratched her cheek, leaving a streak of dirt. "Only thing is, I wish you could go."

So did I. But of course, there was Stephen. Always, always Stephen.

We reached the middle of the lawn. A small, much-needed breeze arose, its fingers tickling the sweat on my face.

And riding on the palm of that breeze was a faint smell.

"Ew, what's that?" Kelly wrinkled her nose.

The back of my neck tingled. "Probably some dead animal down in the woods."

"Oh, great."

"Well, maybe the breeze will carry it away in a minute."

It didn't.

When we moved a few feet over, the smell grew worse. Not enough to be overpowering by any means, but still sweet and cloying, like rotting vegetables.

I knew that smell.

A private projector resides in my head, stubbornly uncontrollable. To say that it makes me a visual person would be like saying water makes the ocean wet. At that moment the smell provided all the encouragement my projector needed to click on, spewing film in vivid Technicolor.

Flash, and I envisioned myself

standing in the morgue last month, my camera heavy in my hand. The fifth victim of the Poison Killer lies before me on the slab, face uncovered. I swallow hard, breathing in tiny tufts of air. The smell is powerful enough to make me shudder. I glance at Chetterling and medical examiner Harry Fleck, hoping they haven't noticed. Before this onslaught of dead bodies, I've never had to enter the morgue for my forensic art work. If Harry saw my reaction, he does not let on.

Chetterling gives me a wan smile. "It never gets any easier, Annie."

I nod, not completely sure that's a comfort . . .

Kelly covered her nose with a hand. "Mom, it's getting stronger."

For some reason I refused to listen to my sixth sense. Illogical, since it had so recently proven itself. Still, on some unconscious level, I knew I *couldn't* listen. Human nature provides a magnificent barrier to fear when you stumble too close to true evil: denial. Whatever tragic thing happened to *her* or *him* can't possibly happen to *you*, because of some differing factor. Our factor was geography. All five victims of the serial killer had been found in forested areas west of Redding, while Grove Landing lay about ten minutes' drive to the northeast of town. Those poor people over there—*they* were living in fear. But *we* were safe.

Besides, hadn't I been praying for protection for me and my family? We'd been through enough crises in the past two years; surely God would spare us now. Particularly since I'd become a Christian a year ago. I was now God's child. Evil could not, *would not*, befall me.

Right?

My heart thumped. "Let's stop here, Kelly. We can do the rest another day." I pushed to my feet, bending over to rub sensation back into my calves. Biting my cheek, I peered into the forest.

Kelly stood up—a lot more easily than I had done. The smell still tainted the air. We looked at each other.

"Why don't you stay here a minute," I told her. "I'll just go in a little ways and check that out. If some animal died in there, it's really going to reek by tomorrow. I'll have to call someone to cart the thing away."

"Yuk. Go right ahead." Kelly hitched her shoulders.

"Gee, thanks." I turned and entered the woods.

The smell led me. Whatever it was couldn't be too far away. A squirrel, I told myself. Or something bigger. Maybe even a bobcat? I'd never seen one, but . . .

I threaded my way around trees and brush, about thirty feet. Saw nothing. The breeze shifted, and the foul scent disappeared. I turned toward Kelly, still able to see her head and shoulders. "You okay back there?"

"Yeah."

I hesitated. Should I go any farther?

My neck tingled.

Suddenly, I didn't like this. Not at all.

My eyes swept the shrubbery ahead of me. Nothing. I looked to my right. Only forest. To my left.

My gaze landed on something white, sticking out from behind a manzanita bush.

I leaned forward, frowning, staring. It almost looked like . . .

The sight registered. A foot, clad in a white shoe. Electricity jolted down my limbs.

No. There had to be another explanation. This couldn't be *here*, so close to my house.

I jerked my head back toward Kelly. She stood at the border of our property, watching me.

"What is it, Mom?" Tension edged her voice.

"Don't move, okay? I just need to . . ." I moved to the left, noticing for the first time signs of earlier passage—the matted grasses, broken twigs. And I knew. My mouth turned cottony. The fickle breeze changed again as if to taunt me, accuse me for denying. It hit me full in the face with the stench.

My limbs froze.

I licked my lips. Managed to take three halting steps. My maddening, visual brain churned out pictures of colorless faces on a cold slab—Debbie Lille, victim number one; Wanda Deminger, number three . . .

He'd been here. No denying, not now. He'd dragged this one right where I now stumbled. I'd entered a crime scene, and I knew what lay at the end. Goose bumps raised on my arms, even as my mind scrambled for rational thought. *Watch, Annie, watch where you step; the detectives won't want anything disturbed.*

The manzanita lay before me, the broken trail sweeping around it. Flies buzzed. I saw the foot, and the lower part of a jean-clad leg. My breath stalled.

I cast a final, nervous glance at Kelly. Then pushed my feet forward until I stood beside the shrubbery, still within sight of my daughter. Steeling myself, I peered around the bush.

The woman lay on her back, neck twisted to one side. Her shoulders dug into the ground, chest arching. One leg drew up toward her torso. Her arms bent and her fingers hooked like frozen claws. Her face . . . Oh, dear God, her face—a mask of horror, eyes sprung wide open, her lips contorted in a nightmarish, silent scream.

My teeth clamped against instant nausea. Air groaned from my throat.

Help me, God! Oh, help us all.

I started to whirl around, then—amazingly—caught myself. *Kelly.* She'd be upset enough without me crashing toward her all wild-eyed. Heart banging against my ribs, I backed away from the bush, throat tight, back rigid, calm slapped on my face like wet plaster.

Far ahead, Kelly awaited me, shoulders hunched. My beautiful daughter. So sweet, so alive . . .

My best intentions melted. Panic swelled around me, shoved at my spine. With a small cry, I flung myself through the forest. When I reached our yard, I grabbed Kelly's arm, dragging her away, pulling her toward home, toward some semblance of safety, the walls of my denial crumbling at our thudding feet.

Chapter 3

June twenty-first—the longest day of the year. Investigators from the Shasta County Sheriff's Department would need the extra daylight.

Detective Chetterling had raced to our cul de sac in near record time, followed by Jim Cisneros in a second vehicle. Matt Stanish, the coroner's investigator, pulled up right behind. More cars, flashing lights, slamming doors, voices. The commotion pulled Grove Landing neighbors from their homes and up Barrister Court to mill in front of my house, shaken and defiled and murmuring all-too-vivid memories of Lisa Willit's murder two years before.

As I watched the scene, the old, familiar guilt settled over me. I'd come so far in ridding myself of it over the past year, and now this. I couldn't seem to get away from the glaring truth: ever since I'd moved to Grove Landing, danger and tragedy had stalked this neighborhood.

As if my guilt had conjured him, Dave Willit drove up in his Lexus with Erin. He squealed tires into their garage, then ran toward me, fear cinching his tanned face. His daughter ran behind him, white-blonde hair flipping against her back.

"Erin!" Kelly hurried down our porch steps toward her friend. Erin swerved in her direction, and they met to hug in the street.

"Annie." Dave gripped me by the shoulders. "Are you all right? What happened?"

I sought his green eyes, my own stinging with sudden tears. "I'm okay. I found a body behind my house. One of *his*." The guilt squeezed my heart. Here I stood again before Dave, flinging vile news in his path.

The next half hour blurred with activity. More officials arriving, Dave taking over the care of a distraught Kelly as I prepared to lead investigators to the body. In the midst of the chaos, Stephen finally returned home from work. He gunned his car up the street, screeched to a halt in front of Dave's house, and jumped out, panic jerking his movements. Thanks to our past experiences, he couldn't help but assume the worst.

Quickly, I took Stephen aside to tell him what happened. He listened to me, jaw flexed, eyes narrowed against the lowering sun. Despite the upsetting news, I could have sworn his first reaction was one of relief. Had I really seen that? If so, he quickly chased it away, replaced with a look of concern. All the same, his spiked blond hair and wide-legged stance, the baggy jeans, the spread of his fingers against his hips, radiated the cocky attitude I'd come to know all too well.

Stephen made a face. "Why can't that crazy guy stay on his own side of town? I'm *tired* of our house being a draw for maniacs."

His thinly veiled accusation struck home. "I didn't ask for this, you know."

"Yeah, I know. But it's another body you might have to draw, right? And now because *you* found it, you'll be all the more involved."

It.

"Stephen, there's a *person* lying back there. Where's your compassion? She can't be older than twenty-five."

His expression half softened. He glanced at the busy deputies and detectives, biting at the inside of his cheek. My indignation melted away, the familiar mother's pain rising in its place. *Oh, Stephen, if only . . .* I understood my son's ambivalence, even as I loathed its cause. Because of the choices he'd made, to him all law enforcement was the enemy. Even when we needed their protection.

"Stephen, I want you to stay in the house. Make sure the doors are locked, and turn on the alarm."

"But—"

"I know, I know, all these people are around. Do it anyway. Kelly's going to stay with Erin. She's pretty shaken up."

He sniffed and turned away. "Yeah, okay."

Before I could stop myself, I touched him on the shoulder.

"What?"

I fixed on his eyes. "Do you know a Blake Smith?"

Something flickered across his face, then was gone. Stephen drew back. "No. Why?"

"He paid us a little visit today."

A second's hesitation. "What for?"

"He said—"

"Annie!" Chetterling's call cut me short. "We're ready now."

"Okay, coming." I looked back to Stephen. "We'll have to talk about this later."

"But what did he want?"

"Not now."

"*Mom!*"

"*Later*, Stephen. Just . . . do what I tell you for once."

With that, I turned on my heel and headed for the waiting men.

Chapter 4

Eight thirty.

I stood at a distance as Chetterling, Cisneros, and Matt Stanish examined the victim. When they gave me my cue, I would join them. I dreaded the thought of looking again at that ravaged face.

With careful steps, the three men sought evidence, first on the ground—any piece of forensic material that could have been left by the murderer. Cisneros photographed the area and the victim from a distance. Slowly, they'd progressed to the woman herself.

All around them, yellow crime-scene tape fluttered. Even amid the trees at evening, the air hung hot, oppressive. In the past hour, everything about these woods had changed. No longer did they seem beautiful, beckoning. Now they reeked with decay and death.

Even if the killer was caught, how could I ever walk back here again?

No. *When* the killer was caught. I couldn't imagine this darkness hovering over us forever, like rain-blackened clouds that refused to break.

Chetterling and Cisneros stood back from the victim, pointing at various marks, taking notes and photographs. Stanish, as coroner's investigator, had the authority to touch the body. All too soon, if they could not identify the woman, I'd be visiting the morgue to take my own pictures of her face. From the photographs I would determine how she appeared in life and draw a composite to circulate in the media. Somewhere out there a mother had lost a daughter, perhaps a man had lost the one he loved. Failing to identify a murder victim only added tragedy upon tragedy.

Stanish squatted near the woman's tortured face. "I'll bet this is our man's sixth victim. Got to be another strychnine poisoning. Only this time we found her soon enough to see how violent the death is."

Despite the warm air, I hugged my arms to my chest. I knew, as did the public, that all the killer's victims had been young women and that they'd died from a lethal dose of strychnine. No visible predeath trauma could be found on them—no signs of sexual assault; no beating, stabbing; no strangulation marks.

But because of my work on the case, I knew more than the public.

While death by poison didn't fit the normal profile of a serial killer, one other feature certainly did. The killer took something from every one of his victims, something expressing femininity. A piece of hand-beaded shirt was missing from the first victim. Locks of thick blonde hair from the second. From another, a gold bracelet. The last two "trophies" were more gruesome. The fourth victim, with long red nails, had the tip of her left index finger cut off. The fifth, with painted toenails, was missing the little toe on her right foot.

I glanced at Chetterling. He looked gray. For all his experience, and for being a huge bulk of a man, he'd proved more than once how much he cared for people. And he'd done more for me than I could ever repay.

He rubbed a hand across his brow. "She can't have been dead long, Matt, not with this amount of rigidity."

Stanish turned aside to cough. "Yeah. Twenty-four hours at the most, despite the smell. The heat's accelerated that. Her muscles will start to relax soon." He took a gulping breath. "But this is what I've been telling you about a strychnine death. I'd only heard about it before, never witnessed it. Pretty rare. See this opisthotonus? The arching of the neck and back? It's caused by powerful muscle contractions. This poor woman convulsed so violently that she finally asphyxiated. And it takes awhile too. It's an excruciating way to go." He shook his head. "That death smile says it all."

Oh, no, here it came. My overactive brain threw out film, displaying gruesome imaginings of the victim's last moments. The convulsions . . . the agony of gasping for breath . . .

I squeezed my eyes shut and willed the scenes away.

"Man." Cisneros tapped his camera. "It's hard to imagine rigor mortis sets in quickly enough to freeze the body in that position."

"Yeah. But it does, pretty much immediately." Stanish pointed to the woman's drawn-up leg. "The intense contractions deplete enzymes in the muscles, so the rigid phase of rigor sets in right away."

Chetterling jotted in a notebook. "Anything missing?"

"Not that I can see yet. Unless there's something on the underside." Stanish tilted his head, peering at the woman. "Wait, though, let me just check . . ." He pulled a tangle of hair away from her face, then looked up at the two detectives, disgust etching his forehead. "Spoke too soon." He pointed toward her ear, and they leaned in to look.

Stanish lifted the woman's head to check the other ear. "Big earring."

From where I stood, I couldn't see what they did. But I could imagine.

The two detectives nodded, their expressions unchanged. Chetterling wrote in his notebook.

Stanish sat back on his haunches, while Cisneros took a picture of the exposed ear. Chetterling raised his eyebrows at Stanish, then tilted his head toward me. The coroner's investigator nodded.

"Annie." Chetterling beckoned. "You want to come on in?"

I'd just love to.

I took as deep a breath as I could stand in the foul air, then ducked under the crime-scene tape. Straightening, I approached the body.

When I'd entered the field of forensic art two years ago, I hadn't thought about having to deal with the dead. Forensic art incorporates so many facets. I started my career by drawing composites of suspects. Then, in the Bill Bland case over a year ago, I drew an updated picture of the twenty-year fugitive to help find him. This year, for the first time, the Poison Killer case forced me into the morgue. I'd drawn three of the first five victims so they could be identified. Like Chetterling said, it hadn't gotten any easier.

I came up beside Chetterling, who touched my arm briefly. The demeanor of all three men seemed to change in my presence. As if they became more solemn, more . . . aware of the devastation, as viewed through my eyes. Not that they were uncaring. But like all in their field, they'd seen so much death, so much tragedy, that they had to clamp down on their emotions out of sheer self-preservation.

My gaze lowered to the woman's face—and stilled at the sight of her right ear. The bottom portion, where an earring would attach, had been sliced away.

"Okay." My voice sounded shaky, and I hated that. I wanted to act like a professional, not a rattled female. I cleared my throat. "She's lost some of the rigidity since I found her, but not much. It's going to be easier for me if I wait until she's fully relaxed. I'll visit the morgue tomorrow to take most of the photos if you haven't identified her."

Stanish nodded. "But you wanted to see her now."

"Yes, because of her hair. By the time I made it to the morgue in the other deaths, the bodies had already been washed, and the hairstyling was long gone. I remembered this woman's hair had a lot of height on top, and I didn't want to lose that."

"All right, I'll get that for you." Cisneros shot a couple pictures. "Anything else?"

From the way the woman's head was twisted, I couldn't see her left ear. I looked to Matt Stanish. "You said she's wearing a large earring? I'll want a good picture of that. May be easier to wait until tomorrow, though, when it's removed."

Distinctive jewelry or clothing could help in identification. I'd drawn the fancy beaded blouse of the first victim, and numerous callers had recognized it.

I wanted to get out of there. The smell was enough to kink my stomach, and the sight of the victim's face too much to bear any longer. I couldn't suppress a shiver. "Okay, I'm done." I turned away from the body, but I still *felt* her. The constricted muscles, the contorted face, threatened to set the movie in my brain running again. "Ralph—" the name squeezed from my throat—"just call me in the morning if I'm not needed. Otherwise I'll come to the morgue."

"Sure. So far, nobody's been reported missing, so . . ."

"Yeah. I know." I nodded a good-bye to Cisneros, and noticed him exchanging a glance with Chetterling. Something about that look made me uneasy.

"Uh, Annie, wait," Chetterling said. "I'll walk you out."

He followed me under the yellow crime-scene tape and back to the trail. There we stopped, and I took the first good look into his eyes. I could see the fatigue. Everyone at the Sheriff's Department had already been working overtime on the Poison Killer case, and now with a new victim, Ralph and his colleagues would likely get no sleep at all for the next few days.

"You okay?" He towered over me with his six-foot-three frame.

I pressed my lips, feeling suddenly vulnerable. Despite our close friendship, I did not want to get teary in front of him. "I'm fine."

He surveyed me. "You don't look too fine."

"Thanks."

"You know what I mean."

"Ralph—" I raised my hands, palms toward him—"I just . . . it's been a long day."

"I can imagine. Two scares in one afternoon." Chetterling glanced toward his colleagues. "Look, I know it's a bad time for you, but I need to let you know a feeling I've got." He brought a hand to his jaw. "Where's Jenna, by the way?"

He was stalling, which meant it was some piece of news he was reluctant to tell me.

"In the Bay Area. She'll be back tomorrow. What is it, Ralph?"

He cleared his throat. "A couple things, unfortunately. First, you can imagine the media coverage we're going to get on this. I'll bet reporters have already come and gone—they've just got time to get this in the morning paper. But you know they'll be back. No doubt they'd have run down this trail if our men didn't stop them. And since you discovered the body . . . I know how much you hate publicity."

Yes, I did. But I was becoming more adept at handling it. How could I not, after the national attention I'd received last year?

"Okay, thanks for the warning, but I'll be fine. The second thing?"

Ralph sighed again. "It's the question I'm afraid they're going to ask. The same question I've been asking myself, Annie." He hesitated. "Looks pretty clear this is another victim of our killer. But why was this body dumped here, fifty yards behind your property? All the other victims were left in woods way on the other side of Redding."

His implication hit with the sting of BB pellets. In all the commotion, I'd had no time to consider this. "You're saying you don't think this was a coincidence?"

Ralph winced. "With your notoriety around Redding? The two times you've helped nail a killer—multiple murderers, both of them? And now you've been drawing composites of this guy's victims. So do I think *this* body, *here*, is a coincidence? Afraid not."

I closed my eyes. *God, not again. Why do I keep getting pulled into these things? I'm just a forensic artist. Why haven't You protected me this time?*

"Annie? I don't want to upset you. But you need to take extra precautions. 'Cause my guess is this madman has purposely changed his tactics. I think he's teasing us by leaving this body practically in your backyard. Jim thinks so too."

Strange, how irritation rose within me. I wasn't quite sure why. Was I upset at Chetterling for his warning—as if I didn't know to be cautious? Or at God for letting all this happen in the first place?

Maybe both.

Quickly, then, the emotion faded, replaced by plain old weariness. My shoulders slumped. I ran a hand over my face, realizing for the first time that I'd never showered after my yard work. I must look a sight. "Okay, I hear you. I'll be extra careful. Thanks for telling me."

A deputy escorted me the short distance up the trail. Then I dragged myself to my house and errant son. My thoughts pinged back and forth, back and forth . . . from Blake Smith's sneer to the horrific grimace on the latest victim's face.

God, please help me. Please help us all.

Chapter 5

Stephen, I need to ask you again if you know anybody named Blake. A big guy, with dreadlocks."

We faced off in the kitchen. I hadn't even taken the time to drink a glass of water. Too much had happened too fast, and I needed some answers.

"I *told* you I don't know who you're talking about." Stephen curled one side of his mouth. "Why do you keep bothering me with this?"

"Well, excuse me for *bothering* you. But this 'friend' of yours walked right into the house and scared us to death. I found him standing over your sister, who was sleeping on the couch. I got my gun, Stephen; I could have killed the guy."

His eyes rounded. "You pointed a *gun* at him?"

I surveyed my son. "Thought you said you didn't know him."

"I don't!"

"Then why do you care so much that I got my gun? You more worried about some stranger than your own sister?"

He blinked. "No."

"Really. Doesn't look that way to me."

"I don't care *how* it looks to you."

Anger stiffened my neck. Why on earth did I waste my time trying to get answers from this kid? He certainly wasn't about to give them. I pointed a trembling finger toward the door that led to his basement bedroom. "Go, Stephen. Just go. I don't want to talk to you right now. I don't even want to *see* you."

He threw me a look as if to say *fine with me* and stalked through the great room. The door to the basement stairs opened, then slammed.

The blaze of my wrath quickly burned itself out, leaving coals of renewed fear for my son. I put a hand over my face and stood in the middle of the kitchen, breathing, praying. Some day this all would pass.

If I lived that long.

The phone rang. I sighed, then moved to the counter to answer it. "Hello?"

"Hi, Mom, can I spend the night with Erin?"

I looked through the window and across the street to the Willits' house. "Sure, Kelly, that's fine." *Can I come too?* "Just borrow a pair of Erin's pajamas, okay? I don't want you running across the street in the dark."

Before Kelly hung up, Dave wanted to talk to me.

"Annie, do you and Stephen want to stay here? You know we've got a bedroom for each of you."

Had he read my mind? I gazed at Dave's house. The front lights were on, illuminating his porch and lawn, and some of the multicolored flowers lining his walk. "No, really, we're okay. You couldn't lure Stephen out of his own room if a bomb hit the house. And I don't want to leave him, so . . ."

"All right. Well. You know I'm here."

"Yeah. Thanks, Dave."

I clicked off the phone and carried it with me into the great room, where I sank onto a couch. A dull ache now pounded my head. Closing my eyes, I rubbed my temples. Stephen's ever-present rap music beat up from his bedroom. The massive log home Jenna and I had inherited from our father sat on a sloping lot, with two stories visible from the front, and Stephen's bedroom and a large rec area visible as a third level from the rear. A sliding glass door off the rec room led to our backyard deck. I would have to make sure Stephen kept that door locked, with the sawed-off broom handle wedged behind it.

And now, more than ever, Kelly and Erin would need to lock the front door as they went back and forth between houses. Either Dave, Jenna, or I would have to watch them cross the street. I didn't want them so much as stepping out on the porch alone right now.

The phone rang again, and I jumped, then glanced at the grandfather clock. Past nine thirty. It was probably Jenna, checking in for the night. I winced. She'd demand my head on a platter when she heard all that had happened—and I hadn't called to tell her. Jenna was seven years younger than I, but I'd swear she was the bossiest mother anyone could have.

I let the phone ring three times before answering it. "Hello."

"Hello, Sister, and what's wrong."

It was more of a statement than a question. How did Jenna *do* that—read my emotions from a single word? I pressed my knuckles against my chin, tired already at the prospect of having to relate the day's events. "Um, it's my forty-second birthday tomorrow?"

"True, but I haven't known you to mourn too much over that. You handled forty-one just fine. Want to try again?"

"Okay, Jenna. It's not been a very good day. Where would you like me to start?"

"At the beginning."

Stupid question. I took a deep breath and blew it out. "Okay. The beginning is, today some huge, creepy-looking guy with dreadlocks and biceps out to here walked into the house and stood over Kelly, who was sleeping in the great room, and about that time I heard him, and believe it or not, instinct took over after all of my trips to the shooting range with Chetterling, and I jerked out my gun and pointed it at the guy and demanded that he leave. Which he did. After threatening Stephen. Sort of."

Silence.

"And by the way, Stephen won't tell me who he is."

I could hear Jenna breathing. Could almost hear her sorting through reactions, a parent seeking logic from a nonsensical child. "Okay. Annie. I am now sitting down. Maybe you'd better start over. A little more slowly this time."

She wanted details, she got them. Everything. How condescendingly cool the guy had been, how threatening. How he'd terrified Kelly and me both. My questions. His demands. The way he'd turned his back on my pointed gun. Truth was, I felt nothing but relief in sharing the burden with my sister. I didn't know what I'd do without her. Then, after all the sordid details, I made sure to inform her how well I'd handled the gun.

"So, Jenna. You proud of me?"

"Oh . . . yeah, Annie. Real proud."

"You don't sound it."

"Well, give me a minute, okay? It's like we just stepped into some scary movie. Right now I can't help focusing on the 'creepy-looking guy with dreadlocks' part." She fell silent. "So you think Stephen's lying?"

"No question. It was all over his face."

"But if this guy and Stephen know each other, wouldn't the guy know Stephen would be at work at that time?"

A rational thought. I'd hardly had the time to ponder such questions. "Maybe he doesn't know where Stephen works. It *is* a new job."

She exhaled. "When did this happen?"

Oh, boy, here it came. "I don't know. Around four."

"*Four?* And you're just telling me *now?*"

"Jenna, you have a life too. What do you think I am, some kid who comes running to you every minute? Besides, I had things to do."

"Annie, we're each others' main support, remember? *Who* was the first person I called when I lost my job? *You.*"

"I know, but—"

"What possibly could have kept you from calling me? Four o'clock was almost six hours ago!"

I pressed my fingers against my forehead, suddenly very weary. "Not much, really. Other than I had to lead Chetterling and his men to a horribly gruesome dead body I discovered in the woods off our backyard. Latest victim of our friendly local serial killer. Who, by the way, according to Ralph's theory, purposely placed the body where *I* might find it. Some kind of new chess game he's playing. Guess I'm the chosen pawn."

That did it. My sister practically came unglued. If she could have reached through the phone, hauled me into some insurmountable castle, and pulled up the drawbridge, she'd have done it. By the time I'd told her the entire story, all of my blithe pretense lay in tatters at my feet. In fact, I was fighting tears.

"Annie, Annie, I'm so sorry. I can't *believe* all this." Jenna exhaled loudly. "This is just—Okay. I'm flying home tonight. Right now."

Jenna stayed in her Redwood Shores town house when consulting for her Bay Area clients. In her Cessna Turbo 210, she could fly to Grove Landing in under an hour.

"What about your software project?"

"It'll . . . I don't know. I'll figure it out. But I'm not leaving you in that house alone."

"I'm not alone; Stephen's here."

"Oh, *that's* a relief."

Dear Jenna. I almost managed a smile. "Okay. Thank you, Sis. I'm really glad you're coming."

"Yeah. Well, just think, I'll be there for your birthday after all."

"Mm. For the best of reasons."

Her absence wouldn't have bothered me. Jenna and I didn't tend to make a big deal of our birthdays. However, Dave and Erin had planned to take me and Kelly out to dinner. Stephen was invited too, of course, but he had to work that day until after seven. Besides, he wasn't interested. Which is why Jenna couldn't go to dinner with us. She had to stay home and "babysit" Stephen when he returned from work.

"Annie. Hey, Annie, you still there?"

I rested my head against my forearm. "Sorry, my mind was wandering."

"I was just saying I'll leave as soon as possible. Hang tight."

"Okay." I checked the clock. Nine fifty. If she left for the San Carlos airport within fifteen minutes, she could be touching down on the Grove Landing private runway before eleven thirty. Not long after that I'd hear her chutting up the extra-wide streets of our sky park. "I'll wait up for you, open the hangar door."

"Well, I should think so. It's the least you can do, considering I'm dropping everything to come back."

"You're not dropping everything and you know it. You'll bring your work with you."

She huffed. "You're an ingrate, you know that?"

"Jenna. Just get home."

The tease fell from her voice. "I'm on my way."

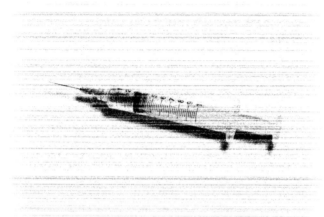

Wednesday, June 22

Chapter 6

How interesting, the way the world turns, one simple event shifting the actions of men. Surely those newspaper people thought they were done for the night. Then, oh excitement! To receive a call and rush to the woods, where deputies mill and strut and bark self-important orders as they shield what should have been shielded long ago.

I laugh at you all. What good is protection after death?

And you, my dear reporter. For all your labor and clamor to learn, you know so little. They play with you, do you know that? Keep details from you, important details. *My* details.

Do they do this to trip me up? Catch me commenting on some aspect of the killings I'm not supposed to know? Do they do it to check those sick people who would claim credit for what I have done? Do they do it just because they *can*?

Do they know how closely I watch?

You authorities, with all your swagger. You, too, know so little. Was the location of the body near a certain backyard purposeful, one of you wonders. What, would you have me act without thinking, like some mindless goat? And six victims in as many months, you say, as if that is important. Am I regulated by the clock? Am I some deranged soul who watches the moon?

I read your words, reporter, and imagine your blood pounding at the thrill of the story. I feed you fodder, and you love me for it. "Come on, telephone," you say, "ring! Call me to another site, another victim, so I can write and record and play reader emotions like a mad fiddler."

Such is your duty, I suppose.

All the world's a stage, and each one acts out his petty life. *Hers*, the most petty of all. Fate took my mother for me, slow in its judgment. If I had known her death would release my power, I'd have killed her myself, and long ago.

I read you again, newspaper article, black words on crisp white page. The depth of your inadequacy! The aroma of my coffee outdoes you, for it carries pungency, tongue-biting flavor. But you are flat, tasteless. Mired in he-saids and she-saids, in the minutiae of bombastic officials and frenetic citizens.

Stand back, all, and admire! Arise and see the beauty of the deed! Who have you lost but another shallow soul?

Women, do not paint yourselves. Do not adorn yourselves. Pretty, pretty, all must be pretty. Where around me is one who is modest? Where is one who would glory in plainness, who would seek the refinement of her own spirit over the lustful affections of men?

Enough, enough!

I smack you, newspaper, and you rattle from my hand. Fall on the table, a corner curling into my full cup, thirstily sucking coffee in your anemia. I watch the dark stain bleed up the page.

Drink your fill.

Yes, and I will drink mine. Away from this kitchen, away from your disgusting insipidity. On rapid feet I stride to my bedroom to revel in the fascination of my deeds. My treasures. I touch them, lift them up, stroke their mewling cries toward heaven.

Heaven hears you, treasures. Yes, it hears.

And your condemnation is its reply.

Chapter 7

I awoke Wednesday morning unrefreshed. My sleep had been fragmented, haunted by dreams of bodies and shadowed men chasing Stephen. I lay in bed for some time, my heavy eyes refusing to open, due both to exhaustion and the shriveling apprehension of what the day would bring. Then a grime-washed crack of light slipped into my shuttered thoughts. This was my birthday.

Happy forty-two, Annie.

Jenna met me in the kitchen, already showered and gunning to tackle the day. Nothing like a challenge to rev my sister's gears. She wished me happy birthday, then promptly insisted I eat something. Naturally. She'd been bossing me ever since she arrived the previous evening.

"All you need to do is faint in the morgue, Annie." She shook her head at me, hands on her hips, then turned to slip a bagel into the toaster without waiting to ask what I wanted.

At least something in the world hadn't changed.

Jenna had brought in the paper. It lay on the counter, daring me to read its coverage on the latest victim like a flame taunting a moth. I did not pick it up.

I hit my office, coffee in hand, by eight o'clock. For half an hour I read the Bible and prayed. I dared not cut my devotions short at such a time as this. One thing I was learning in my new walk with God: the greater my difficulties, the more time I needed to spend with Him in preparation.

My prayers for discovering the killer, bringing him to justice, bordered on begging. I asked God to keep all I knew and loved safe. *No more victims, God, please no more.* I prayed for wisdom to deal with Stephen, and for his protection. Finally, I thanked God for Jenna and her help with the kids.

Actually, my sister would have a lot of time to work on her project. Kelly planned to remain with Erin for the day. Stephen would have to be at the video store by ten. Jenna informed me she would grill him before he left about our unwanted visitor. Even with her tenacity, I didn't expect her to get very far.

Nine o'clock. I entered my least favorite place in the world: the morgue. Cold, shiny tables; cold, shiny pans and instruments; the biting scent of cleanser and the clawing odor of death warring like two beasts over prey. I carried my purse and digital camera. During the drive into Redding I'd prepared myself for my task. *Focus on the parts, Annie, not the whole. Think clinically, not personally.*

"Hi, Matt." The coroner's investigator already stood at his post, ready to assist me.

"Morning, Annie."

I rested a reluctant gaze on our newest Jane Doe, victim number six. She'd been washed. Her body now lay relaxed, her skin the normal blue-white of death. Her mouth hung slightly open—a typical slackness.

Matt and I set about our work, thorough yet efficient. As soon as we finished, the autopsy on Jane Doe would begin.

Anytime now, Chetterling and Harry Fleck, the medical examiner, might arrive to prepare for the autopsy.

If one fortunate side to this whole ordeal existed, it was my close working relationship with Ralph Chetterling and the others at the Shasta County Sheriff's Department. Many forensic artists would not have been afforded such easy access to the victim. They'd have to rely on pictures taken by someone else, such as the coroner's investigator, who likely wasn't thinking of the artist's needs. As a result, the drawing process could be much harder.

When taking pictures myself, I followed a set procedure as I'd learned in my forensic art classes. I positioned a scale perpendicular to the camera lens, taking photos from directly above and straight down upon the face. Incorrect angles can skew the appearance of features in various ways, such as making the face look too long. Correct lighting is also critical. In some cases, such as with the elderly or someone heavy, the most natural-looking pictures would be taken from a body that is propped up, so the facial features fall naturally with gravity. But our Jane Doe was young and slim enough that this wasn't necessary.

Matt Stanish and I spoke little as we worked, other than my asking him to help set up the shots. But inside me, emotions shouted and roiled. Another life stolen away through violent death. And mere inches from her, I stood whole and vibrant. Two days ago, she'd been as alive as I.

How fragile the membrane between life and death.

God, please help us find this killer. And in the meantime— spare my family, my friends.

I leaned over Jane Doe, aiming the camera. *Click*, and her death-painted face froze in my picture frame.

One photo at a time, Annie. Think of the parts, not the whole.

I turned off my mind, somehow managing to pull the plug of its ever-ready film projector. *Aim and shoot. Change position. Aim and shoot. Just perform the task.*

"Okay, Matt." I straightened, took a step back. "All I need now is to photograph the earring."

"Yeah. I've got it here for you."

We set it in a well-lit area, and I stood directly above it, focusing down. The earring was a gaudy blue crystal teardrop surrounded by small white stones. Cheap jewelry that cried for attention. Who was this woman who'd worn it? Would she turn out to be another hitchhiker like Alicia Franz, victim number four? Was she a young mother like the last woman, Christine Ballermo?

Who loved her; who now missed her? Who would want her dead—and why?

Point. Zoom in. *Click.*

Done. I placed my camera back in its case. Matt handed me a manila envelope. "Here are my shots from last night."

"Thanks." I lay the envelope on a nearby counter.

Chetterling and Harry Fleck arrived. Harry and I exchanged greetings before he turned to talk to Matt. I gazed at Chetterling. An almost tangible weight hung over him, a miasma of fatigue and responsibility. Dark circles stained the area beneath his eyes.

"Morning, Annie."

"Hi." All I could muster was a wan smile. "I'll bet you didn't get any sleep last night."

He shrugged. "Not much. And I'll tell you, ever since people started reading their papers this morning . . ." He closed his eyes, ran a hand across his forehead. "It's getting bad with this latest one. Calls have flooded the station in the last couple hours. People demanding to know what we're doing, why haven't we located the perpetrator, and on and on. Like we're sitting around eating chocolates."

I shouldered my purse, my heart quelling at his words. The last thing Redding needed was a firestorm of misplaced anger, fueled by citizens' fear. "Don't worry about everyone out there. All you can do is your job. And you've always managed that very well."

"Yeah, well, I'm beginning to wonder."

"Ralph, *don't.*" The words bounced from my mouth, rough at the edges. Without thinking, I reached out to press my fingers into his thick arm. Never had I heard Chetterling utter a comment even bordering on defeat. He *was* tired. I searched his ragged face, easing my hand away, back to the safety of my purse. "Look, I really . . . I know this is hard on you. Please just . . . remember I'm praying for you."

Did I see the lines in his face flatten, just a little? We regarded each other, a new remorse wriggling in my stomach. I'd never so much as mentioned prayer to him before, never once in the past year had even told him about my newfound faith. What kind of a Christian was I? And now that I had spoken, how would he take it?

"Thank you, Annie. That's something I can always use."

I nodded, focused on the floor. "Um, bad time to ask, but did you get a chance to look at that fax I sent you?"

"Yeah, before this body turned up. Sorry to say I don't recognize him. But we'll keep an eye out." Chetterling looked at me askance. "You didn't tell me about pulling a gun on him."

"Yeah, can you believe it? You taught me well. I barely had to think. It's like you said—if you've practiced enough, pure instinct takes over."

He shifted his weight, one hand finding his hip. "Glad to hear it, but I'm sorry it needed to be done." He thought a moment. "I didn't get to run the name Blake Smith through our system. I'll do that when I get the chance."

As if he had time to do this for me. "Thank you." I smiled at him. "Well, I need to go now. Need to get this Jane Doe drawing done."

And I would need to work with laser concentration, if I was going to make dinner with Dave and the girls that night.

"Okay. Oh, by the way." Chetterling touched my shoulder. "Our task force is planning to meet tomorrow afternoon at three. We'll be going over everything to date—profile of the killer, information about strychnine, all of it. And, of course, we'll have to revisit the geographic profile, now that the perpetrator's decided to move his operation across town. I'd like you to come."

My head drew back. His invitation intimated an unexpected level of trust in me, a person outside law enforcement ranks. "Why?"

Chetterling tilted his head. "You're in this, Annie, more than just as an artist, whether you want to be or not. Especially after last night. It's not that I expect you to *do* any more, you understand. I just thought you might feel more comfortable if you at least know what we know."

He read me all too well. "Yes, I would. Thanks, Ralph, I'll be there."

I called a good-bye to Matt Stanish and Harry Fleck. The door to the autopsy room closed behind me, and I walked down a hall toward the lobby, eyes focused downward, thoughts already turning to bone structure, to the unique features and asymmetries that melded to form the face of Jane Doe.

"Hey, Annie!"

I glanced up at the familiar voice to see Gerri Carson, wearing her wide smile. I'd met Gerri through her chaplain work with the Sheriff's Department. I knew her genuine empathy, her soothing, efficient demeanor as she came alongside victims in tragedy. The first time I'd laid eyes on Gerri, she was comforting a gurney-born, shock-ridden Erin on the night of Lisa Willit's murder.

"Gerri, hi." We hugged each other. "It's so good to see you."

I hadn't seen her for a number of months. She'd let her curly gray hair grow a little, but otherwise looked the same, with her warm brown eyes and aura of serenity in the midst of a storm. Gerri was in her midsixties but had the energy of a much younger woman.

She glanced at the empty front desk. "It's so quiet in here. Where is everybody?"

"I don't know." The desk had been manned when I arrived. "He probably just stepped away for a minute."

"Well, anyway." Gerri studied my face, her eyes mixing compassion and astuteness. "I called your house and heard you were here. Thought I'd stop by and see how you're doing."

I nodded, a telltale flush heating my cheeks. Something about Gerri—I never seemed to be able to hide anything from her.

She squeezed my arm. "I'm so sorry. Please know I'm praying for you. This case is a tough one, Annie. But this time you'll know to rely on God's help. He won't let you down."

"I know." I bit the inside of my cheek, wanting to say no more, yet unable to stop myself. "All this . . . madness has been bad enough, but last night it hit so close to home. I don't really understand why. I guess I just assumed, now that I'm a Christian, God would spare me from this kind of trouble. Know what I mean?"

Gerri nodded. "Oh, yeah. It's a hard question to answer— why God lets trouble come to His followers. All we can do is fall back on Romans 8:28. That God uses even the worst of circumstances to make us stronger. One day Jesus will come back, and the world will be perfected again, like when He first made it. But until then—think about it, Annie. For now, God uses *evil itself*, which wants to push us away from God, to bring us *closer* to Him. Hah! What a clever victory." She shot me a smile full of wonderment.

I could only smile back. "Okay. Guess I never looked at it that way before."

Her sunny expression waned. "But look, I don't mean to make light of your fears. All of us are scared. Still, we can do something about it. My church is having a prayer meeting tonight to pray for God's intervention in these killings. You may have seen the little article in the paper this morning, inviting anyone who wants to attend. I know some people from your church are coming. Think you can make it?"

The morning paper. I'd avoided it like the plague. "Oh, how I wish. But I can't. I have dinner plans tonight, and it's not something I can break."

"No, of course not." She firmed her mouth with that take-on-the-world Gerri confidence. "That's just fine, you go to your dinner, but know God's people will be praying. And I mean up a storm!"

"Good. I'll tell—"

The building's front door thrust open. A man and woman hesitated on the threshold, terror in their eyes, as if teetering on the edge of hell. Trembling, they forced themselves inside. The woman gripped the man's arm, her fingers white. Her brown hair looked uncombed, her eyes and cheeks red, swollen. The man's thick hands clasped and unclasped, his face looking blanched and weathered. Together, they stumbled toward Gerri and me.

"We heard . . ." The man's words curled and fell away, like discarded shavings from hard-whittled wood. He swallowed, his eyes searching mine. "We think you might have our daughter."

Chapter 8

In the second that I searched for a reply, Gerri took over. She reached both hands out to the couple. "I'm Gerri Carson, a chaplain with the police and Sheriff's departments. Let me help you."

The man nodded, a raw, worn gesture. "We read in the paper this morning that you found another . . . someone. We live south of Red Bluff and came right away to see for ourselves if . . . Our daughter, Julie, she's twenty-five. She drove away two days ago to visit some new boyfriend, she said. We haven't heard from her since, and she's not answering her cell phone." The man's voice cracked.

Air pooled in my throat. *Oh, Lord, help these poor people.*

Gerri's voice remained tender but steady. "Okay, let's find out what we can for you. Would you like to have a seat for a minute? Maybe some water?"

The woman shook her head. "No, please, we just want to go in there. We have to see. We have to kn—" Her face crumpled.

"All right, I understand." Gerri looked over her shoulder, mouthing for me to "go get someone." I set down my belongings, then scurried away, the voices like fire brands at my back. I could only thank God the three men would still be in the first, external stage of the autopsy. As my feet scurried down the hall, I heard Gerri pulling names from the man and woman. George and Diane. I slipped through the door into the autopsy room and called for Chetterling. He, Matt, and Harry looked up from their work, a notebook and pen in the detective's hand. Jane Doe—Julie?—lay uncovered before them on the stainless steel table. Exposed and pitiful. She had not yet been cut.

"A couple's here. Wanting to see her." I averted my eyes from the body. "They think she may be their daughter."

The men exchanged a glance.

"Okay." Chetterling set down his notebook and pen. "Be right there."

I escaped back into the hallway, leaving the wrenching sight of the autopsy room for the fearful moan of parental voices that could soon swell to full mourning. As I drew closer to the lobby I could make out Gerri's soothing words. She was asking George and Diane about their daughter—her hair and eye color, her height. By the time Chetterling introduced himself to the couple, she had enough information to take him aside and compare descriptions.

Chetterling gave a slow nod. "Sounds like I'd better let them see her. Do you think they can handle it?"

Gerri glanced at the couple. "I don't think they can handle *not* doing it. No amount of description you give them is going to suffice."

"All right. We'll get her ready."

As Chetterling disappeared, I introduced myself to George and Diane. Then we waited, a clock on the wall ticking interminable seconds. The projector in my head spooled out variant endings to this real-life drama—the shocked despair of recognition, the collapsing relief of seeing a form unknown.

"Will you come with us?" Diane's pain-filled eyes looked to Gerri, then me.

"Of course," Gerri said.

Chetterling beckoned. Gerri and I ushered George and Diane down the hall toward the viewing area. None of us spoke.

We drew up to a window, covered on the other side by a thick curtain. Beyond the glass, I knew, lay the small viewing room.

Diane faltered, knees buckling. George and Gerri held her up. All I could do was hang back and try to pray. But my prayers tore away, midsentence, as I focused on Diane's hunched and quivering back, her spine showing through a cotton blouse. The clench of her fingers around her husband's wrist, her trembling, spoke more than any words could say.

Anger seared through me, trailing the smoke of hopeless injustice. *How* could one person kill six innocent women? How could he cause so much grief to so many people?

Why was God letting this happen?

"In just a minute—" Gerri's tone was low, calm—"they'll pull the curtain open."

"Okay." The whisper leaked from Diane's mouth.

I hovered near George, focusing on his gray face. Trying to imagine myself in his and Diane's position, weak-kneed at the door to hell, wondering if my Kelly lay vulnerable and forever broken on the other side. At the mere thought, my throat cinched tight.

George reached hesitant fingers to touch the glass, as if through it he might somehow sense the presence—or absence—of his daughter. His hand shook. I heard Diane shuddering as she breathed.

The curtain drew open.

Diane gasped, the sound rattling down her throat. A low moan escaped George. "It's not her." He looked away, then at Gerri, eyes half-focused. "It's not Julie."

They both erupted in sobs.

The curtain closed, its swishing barely audible through the glass.

George and Diane turned away. Suddenly, they couldn't leave fast enough, as though the truth might change if they lingered a second longer. Clutching each other, they stumbled from the nightmarish window, all the way up the hall, and out the front door. Gerri stayed close behind. I knew she wouldn't leave them until they were calm enough to drive.

I lingered near the entrance, retrieving my purse and camera and envelope of photos with trembling hands. My heart would not stop fluttering.

"Annie?"

Through a blur of tears, I looked around to see Chetterling. "Oh, Ralph." I brought a hand to my mouth. "That was terrible. That was just . . ."

He stood close, looking down upon me with knowing empathy, hands low on his hips. "I know. I'm sorry you had to see that. At least they—"

"But it doesn't matter!" I gestured vehemently toward the door. "No, I don't mean that. I'm really, really glad for them. But their gain is someone else's loss. Some other mom and dad's grief!" I jerked my purse strap up my shoulder, my throat thickening. "We have to catch him, Chetterling. We have to catch him *now*. I swear, I want to shoot him myself!"

Chetterling said nothing, just let me vent. I clutched my camera and glared out a window until my breathing steadied. "Okay. Thanks." I faced him once more, my taut jaw slackening. "I'm through now."

He nodded, his expression placid, as if he'd have waited me out all day. Sometimes it was obvious he'd grown up with sisters. Then, unexpectedly, he gave me a lopsided smile. "All right. Well. Guess you better get on with your work, and I'll get back to mine."

Poor, tired Chetterling. My work would be a whole lot easier than his. "Yeah."

"Hey," he called as I was halfway out the door. "I almost forgot. Happy birthday."

I eyed him askance. "Who told you?"

He shrugged. "Nobody. I just remembered from last year. Birthdays do happen like that, don't they? An annual thing?"

I gave him an *oh, ha-ha* look and pushed myself out of the building. Halfway across the parking area, Gerri stood talking to a calmer George and Diane. I gathered myself, knowing that I should say good-bye to them, express relief and happiness. I needed to tell them I hoped they would find their daughter safe and well. The words took up rehearsal in my head as my feet headed in their direction. But the scenes in my mind fast-forwarded—to my going home, to meticulously drawing Jane Doe's face.

So her real loved ones could visit the morgue with tenacious hope . . . only to stagger away, all dreams crushed.

Chapter 9

Eleven thirty.

I pulled my SUV into the garage and shut off the engine. For a moment I rested my head back against the seat, regrouping. The drive home hadn't been long enough to cool the simmering waters of the morning's memories. With a sigh, I gathered my things and slipped out of the car. I had precious few minutes to waste. My work beckoned. If all went well, I'd have time to complete my drawing, return it to the Sheriff's Office, then dress for my birthday dinner.

Dinner. I tried to grasp the concept of relaxing, enjoying a night out. The idea enticed yet eluded me, an out-of-reach butterfly airing its wings.

I found my sister hunched over the computer in her spacious bedroom, working on her project. I knocked on her open door. She jumped.

"Hey."

She flexed her shoulders. "Hey, back. How did it go?"

If she only knew. "Terrific. A trip to the morgue is always a great way to start the day."

Jenna's mouth twisted in sympathy.

I walked over to her bed and sank upon it. "Chetterling wished me happy birthday. Nice of him, huh?" As soon as I'd spoken the words, I wondered why on earth I had. Knowing Jenna, she'd make something of it.

Then again, maybe I wanted her to. After this morning, I yearned for a few minutes of light conversation, even if it thumbed a nose at reality. Words that focused on life, on hope, not death and tragedy.

"Yeah, nice. You tell him it's your birthday?"

Here it came. I lifted my shoulders. "No. He just knew."

"Just knew."

"Uh-huh. Like he said, they happen every year."

She shook her head, as if not quite believing my naïveté. "Annie, you just don't remember somebody's birthday for nothing. You have to *think* about remembering it."

"Okay, Jenna." I held up both hands, suddenly sorry I'd started this. I was too tired. "Just stop right there. We're not going down this road again."

She flicked a look at the ceiling. "What do you mean *again*? More like *still*. More like—this is the slowest movie I ever saw in my entire life."

My work awaited me. I pushed from the bed. "Maybe it isn't a movie at all. Maybe you just think it is."

"I know what I see. And *that* is a man who cares for you. A man who sent you flowers last year. *After* you nearly got him killed, I might add."

I made a little *tsking* sound. "Actually, you didn't need to add that part."

"Okay, you're right. Sorry." She tapped a bare foot on the carpet. "But really . . . when are you going to do something about this?"

"Just what am I supposed to do?"

"I don't know . . . *say* something. Show him . . . you care."

Images of Chetterling flashed on the walls of my mind. First meeting him two years ago, the night of Lisa Willit's murder. The bulk of the man, his large, chiseled face, the small, dark brown eyes and thin mouth, formed a package that cried *authority*. Without even trying, he'd intimidated me. Fast-forward to the way he'd looked at me last night in the forest. And this morning. Both times he'd been concerned, compassionate. I knew he respected and cared for me as a friend and colleague. But I'd never sensed anything more from him. I wasn't sure that I wanted to.

"I *don't* care, Jenna. Not the way you mean." I ambled over to stand by her desk, closing my eyes. The events at the morgue still nibbled at my nerves. "The thing is, what if he *did* make some kind of move? Maybe said something. Or what if I did? And the other one didn't respond? Our working relationship would never be the same. There'd be this new awkwardness and embarrassment between us. I don't want that, ever. I *really* don't."

She surveyed me, biting her lip. "So out of fear, you'll do nothing. Forever."

"Guess so." I hitched my shoulders in a *so what?* gesture. This made no sense anyway, my sister trying to match me up when she's never even been married once and was ten times prettier. Jenna has a great figure, gorgeously thick hair and velvety brown eyes with long lashes. My eyes are somewhere between hazel and gray, my face too round, my waist too wide. Besides, Vic, my children's dear father, unceremoniously dumped me four years ago for a model-faced husband-stealer eleven years my junior. That hadn't exactly pumped me up in the self-esteem department.

"Anyway," I rubbed the back of my neck, "this conversation is off the subject. I came in here to talk about two things. First, did you get anything out of Stephen before he left for work?"

Jenna leaned back in her chair with a sigh. "Nothing. Not that I didn't try. But that kid . . . Annie, I don't know what's going to become of him. He's nothing but belligerent. Bent on self-destruction."

"I know." My personal projector kicked on, spewing scenes of Blake Smith lowering his hands in defiance, even as my gun pointed straight at him. Forcefully, I pushed the thoughts away. I had enough to handle right now. "Okay. Well, thanks for trying. The second thing is, I just wanted to say thank you again for staying here with Stephen while Kelly and I go out to dinner tonight. I wish you could go with us."

"Go with you?" Jenna folded her arms. "Well, I guess I could have. Since this is only a birthday dinner, with the two girls between you and Dave. All nice and safe, so nobody has to say it's a date."

Good grief, what was wrong with my sister? If she couldn't hitch me up with one man, she'd turn around and try it with the next. "Oh, for heaven's sake, Jenna, it's *not* a date."

"Okay, it's not a date." Jenna's smug smile made my jaw clench. "Don't worry, I'll say no more. I'll just stay home with Stephen, like you need. Make sure he doesn't burn the house down."

"Thank you." I headed toward the door, then stopped, afraid my actions seemed a little too abrupt. "Really, Jenna, thanks a lot. You're the best. Even if you are a pain in the neck sometimes."

She shook her head and turned back to her computer. "Like you could do without me."

I left Jenna's room, prepared to set to work. But once in my office I hesitated, my gaze wandering out the front windows toward Dave's house. I really should check on Kelly after all that had happened yesterday. And I should call Stephen at the video store, just to make sure he was okay.

First I phoned the store and was grateful that my son answered rather than the manager. "Yes, I'm fine, Mom." Stephen's impatience was painfully evident. "I don't know why you keep calling."

Was that false bravado in his voice? "Just listen to me and be careful, okay? Don't go very far at lunchtime, and come straight home when you get off."

"Yeah, Mom, okay. I gotta go now. I have a customer."

With a sigh, I hung up the phone, then left my office to walk across the street. The sun beat mercilessly on my head as I crossed Barrister Court. Our sky park was quiet, no distant roar of a private plane preparing to land. *God, please keep things this way. Quiet. No more bodies here, okay?*

In the Willits' kitchen, pop music thudded from the stereo in Erin's room. The girls were baking chocolate chip cookies, remnants of flour and butter smeared upon a counter.

"I'm fine, Mom, stop worrying." Kelly wagged her head at me in time to the music. Erin laughed. For the thousandth time, I thanked God for their friendship.

Dave wandered in. "Hi. Thought I heard the doorbell."

I smiled at him. "Good morning." The light green knit shirt Dave wore accentuated the color of his eyes. For some reason my hands suddenly wanted something to do. I picked up an errant chocolate chip and tossed it into the sink. "How in the world do you work with that music going?"

Dave owned commercial real estate in Redding and managed his accounts from home. His office was down a long hall, just on the other side of Erin's room.

He grinned at the girls. "I've gotten used to it."

"Well, if you want to send them to our house for a while, that's fine. I'll be home working all afternoon. Jenna's there too."

"Annie, remember you have to dress up tonight." Erin scrunched her shoulders with anticipation. "We're all dressing up 'cause we're taking you to a fancy place!"

"Okay, I can't wait." I ran my fingers through her silky hair, then looked to Dave. "Thank you again."

"Hey, believe me, the pleasure's ours."

He held my gaze for a brief moment. I nodded, rather abruptly, and turned to leave.

"Mom." The hitch in Kelly's voice stopped me. "This morning, did you go to . . . Did you see . . . ?"

Ah, here lay the truth. Despite her blithe teenage veneer, Kelly hadn't forgotten yesterday. "Yes."

"So you're going to be drawing now?"

Inside, I cringed. If Kelly were home while I drew, she would know not to enter my office. My rule stood firm. She didn't need to visit the murky pool of death in which my recent work forced me to wade. But sometimes I wondered if her imagination proved just as chilling.

"That's right." I pulled my daughter into a hug, whispering in her ear. "Don't worry, everything will be fine. Nothing else is going to happen today, Kelly."

She gave me a squeeze. "That's right. Nothing."

How wrong we would prove to be.

Chapter 10

I bent over the worktable, my concentration fluttering like curtains in an open window. For stretches of time I could focus on Jane Doe's face, looking from photographs to my drawing pad, sketching her features, slowly filling in details. One of the hardest things I'd had to learn—was still learning—lay in enlivening slack, lifeless features. Until these serial killings, I'd never realized how important a role animation plays in someone's face. Now I struggled to reconstruct vitality, drawing Jane Doe's glassy eyes as open, alert, the flatness of her mouth as one held by quickened muscles . . .

My thoughts paused, shifted. My movie projector clicked on, spinning out the scene of finding her body. Spinning imagined sequences of her killer standing back in warped fascination to watch her contort and die.

What kind of man could do that to a person?

I shook the morbid thoughts away, only to envision disturbing pictures of Stephen. My son in the shadows, taking money from an outstretched hand, sliding a bag into an open and waiting palm. Then I saw Blake, hulking over Kelly, flinging his insolence at me.

God, what is happening? Everything's coming down on us at once.

I checked the clock. Two twenty. I pushed from the table and flexed my head back, kneading the muscles in my neck. Time to take a few minutes' break, get a drink of water.

As I pulled to my feet, the phone rang.

I crossed to my desk to answer it. Maybe it was Chetterling with an identification on our victim. But no. The caller ID showed Stephen's cell phone number. I stared at it for a second, then picked up the receiver. "Hi, Stephen."

"Mom." His voice was thick, raw. "Look, don't freak out. And I don't have time to answer questions right now. But I need you to come get me."

Come get him? "What do you mean, aren't you at work?"

"It's my lunch break." Air pumped his tone, as if he was walking fast. "Please, Mom, just come."

"I—where's your car?"

"*Mom!* Would you listen to me? I need you here, *now*. I'm in trouble. And I *don't have time to answer questions!*"

Fear washed through me. Was Blake chasing him? "Okay, I'm coming. But where?"

His breathing gusted. "Start driving to Redding and call me back on your cell phone. I have to keep moving. I'll tell you where to meet me."

Seconds later I pulled out of the driveway, my heart in my throat. I hadn't even stopped to tell Jenna I was leaving. As I turned out of Grove Landing sky park, I pressed my cell to my ear, listening to the first ring of Stephen's phone, praying for him to pick up. On the second ring he answered, sounding winded.

"Okay, you know the Safeway at Shasta Station?"

Shasta Station—a shopping center Dave owned. "Yes."

"Drive around to the back. Where they throw out boxes and stuff. I'm there right now, waiting for you."

My breath hitched. "Stephen, what happened?"

"I'll tell you about it when you get h—"

"No, Stephen, *now*. You're scaring me to death."

"Okay, okay, don't have a fit." Muffled movement of the phone. "I met up with some friends for lunch. I was talking to them, and this van drove up, and they all told me to get in it. I really didn't have a choice. They started accusing me of owing them money, and they took me to this guy's house and wouldn't let me go. They took my wallet. Then some of them left and said they'd be back. They left me with two of the guys. I went to the bathroom and crawled out a window and ran."

Heaviness sank over me. *Accusing me of owing them money*. No doubt for every detail Stephen told me, he'd left out a dozen more. My son was in serious trouble. *Please, God, keep him safe!*

"Are these 'friends,' as you call them, still after you?"

He hesitated. "Yeah."

I drew close to a car driving far too slowly, with no way to pass. *Come on, move!* "But you're safe until I can get there, right? They don't know where you are?"

"I'm okay. But they know where I left my car. And now they know where I work, so . . ."

"Stephen. Who are they? Is one of them Blake?"

"Mom, you ask too many questions."

"Too many questions! I'm worried *sick* for you and I want to know what's going on!"

"I'll tell you when you get here. Please just come now."

"I am, I am! I'm trying to hurry."

"Okay. Thanks."

How grateful he sounded. Like he used to when he was a little boy and I tended a skinned knee or banged arm. Where had that little boy gone? How had we gotten to this?

"Stephen, don't hang up. Even if we don't say anything, I just want to know that you're still there, waiting for me. I'm behind this really slow car, and . . ." The words choked.

The minutes limped by, my fingers curling around my cell phone, the steering wheel. My foot poised above the gas pedal, awaiting the slightest chance to go a little faster. After what seemed an interminable time, the car in front of me turned. I surged forward and finally hit the northeast side of town, going well over the speed limit. Shasta Station lay at the south end of Redding. I forced my foot to ease up. While I drove and fretted, I decided what I would do.

After an agonizing trip, I pulled into the back of Safeway and stopped, eyes frantically searching the area. "Stephen, I'm here. Where are you?"

He stepped out from behind a blue dumpster, cell phone in hand. *Thank You, God!* I clicked off our call and drove forward to meet him. When I drew near enough to see his face, I gasped. He'd been *hit*. More than once. One eye gleamed purple-black. Another bruise stained his left jaw, and dried blood crusted his lip. The sight cut right through me.

"Oh." I brought a hand to my mouth, tears stinging my eyes. Stephen slipped into the car.

He tilted his head, trying with all his might to look cocky. "I'm okay, don't get all trippy. Just get me out of here."

I turned the SUV around, feeling the beat of my heart, questions ripping through my head. We drove across the Shasta Station parking lot, and I looked helplessly at the street. "Where do I go?"

"Turn right."

We'd gone a few blocks before I could find a steady voice. "Stephen, why did they do this to you? What do they want?"

A sound of disgust pushed from his mouth. "They're crazy, that's all. Don't know what they're talking about."

"And you call these people your *friends*?"

He turned away to stare out the window.

I flicked paranoid glances at everyone we passed, looking for who knew what. "Where's your car?"

"At the 7-Eleven, around the corner from the video store." He checked an empty left wrist. "Oh, man. I keep forgetting they took my watch too."

My teeth pressed together. That watch had been a Christmas present.

We hit a stoplight. The 7-Eleven and the video store lay a couple miles down the road, straight ahead. I turned right.

"Hey, what are you doing?"

"Taking you where you need to go."

He pointed a finger diagonally across his chest. "My car's that way."

"And the police station's this way."

"The pol—No, Mom, no! You can't take me there!"

"Stephen, I can't take you anywhere *but* there. A group of people have beat you up, taken your watch and wallet. Are apparently still looking for you. And you think you're just going to pick up your car and go back to work like nothing happened? How are you going to explain your face to your boss?"

"I didn't say I'd go back to work, but I gotta get my car! I already called the video store and told them I had an accident.

Won't be back this afternoon. But I just need to get to our house for now, get out of town."

My tone flattened. "These people, whoever they are, they know where you work. They know where your car is sitting right now. They know where you live. They're obviously out to hurt you. How do you propose to stay away from them?"

He glared at me. "So what are the police supposed to do?"

"Protect you, how's that for an idea? And while they're at it, protect all of us. Don't forget that one of your *friends* showed up in our house yesterday, uninvited."

Stephen pushed hard against the back of his seat. He held up a hand, palm out. "Okay, Mom, listen to me now. Just chill and listen. I *can't* go to the police. All they're going to do is ask questions, and *I can't answer them.*"

"Yes, you can. It's very simple, Stephen, just open your mouth."

"What—" He sank his head in his hands. "You don't understand. I *can't* tell this to anybody. I can't go running to the cops."

"Really. So what's your plan? What's *our* plan, since you've now dragged your whole family into this?" I thumped the steering wheel, frustration cinching my throat. "And I don't even completely know what *this* is."

My cell phone rang. I ignored it.

"Aren't you going to answer that?"

"No. *I'm* the one who wants answers right now. From you."

No response. The phone rang four times, then stopped. I knew I should answer. It could be some news about the case, or Jenna, wondering where on earth I'd disappeared to. No matter. I'd check the message later.

We reached the Redding Police Station. I pulled into the parking lot and stopped the car, praying that Stephen wouldn't bolt. From the look on his face, he considered it. But then what would he do? Where would he go? Right now, I was his only deliverance.

I opened my door. "Come on."

"Mom, *pleeease*."

"Stephen. Come."

He looked away and shook his head, uttering a curse under his breath. I took the opportunity to pick up his cell phone from the console and slip it into my purse.

"Oh, great. Terrific." He spread his hands. "Now you're taking my phone."

I surveyed my son and his battered face, seeing the fear he tried so hard to hide. If he'd had any other choice, he'd have already run. The cops and Sheriff's deputies were the ones who'd busted him for drugs. A part of me quailed at the thought of walking through the department with my belligerent and bruised son. I'd worked with the officers on many a case in the last two years. Meanwhile, Stephen's growing record had been a source of embarrassment and shame in their presence. On two occasions, for some forensic art assignment, I'd had to interview the very officer who'd arrested my son just days earlier. I knew my reputation as a professional ran high. But my reputation as a mother? Surely, the officers saw me as a complete failure.

God, I don't want to fail my son as a mother. Help me.

"Stephen. Let's go."

With the drooping reluctance of the doomed facing a firing squad, he dragged himself out of the car and followed me into the station.

Chapter 11

The woman behind the receiving desk at the police station greeted me by name, her smile fading with her first glance at Stephen. Slumped and dejected, his battered face scowling with indignation, he looked like some creature the cat had dragged in. "Hi, Kathy." I worked to keep my expression placid, but I could feel my cheeks flush. "We need to talk to somebody. Maybe an officer involved in drug cases?"

"Oh, great, Mom." Stephen narrowed his eyes at the far wall, jaw flexing.

"Sure, no problem." Kathy fairly chirruped the words as she picked up the phone.

We didn't have to wait long. Frank Nelson appeared, a burly young officer whom I knew by acquaintance only. Fortunately, he'd never had to arrest Stephen, or no doubt my son would have run for the door. Nelson invited us back into a small, cluttered office to talk, the equipment attached to his belt squeaking as he settled into a well-used leather chair behind his desk. Stephen slouched against a wall, arms folded, looking around the office with a curl of his lip. I could almost reach out and touch the noxious cloud hanging over him. Wordlessly, I motioned for him to sit in one of two wooden chairs facing the officer's desk. He threw himself into a chair with a huff. I sank into the other one, feeling the tremble of my ankles, the familiar knot in my stomach. Every time I witnessed my son facing a policeman or judge, it was the same. Utter fear for him, for our family.

"All right, Stephen." Nelson leaned back in his chair, a calculated casual move to help set us at ease. "Tell me what's going on."

Stephen cracked his knuckles, focusing on the floor. "I got in a fight with some friends, that's all."

"Really. Your mom bring you down here just for that?"

He shrugged. "She won't leave it alone."

A rebuke formed on my tongue. Nelson gave me a look, his message clear: *I'll handle this.* I bit the rebuke back.

"Okay, just a fight. What are the names of the other guys involved?"

Silence.

"What were you fighting about?"

Stephen firmed his lips. His right leg started bouncing up and down. The floor beneath my feet shook.

Enough of this. "He won't tell me who it was. He did say they took his wallet and watch."

Nelson stuck his tongue between his lips, assessing my son. "You want to report the theft?"

Stephen shook his head.

The officer slapped his palms on the arms of his chair and leaned forward, air seeping from his throat. "Okay. We're getting nowhere real fast." He looked to me. "Will you let us talk alone for a minute?"

Dully, I nodded. With a glance at Stephen, I rose and tottered from the office.

For ten minutes I paced the hallway, occasionally exchanging greetings with officers who walked by. Fortunately, none asked why I was there. The air-conditioning turned too chilly. I rubbed my arms. My thoughts began to flit from one problem to another with no place to land. What would happen to Stephen? How could I keep him safe? And Jane Doe—I hadn't finished drawing her yet. How would I ever concentrate on that? *Dinner.* Oh, no, I'd almost forgotten. How could I go now?

I rested my head against the wall, defeated and frightened. *God, You'd better help me through all this. I don't know what to do! And please, protect my son. Most of all, change his heart . . .*

The office door opened, and Nelson stuck his head out. "You want to join us again, Mrs. Kingston?"

With a nod I followed him inside and resumed my seat. Stephen still stared at the floor, fingers picking at his jeans. His jaw seemed even tighter, new creases in his forehead.

Officer Nelson cleared his throat. "Mrs. Kingston, I'm going to have to tell you the truth. I'm afraid there's nothing I can do for you or your son."

I stared at the man, feeling the weight of my body in the chair, as if someone had turned up the gravity level.

He spread his hands. "Stephen won't tell me anything. And if a person won't talk, then . . . what am I left with?"

My eyes closed. If only I had a copy of my Blake drawing with me. "But *I* can tell you. Like about the guy who walked into our house yesterday, demanding to see Stephen. I found him standing over my fourteen-year-old daughter while she was sleeping on the couch. He was . . . scary. Big guy, muscular, with dreadlocks. I drew a picture of him I could show you. I'll bet you anything what happened today has something to do with him."

Nelson's eyes shifted toward Stephen, the officer's expression hardening. "You sure you want to keep so stoic, man? Sounds to me like this is starting to spill over to your family. If you're in danger, they could be too. Or does that even matter to you?"

Stephen shot him a look to kill, then shoved to his feet. "That's it. I'm *out* of here." He threw the door open and stomped away.

Before I knew it, I was on my feet, clutching my purse. I needed to hurry after him, make sure he didn't run down the street and disappear. He didn't even have his cell phone. How would I reach him if he took off? How would I know he's safe?

Officer Nelson must have read my thoughts. He shifted in his chair. "My advice is to let him go. Maybe a few more lessons from the street are exactly what he needs."

I whirled on the policeman. How young he was. Probably unmarried, no children. He had no *idea*. "You have to do something!" The words shot from my mouth. "We can't just let him go and walk back into danger."

"What am I supposed to do if he won't talk?"

"I don't know—*something*! Lock him up for his own safety, if you have to."

"Mrs. Kingston, I can't lock him up when he hasn't done anything. I'm not the boss here, you know; I'm the little guy. I have to follow the system."

"Then there's something terribly wrong with your system."

He spread his hands, as if to say, *yeah, tell me about it.*

My vision blurred. I would get nowhere with this man. "I want to fax you the picture I drew of Blake Smith. Will you at least look at it? Maybe he's someone you're already look-ing for."

He stood up behind his desk, a sign that our meeting was over. "Sure. Fax it to my attention. I'll let you know if I rec-ognize him."

If he looked at the drawing at all.

"Thank you." The words were cold, tight. And I didn't care. "I need to go find my son now. *Somebody* needs to make sure he's safe."

I turned on my heel and hurried out the door.

Chapter 12

There is no God, there is no God, there is no God, *there is no God!*

So now you want to pray against me, do you, Christians? You who go to church and profess your cleanness. You who talk to a God you can't see and live by a faith you can't touch, while the evil of this world corrupts and perverts, and no one stands in its path.

My mother went to church too. Oh, yes. Sought God in the heavens, in hell, in this religion and that one. Sought all her life, looking for Him in the faces of men, in the touch of their fingers, the brush of their lips. Sought Him in this country and that one, her "divine mission" as sole truth-finder, her words webbed lies spun from a black heart. And I, frightened, neglected child, could not get away. Had to pray to her succession of gods. Had to help her get ready for her "ceremonies" with men.

The town weeps and staggers like a woman in labor, wailing "no more!" But like *her*, you reap the harvest of your own sowing. You want me to stop, even as your women continue to adorn themselves as she did, painting and plucking, sashaying their wares through the streets. Beautiful on the outside. Vile within.

So seek. Pray. Plead, beseech! Stretch your arms to the sky, crying tears from your self-satiated souls. Cry to your God, see if He hears. God on His platform, God on His throne. And far, far away your wailing reaches His consciousness, no more than the whine of mosquitoes.

While you pray, what will I do? Yes, what, what? Sit back, eat, drink, watch the news on television? Walk your streets, mingling among you, seen but unseen, known but not known?

Ah, no.

I will teach you the benefit of your prayers.

Chapter 13

My heart swelled when I saw Stephen slumped against my car in the police station parking lot. "Oh, I'm glad you're here." The air in the SUV was stifling as we climbed inside. I started the engine and blasted up the air-conditioning fans.

"Okay, Stephen." I turned to him, taking in his still-defiant expression, the beading sweat on his forehead. "Thanks to your actions in there, we're on our own. So you're going to tell me the whole story. Now. We're sitting here until you do. Apparently, you know you're in deep trouble, because you didn't take off down the street."

Stephen's jaw flexed back and forth. He glared out the windshield at a policeman getting out of his squad car across the lot.

"Fine. They said I took some money."

This I already knew. "Who's they?"

"Just some guys I hang out with. Kenny and Dwayne. And Al and Eddy."

I pondered the names. "I don't know any of them."

He shrugged. "Yeah."

"So . . . how did they say you took this money?"

He cinched his mouth into a sneer. "I don't know, some drug deal they did. They came up short or something."

Drug deal. I forced my voice to remain calm. "Were you in on this . . . business?"

He flicked at a piece of lint on his jeans. "Not really."

"What does *not really* mean?"

"I was—would you stop looking at me like that? I talked to somebody on the phone, that's all. Like a messenger."

In other words, he was involved. My insides curled into a little ball, hard and protective.

"I see. And how much money was somehow missing?"

"I didn't take it, Mom."

"I'm glad to hear that. How much do they *think* you took?"

He focused out the window for a long moment, thumb and fingers hitting against one knee. "Two thousand dollars."

My mouth dropped open. I don't know what I had expected, but it wasn't anywhere in that ballpark. *"Two thousand dollars?"*

"Like I told you, they're crazy."

"But . . . but that's a lot of money! And they're drug dealers. And if they really think you took it . . ."

No, this could not be happening. People like that, with this kind of money involved—they weren't just going to pat my son on the head, say *don't worry about it.* "Stephen, what are you going to do? They won't leave you alone."

For the first time, I saw a corner crumble in the wall of his defense. He looked down at his lap, even as that one hand kept slapping his leg.

"I suppose they expect you to pay the two thousand back?"

His hand stilled. He pressed his lips together and glanced at me from the corner of his eye. "They want four thousand. They say it's *interest.*"

My breath caught. *Interest. Of course.* That's what the bad guys did in all the movies, didn't they? Charge double pay-back? And if they didn't get it when they wanted it . . . I leaned against my window, head on the glass. I could not believe this was happening. This wasn't some movie, this was my life. My *son's* life.

"Stephen. Was one of the people who beat you up the guy who was at our house yesterday? Who called himself Blake?"

Slowly, he shook his head. "No. But I know he told them to do it. Blake runs things. He's up the chain, second guy from the top."

Up the chain. More like chain gang. The air-conditioning fan suddenly hurt my ears. I smacked the dial to turn it down. Then sat staring into the distance. What to say? What to do?

"We need to go back inside the station. Find Officer Nelson and tell him all this. They *have* to protect you. Arrest these guys."

"Mom, there *is* no protection, don't you get it?" Stephen sighed at the heavens, as if searching them for some sense to imbed in my brain. "It's not like some cop could follow me around all day. And you want to know the truth? If I give the cops names, and they start looking for these guys because of *me*—I'm dead. I mean it. No drama, just the facts."

Okay, this *was* a movie. Somehow I'd fallen into it, had entered a wrong door and shrieked headlong into blackness. Or a nightmare had caught me, wrapped me in its dank, embittered web like a spider enveloping his prey. In rapid sequence, my brain flashed scenes of Stephen

hunched in Officer Nelson's office, hands fiddling with the hem of his T-shirt as he mumbles the names and deeds of all his former friends . . .

glancing furtively over his shoulder as he scuttles to his car after work . . .

hiding at home day after day, afraid for his face to be seen . . .

perched on the witness stand, star testimony for the prosecutor against Blake, his eyes avoiding the man's murderous and revengeful glare . . .

I'd been in forensic art for two years. A courtroom artist for a decade preceding that. I'd seen enough violent crime as a result of drug deals to know the danger Stephen faced. The threat was bad enough now, but if he started "ratting" on his friends . . .

God, help us both! I don't know what to do.

I could go back to Officer Nelson, tell him the story. Give him the first names of the four boys. But that wouldn't be enough. And even if it was, if those boys were picked up, wouldn't Stephen still refuse to talk? Bottom line, without his cooperation, what could be done?

Did I even *want* him to cooperate? How could I insist on it now, knowing it would place his life in danger?

Suddenly, all I wanted to do was get Stephen home—behind locked doors.

A whirlpool set in motion in my stomach, my emotions sucking down, down. Until nothing but a strange calm remained.

"Put your seatbelt on." With robotlike movements, I fastened myself in, backed out of the parking space. We headed down the road without speaking, Stephen scanning the sidewalks. I drove to the 7-Eleven, where he'd left his car. The used Chevy Blazer sat unharmed, its interior no doubt roasting in the heat.

"See anybody that worries you?"

Stephen looked around. "No."

I pulled into a parking space away from the store's entrance. "I don't want *you* driving your car home, because someone might recognize you in it. So I'm going to drive it, and you're going to follow in this car. *Don't* fall out of my sight, okay? I'll give your cell phone back just for the trip, and I want you to keep it on."

He nodded and reached into his pocket for the Blazer keys. As he handed them to me, ghostly fingers squeezed my chest. That one, silent action of Stephen's told me more than any amount of words. Finally, my son was not fighting me. Not because of a change of heart. He simply had nowhere else to turn.

Chapter 14

We made it out of Redding without mishap.

As Stephen and I turned our separate cars onto the road toward Grove Landing, I picked up my cell phone to call home. Jenna answered on the first ring. "Annie! I tried to call. Where *are* you?"

Where to begin? I told her the bare-bones version of what had happened. Which, of course, wasn't enough for my sister. By the time I neared the sky park, my eyes constantly flicking to the rearview mirror to check on Stephen, I'd related everything. My throat ran dry, my voice was pinched, and my eyes felt like they'd been sandpapered.

For the second time in twenty-four hours, I'd succeeded in rendering Jenna speechless. When she did respond, it was with inane words meant to soothe. "Okay. Fine. Another problem. We'll work it out."

Sure. Didn't we always? But this was just a little too much at once.

"Look, Jenna, the first thing is to get Stephen home and safe. He can't answer doors or phones. He's not going anywhere, and we never leave him alone. Second, somehow I've got to finish my work. I have no idea how I'm going to concentrate, but the drawing has to get in tomorrow morning's paper. Which means I have to take the original into the Sheriff's Office."

"Yes, okay." Jenna pulled her act together. "I'll do whatever you need to help. I can take the drawing back into Redding for you. How long will it take you to finish it?"

I drew a deep breath. "I don't know. I don't know much of anything right now. Maybe two hours. If I can just . . . put my mind to it."

"I swear, that Stephen—I'm going to strangle him."

"Jenna, stop. I just . . . I know what you mean, believe me. But right now I'm more worried about *him.*"

"I'm sorry. You're right." She paused. "Are you going to make your birthday dinner tonight?"

Dinner. Once again, I'd forgotten all about it. "Oh, I can't. I can't leave Stephen right now."

"Yeah." She paused. "On the other hand . . . do you want Kelly to know about all this?"

"No. It'll scare her way too much. She's already been scared enough with the little she does know."

"I agree. So maybe you *should* go to dinner."

"How can I? I'd be worried every minute about Stephen. And you'd be left there alone with him."

"Don't worry about me; I can handle myself. If anybody came to the house, I have my gun, and you know I'd use it. As for you, you'll go to dinner because you need to do it for Kelly. Erin too. Let's keep all this from them as much as possible. Which means on the surface, life is going to have to go on."

I could see her point. Still . . . "I don't know. I'd never be able to get ready in time."

"Yes, you could. You might have to move your reservations back a little, but Dave will do that for you. And we can just tell the girls it's because of your work. Which is true."

"But what will we say about Stephen's face? It speaks for itself, let me tell you."

"He got into a fight with friends. Period. Kelly knows his friends. That shouldn't surprise her all that much."

I'd run out of arguments but still wasn't sure I should go.

I turned onto Barrister Court. Stephen followed. My mind spun with all the have-to's and unknowns. "Jenna, we're home now. See you in a minute."

Leave it up to my sister. Once I stopped arguing, she just assumed she'd convinced me, and that was that. In the two minutes it took for us to walk into the kitchen, she had all the details figured out.

"Okay, Annie." She took my purse from me while Stephen slouched into a seat at the table. His eye and jaw were now swollen, the black-purple bruises eliciting a wince from her. "You go draw. Don't even stop to call Chetterling to tell him the drawing will be late; I'll do that. I'm also going to call Dave and ask him to move your reservations back until, what, seven thirty? When you're done with the drawing, I'll take it in—" she flicked a hard look at Stephen—"while your mom stays with *you*, since you apparently need so much babysitting." She turned back to me. "Tonight, you go out, and I'll stay with him. Stephen, you are going nowhere. In fact, I'll take those Blazer keys right now." She held out a waiting hand. I dropped the keys into her open palm.

Stephen muttered under his breath. "You don't need to tell me not to go anywhere; I'm not *stupid*."

Jenna made no reply. The look on her face said it all.

"And tomorrow—" she turned back to me, expression softening—"we will all three sit down and figure out what we're going to do. All right?"

I nodded. "But, Jenna, let *me* call Chetterling. I need to talk to him myself about my drawing deadline and . . . all this."

"Okay, fine. Go on now."

I turned to Stephen. "I'll take your cell phone again."

He handed it to me without protest.

In my office, I shut the door and leaned against it, pulling my random thoughts into some semblance of order. Even before I called Chetterling, I knew there was something else I needed to do.

Sinking into my desk chair, I lowered my face into my hands and prayed. I begged God to help me with Stephen, to give me wisdom and strength. "And please, Lord, turn him around, like You did for me. He's stubborn and awful, and sometimes I hate him, but You know how much I love him, God. You know how much good is in him, underneath all that anger and pride. Somehow, just see me through. I'm not good at this. Not at all."

Tears threatened, but I held them back. Maybe I would cry later. Maybe when I lay in bed, with this horrible day behind me, I could let go. But now, all I could do was pull myself together.

When I finished praying, I felt no better. Still, over the last year I'd been trying to trust God regardless of my feelings. As Dave once pointed out to me, God's truth remains truth no matter what. Would I really want to serve a God whose reliability depended upon how I felt any given day?

Before I phoned Chetterling, I faxed my drawing of Blake to the police station, attention Officer Nelson. On a second piece of paper I wrote my business and cell phone numbers, asking him to call me as soon as he'd seen the drawing. If I didn't hear from him soon, I'd be bugging him.

Then I dialed Chetterling's direct office line, wishing I didn't have to burden him with my problems, even as I hoped he could do something to help. But who knew if he would even be available right now?

Fortunately, he picked up the phone.

In a dulled tone I told him I was sorry to be so late with the drawing but would have it to him in a couple hours. Then I related the story about Stephen. "He seems so scared, Ralph, and for once I don't think he's trying to manipulate me. I really do think he'd be in more danger if he talked to police."

Chetterling took a moment before replying. "You're right to be concerned. If this involves some circle of drug dealers— and we've got them in Redding—they're not going to let it drop. It's not just the two thousand dollars at stake. These guys have a reputation to maintain in order to keep their people in line. They operate on intimidation. And word will get around the streets real quick about what they think Stephen's done. You'd be amazed at the networks these people have."

I rubbed my temple. Maybe if I pressed hard enough, I'd rub myself right out of this mess, a genie released from a prison bottle. "What should I do?"

"Think he'll talk to me?"

"No. He's scared to talk."

"We need to work on that. This thing's already too far gone. If the guys he's been running with, and this Blake guy, aren't taken off the streets, when will it be safe for Stephen again? For now . . . can you send him away for a while? Maybe he could go to his father's."

Oh, I could just imagine calling Vic. He'd been nothing but accusatory about Stephen's behavior over the past two years. How could I have let *his* son—whom, by the way, Vic had abandoned and hardly ever saw—become involved with drugs?

"Well, I can try. But I don't expect much help."

Ralph grunted. "Understood. Maybe send him to a friend's house or some—Wait, Annie, can you hold on a minute?"

I heard a sound like a hand covering the phone, muffled voices in the background.

"Okay, I'm back. Sorry, but I need to go. Let's talk about this later. For now, do what you're doing. Keep Stephen home, with no talking to friends. He'll get bored of that real quick. Maybe tomorrow he'll be ready to talk to me."

"Okay. Thank you, Ralph. And I'll . . . get that drawing to you soon."

I hung up the phone and stared across the room at my drawing table. *Send Stephen somewhere.* Yes, that was what I should do. It would buy us some time. But I doubted his father would take him.

The phone rang, making me jump. It was Officer Nelson. My heart lurched.

"Sorry to say I don't recognize this guy," he told me, "but I'll show it around to the other officers, see if somebody can tell me about him."

Well. Sounded like the young policeman had found a little heart. "Thank you," I said, meaning it this time. At least this was something.

And thank You for this much, God.

I reported to Jenna about the two conversations, then checked on Stephen. He was in his bedroom, rap music pounding. He did not want to talk. I started to urge him again, then remembered Chetterling's wisdom. Stephen was a teenager. Staying in his room with no one to talk to would soon become unbearable. No cell phone, and last year I'd taken his computer keyboard to keep him from online chatting. Plus I'd taken out the home phone extension in the rec room. He'd have to come upstairs to make a call.

Tomorrow, I told myself. *By tomorrow he'll be tired of this.*

I mounted the stairs and headed to my office to work.

For the next hour, through sheer willpower I forced myself to concentrate. Slowly, the drawing began to emerge. I had to admit it was a good thing I'd visited the crime scene. The photos of Jane Doe's hair as it had been styled would make a big difference in the final result.

Sometime around five, I heard Kelly and Erin returning. Kelly's room lies directly above my office. It wasn't long before their voices and music filtered down from the ceiling. I knew they were getting ready for dinner. Probably trying on a dozen outfits, deciding what to wear. Doing each other's hair. Putting on makeup.

I hoped Stephen had stayed in his bedroom, that the girls hadn't seen his beat-up face. Tomorrow would be soon enough to explain it.

At six thirty, the Jane Doe was ready. I'd also completed a close-up drawing of her earring. For a few minutes I could only stare at the woman's face. Trying to imagine who she was, what kind of person she'd been, pushing away the gruesome memories of the contorted features I'd first seen.

Lord, here she is. You know her. You died for this person. Please help us identify her.

At six forty, I climbed the stairs toward my bedroom. Jenna was already on her way toward Redding, drawings in hand. She'd be back by the time we had to leave.

I hit the upstairs landing and stood outside Kelly's door, trying to force happiness into my expression. I needed to stick my head in the room, see how the girls were doing. Show them how much I anticipated the dinner. Thirty minutes remained. In that time I'd need to shower, dress, and try to make myself look presentable.

Time to celebrate.

Chapter 15

I chose a sleeveless black silk dress with a V-neck collar. A simple pearl necklace I'd inherited from my mother. Thank goodness my brown shoulder-length hair could be blow dried and sleeked with little trouble. I reapplied my makeup, using extra eye shadow and mascara. Some lipstick and gloss, and I stood ready. When I descended the stairs at ten past seven— miraculously on time—the girls hovered in our great room, impatient. Erin glanced around at me and grinned.

"Wow, Annie, you look so pretty!"

"Thank you. So do both of you." I walked over to hug them. Erin's white-blonde hair and fair skin stood out against a pink blouse. She carried a small white purse. Kelly wore a cream-colored dress, stunning against her tanned face and long brown hair. And their light amount of makeup—how did girls that young learn to apply it so well these days?

"Come on, let's go." Kelly fairly rose up and down on her toes.

Jenna emerged from the basement stairs. She smiled at me. "You look great."

"Thanks. Stephen okay down there?" I kept my voice light.

"He's fine. Go on, now. See you in a few hours."

The girls hurried out the door, and I trailed behind them, turning to Jenna. "I'll have my cell phone on," I said in a low voice.

She nodded. "Can you believe he just asked me to give his phone back?"

I closed my eyes. Stephen was getting bored a little too quickly. He'd want to talk to other friends, people he thought he could trust. Didn't he understand that right now he couldn't trust anybody?

You'd be amazed at the networks these people have.

At the last moment, I almost wanted to call the dinner off. Stay home with my son. Jenna saw my expression and nudged me outside with firm hands. "Good-bye. Have a good time."

I heard her lock the door behind us.

Dave, ever the gentleman, was turning his car around in the cul de sac to pull up to our curb. Evidently a birthday girl shouldn't be required to cross the street. He got out to open my door for me. Wow. He looked so *good*. Even in my preoccupied state, I couldn't help but notice. I hadn't often seen him dressed up. Even at church the unspoken code tended toward casual. Now he stood before me in suit and tie, green eyes vivid against his tanned features. Dave had a pronounced jaw in a squared face, and a mouth that had so often appeared sad since Lisa died. But now he smiled at me with real warmth.

At that moment, the strangest, most unexpected thing happened. The sight of him hit me in the chest, as if all air had been pushed from my lungs. I smiled back, opening my mouth to say something, anything. Some natural, witty word to hide my sudden self-consciousness. And wouldn't you know, the girls noticed as we stood there and ogled each other. Out the corner of my eye I saw them exchange a look.

Dave took my hand. "You look beautiful."

"So do you. I mean . . ." I shook my head and slid into the car. *Real good, Annie.*

When we reached Redding, the streets looked so empty. I told myself it was only due to this being a Wednesday night. But no. The town lay under siege, and residents were understandably scared. Weekend business, even in this usually busy summer month, would be poor too. Even as the girls chattered in the backseat, that sobering knowledge sent my thoughts scurrying down dark tunnels. Who *was* the killer? Did he walk among us, look like anyone else during the day? Had we passed him even now, waiting to cross the street? And what about the people after Stephen? Had we seen them?

How many times had I walked past evil, maybe even brushed its shoulder, and not known?

A sudden shiver ran through me.

"Is this too cold on you?" Dave adjusted the blades of an air vent.

"No, no, I'm fine."

Dunnings' Restaurant is the finest in Redding. That I knew, although I'd had no previous occasion to go. Kelly sucked in a breath as we entered, gazing at the wood paneling on the ceiling and walls. "Ooh, this is nice."

Erin looked around, nodding with a muted satisfaction. "I was here once before. For Mom's last birthday."

The comment sliced through me. Dave gave me an awkward smile, but I looked away, not knowing what to say. That he'd brought his wife here, and had now chosen to bring me . . .

The maître d' ushered us to our table, his eyes lingering on my face. I'd noticed the expression among Redding citizens many times in the past year—the *where-have-I-seen-her-before?* puzzlement. Amid the nationwide media attention following the Bill Bland fugitive case, my picture had been splashed on newspapers and magazines across the country, not to mention the extended publicity here in the area.

Dave pulled out my chair, Kelly's and Erin's as well. My heart tugged at the gesture.

"Well, look who's here. Hello!" Our young waitress appeared before us, a smile on her pretty face.

"Karen! I didn't know you worked here." I smiled back at her, but cringed inside. Karen Fogerty and her parents attended our church. I didn't know her parents well, but Karen helped out with the girls' youth group. I knew the girls adored her. But what must she be thinking, seeing the four of us out to dinner? Would she assume something between me and Dave? Would she tell people at church, her family?

Annie, get a grip. If only this was the worst of your worries.

"Hey, Karen!" Kelly and Erin said almost in unison.

We chatted with Karen as she handed out menus, her warmth sparkling as much as the topaz ring on her little finger. Erin told her we were there for my birthday. *Thank you, Erin,* I wanted to say, *hope that explains it.*

"All right now, I'll leave you all to your celebration." Karen beamed at us all once more. If she thought anything about Dave and my having dinner together, she didn't let on. "I'll be back soon to take your orders."

Somehow as that dinner progressed, I managed to turn away the anxieties coursing through my mind. Dave and I coaxed the girls to talk about their friends—who was "going out" with whom and their summer vacation plans. Erin told lavish tales on her previous science teacher, Miss Beech, a rather free spirit who couldn't decide whether she wanted to be a blonde, brunette, or redhead. Which led Kelly to talk about her lab partner, a boy named Elvis, poor thing, who couldn't perform even the simplest of experiments without making a complete mess. When they'd cut up a frog, he'd fainted right over onto Kelly's lap.

Dave and I both laughed probably far more than we had in a long time. The laughter felt good, cleansing, like a fresh breeze sweeping through a long-shut room. I knew when the evening was over, as soon as I stepped back into my home, my fears and worries would return with a vengeance. But for a short time, with the glistening joy of our two beautiful girls, and the sparkle of Dave's eyes when he looked my way, a semblance of peace bubbled within me.

Karen served us dessert, smiling and bantering with the girls all the while. As she walked away, something in the air around our table shifted. Kelly and Erin exchanged looks, then glanced meaningfully at Dave. I could have sworn I saw him give the barest of nods to his daughter. I busied myself with pouring cream into my coffee, pretending not to notice. Erin bent down, perhaps to get something from her purse. She fiddled for a minute, then rose up in her seat. She appeared to hand something to Dave under the table.

A present. They were going to give me a present.

I caught Kelly's eye, and she raised her brows in anticipation. Whatever was happening, she was in on it.

"Annie." Dave brought a small, gold-foil wrapped box from his lap and held it out to me. "Erin and I wanted to get you something for your birthday. We wanted it to be something special, after all you've done for us these past two years. So we went looking together. Erin actually found this. And Kelly approved."

Wordlessly, I accepted the gift. All I'd done for them? Erin had been like my second daughter since Lisa died. I'd done nothing but love her as she deserved to be loved, tried in my own tiny way to make up for a loss that could never be mitigated. "This is really . . . unexpected. Thank you."

Kelly twirled a strand of hair around her finger. "Go ahead, Mom, open it."

I began working at the bow. "So you've seen this, huh, Kelly?"

"Oh, yeah."

Like three eagles, they watched me untie the ribbon, slide it away. Then stick a finger under one taped end of the box.

Erin sighed with impatience. "Annie, you don't have to save the paper."

"I know, I know."

The box soon rested in my hand, unwrapped. From its size, it had to be some piece of jewelry. I opened the top, and inside lay a small blue case. "Ooh, wow, velvet." Self-consciousness curled once more around my shoulders. I took out the case and carefully flipped back its top. Then let out a small gasp. Inside lay the most beautiful necklace I'd ever seen. A gold filigree basket with three small flowers, their petals an intricate array of sapphires and rubies, their leaves made of emeralds. The pendant hung on a serpentine gold chain.

I couldn't say a word. Could only stare at the necklace. My eyes would not rise from the sight. It shone and sparkled . . .

and was far too expensive. How would I begin to thank Dave for spending so much money? On *me*? How could I even accept it?

How could I not?

"It's . . ." I turned to Dave, feeling the sting of tears, embarrassed that he would see. "It's *beautiful*. I can't . . . I don't even know what to say."

"Just say thanks, Mom!"

Oh, Kelly. The insouciance of a fourteen-year-old.

Gently, I fingered the stones. "Erin, this is so lovely. You certainly have very good taste." I gave a little laugh. "Thank you so much, both of you. I never . . . I just wouldn't have expected something like this."

I lifted my eyes to Dave's again—and air backed up in my throat. I read something in those eyes, something I hadn't seen before. And I knew then. The truth stilled me, like wind-ruffled rushes suddenly at rest. This chosen, expensive gift was his way of expressing what he had not been able to say. Perhaps what he had not yet even fully admitted to himself.

He nodded. "Would you let me put it on you?"

"Yes. Absolutely."

I fumbled with the clasp of the pearl necklace I wore, my hands trembling. As I lay it on the table, Dave rose to stand behind me. I felt the warm brush of his fingers on the back of my neck as he swept my hair aside, fastened the necklace.

"There." He sat down again, leaning toward me. "Now let's see."

I turned to him, letting him look, then to the girls.

"It's so pretty," Erin and Kelly breathed.

"Even better on you than in the box." Dave smacked his palms with delight.

Erin couldn't stop smiling. "So you're going to wear it now, right?"

"Of course I'm going to wear it."

"I mean like all the time."

"Now, Erin," Dave chided, "don't put her on the spot."

"No, no, she's not putting me on the spot." I ran my fingers over the gold chain. "Really, I will wear it every day. Even though it's so expensive." I attempted a grin. "How do you think it will look with a T-shirt?"

"Great," Kelly pronounced.

Briefly, Dave laid a hand over mine. "It'll look stunning."

Later that night, when I undressed for bed, I took off the necklace and stared at it for a very long time. Jenna's reaction to the present still rang in my head. "Oh," she'd said. Just like that. "Oh." Then she'd looked at me in that Jenna way, lips pressed, one brow slightly raised, head nodding in sage prescience.

With great care I lay the pendant in its velvet box, then climbed into bed and drew up the covers, all energy spent. Yet sleep remained tauntingly elusive. I lay blinking up at the high-beamed ceiling, scenes and voices swirling in my head. Jane Doe lying on the cold slab, Stephen's bruised and swelling jaw. Chetterling's question, *"Can you send him somewhere?"* The shaking limbs of George and Diane. Officer Nelson's hardened expression at Stephen. Erin and Kelly's anticipation.

The look in Dave's eyes at dinner.

Two thousand dollars missing.

Six women dead.

Words and snatches of movement flowed, flowed through my brain, intermingling into one current, one stream.

Turning warm . . . washing over my limbs . . . pulling me down.

A final word from the day lingered as the waters of sleep tugged me under.

"*Oh.*"

Chapter 16

How silent you are.

Cars fill the church parking lot, the proof of your gathering. I might even dare step inside, watch, listen, if I could withstand the saccharine.

Pray, all you deceived ones, pray. And my work beckons. This one will be different from the last.

All are different, in their own way.

I drive the town. Up and down its streets, alert, watchful, a sentry on duty, a stealth soldier. I will judge. I will choose—

Look now, there. A familiar face. Out on the town, are we? What a portent, what a sign! Yes, I shall wait here.

The waiting takes patience.

Patience . . .

Patience . . .

Here now the one comes again. And goes. Here now I continue to wait.

Finally . . . ah.

Yes.

You wonder how I lure them. Do you not see they come to *me*? They are sent by the forces that would see them pay, see them fall as their souls have already fallen. She prances across the parking lot, slides into her car, skirt riding up her leg.

Shakes her hair, turning her head sideways before the flipped-down mirror to check her face, the veneer of her emptiness.

They are all the same.

Her window is down. The night is hot.

She starts the car.

I follow.

Now begins the game of mouse and cat. She turns through the streets, pulled by her dark desires, one hand on the wheel, fingers in her bronzed hair. Reaches the end of town and pulls out on a highway. Of course. Had I not known she was the one? She is headed north of town. I do not care where she goes.

My palms itch. It is always this way. And my heart beats the steady pulse of justice striding in robed finery. Later I will drink much water and cleanse myself of the woman's touch. Now I lack nothing but to watch as she dies.

She turns right, houses grouped in the distance.

Her time has come.

I roll down my window. Push the accelerator until I pass her, willing myself not to swivel and look. I drive until her lights begin to fade behind me, and then my car slows, slows, the wheel wobbling, road undulating beneath my tires. I swerve over the yellow line and swerve back, knowing she watches, reveling in the rhythm of our pas de deux. At last my car drags to a stop, midroad, and I lean back against the headrest, eyes closed, mouth open. Breathing. Listening.

Waiting.

Behind me, a car stops. A door clicks open. Footsteps approach, cautious and timid in this age of evil. Bracelets tinkle. An intake of air as she sees my cinched face, the clutch of hand to chest.

"Um, are you okay?"

"Something . . . my heart, it's never been right. Need my pills. I live just ahead in those houses. Can you help?"

"Yes, sure. I live up that way anyway."

I stumble out onto pavement, moaning, mumbling. In a feigned moment of alertness I tell her to pull her car well off the road, where it won't be hit. I will bring her back to it as soon as the pills are taken. I slump against the car as she complies, her stupidity as fatal as her sins. Finished, she helps me into my own passenger seat. She slides behind the wheel and drives.

Ah, no, but I will be sick! Pull over, pull over, please, and allow me my purging. She halts our chariot and hurries around the front to open my door, the princess become the servant. I reach under the seat, extract my magic wand. The door opens. She holds out her hand, her bare arm tanned and pulsing under the nascent moon.

I jab home the needle.

Her eyes round, mouth forming a silent O. I shove from the car, wrap her in my arms, and push her inside. Shock renders her witless, pliable. I jog around to the driver's seat, and off we go. Toward eternity. We turn from the road, into a dusty lane, down, down. I flick off the headlights, pull her from the car and to the ground, dirt and pebbles her final feel of earth.

She tries to get away, flee her fate. I hold her down, tell her it is too late; the Grim Reaper has come riding, riding, and his sickle has struck, and she will fall as his harvest.

Besides, I whisper, running will only pump death through her veins all the faster.

In time, the countdown minutes reach zero.

By the light of the moon, I watch her dance.

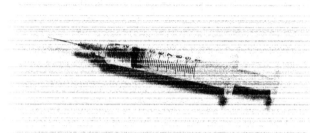

Thursday, June 23

Chapter 17

My Jane Doe drawing appeared in the morning paper, large and in color. I knew the sketch had also been faxed to Bay Area papers and would appear on TV news as well.

Lord, help us find out who she is.

The accompanying news article mentioned that the regularly scheduled Redding City Council meeting would be held that night at seven o'clock. Members of the task force would be there to answer citizens' questions about the case. I knew the move was designed to calm people, let them know law enforcement was doing all it could. But something in my gut told me the meeting would be anything but calm.

I could not get moving. I hung around the kitchen, drinking coffee, spinning my wheels, worrying. My mind clashed with thoughts, like strains of music from battling radios. Worries about Stephen . . . fear and anger over the serial killings . . . memories of last night, of Dave, my present . . .

"I see you've got your necklace on." Jenna leaned against the counter, the sun highlighting her hair. She held a mug of coffee, perching one bare foot on top of the other. Not a stitch of makeup covered her flawless, lightly tanned skin. And as always, that aura hung about her—the one of efficiency, the *I'm-in-control-no-matter-what* attitude that firmed her cheeks and mouth and posture.

Good grief, just look at her. Everything a man could want. Why is Dave interested in me?

My fingers automatically sought the necklace.

"Annie, don't put your fingers on the stones, that just gets 'em dirty."

I took my hand away, then gave her a look. "I swear. Is there *one* thing you won't boss me about?"

She drew her head back, seeming to ponder my question. "I guess I do that a lot, huh."

I made a little snort.

"Okay, okay, I do." She gazed out the window, eyes focusing on the distance. "Guess that's why I can't keep a man. They all think I'm too . . . I don't know, capable or something."

"*You* can't keep a man? You've dated more men than I can count."

She tilted her head. "That's just what I mean."

What was this? A vulnerable side of Jenna, having to do with *men*? "Well . . . I didn't think you wanted to settle down. You've always liked your independence."

"True."

"So then?"

She raised her shoulders and looked me straight in the face. "So sometimes it gets old, you know? Even if I don't really believe in marriage, sometimes the thought of someone steady sure seems nice. But as you well know, most men aren't steady. Look at our parents, how Dad ran around on Mom all the time. Look at Vic and what he did to you." She glared at the floor. "Most men are just jerks."

Click, whir. The projector in my head spun out pictures of Dave and Lisa when we'd first met them. How happy they were. The difference in their lives was one I'd come to know personally. They'd placed Christ in the center of all they did.

I blinked. How about that. Somehow, somewhere along the past year, my attitude of marriage had evidently changed. Annie Kingston, bruised and bewildered by a childhood of watching her unhappy parents, then by faithless husband Vic, now saw hope in the God-ordained institution. Who would have thought?

Now here I sat, my life, my purpose, reawakened like some phoenix rising from the ashes. But whenever I'd talked about my faith to my sister, she rejected the notion. And she needed God's help in her life. As we all do.

Jenna set her coffee mug on the counter and folded her arms. "Speaking of jerks, what are we going to do with Stephen?"

I rubbed a hand over my eyes. "I have to call Vic, that's what we're going to do."

"Now there's a happy way to start the day." Jenna tipped back her head, surveying the ceiling.

I drank my coffee in silence, half hoping she'd try to talk me out of it.

She heaved a sigh. "Well. Might as well get it over with."

My head nodded. Everything within me dreaded phoning my ex-husband. Still, everything within me hoped, *ached*, for his help. The serial killings were enough to deal with. But now all this trouble with Stephen ... And there was something else, something I hardly wanted to admit to myself. Imagine this house, our lives, with Stephen gone for the summer. I could hardly picture the freedom—days, weeks, expanding like long asthmatic lungs suddenly cleared. I wouldn't have to worry about my son's safety. Wouldn't have to constantly protect myself against his withering attitude, the blister of his scorn. Kelly could relax. Maybe have old friends over once again.

Please, God.

As I rose to get the phone, my mind treated me to a happy little scene. Vic's voice in a warm thrum over the line: *Sure, I'll take our son for the summer, of course I'll help. Haven't you done more than your share of raising him?*

I blinked the fairy tale away, sank back into my chair, and punched the hated number. Jenna watched me, one hand curled into a fist and resting under her chin. First ring. Okay, maybe if not for the summer, Vic would at least agree to taking Stephen for a few weeks. Surely he wouldn't let his son stay here under these circumstances.

The second ring cut off abruptly. "Vic Kingston."

His voice did it to me every time. I felt the glacial surge of something inside me ripping away, like crusted snow hurtling down a mountain. "Hi, Vic, it's Annie."

"Oh, hi. Look, I'm about ready to go into a meeting, can we talk later?"

Vic was always headed for a meeting. "Then I'll be quick."

In about sixty seconds I summed it up: Blake Smith, Stephen's bruised face. Oh, and by the way, our local serial killer's sixth victory found not far from our house. Not that the two had anything to do with each other—except wear our nerves to a thin frazzle.

At the last piece of information, Vic made an impatient sound in his throat. "Annie, why do you always get yourself into these situations? I told you, you should never have started that forensic art stuff."

I clamped down my teeth and said nothing.

"Look." Shuffling sounds filtered over the line, papers, files, being moved around. "I don't care what Stephen says, the best thing you can do is go to the police. Let them handle this. What does Stephen expect to do, hide in your house the rest of his life?"

"What he needs to do is get out of here, Vic. Just for now. Until we can sort this out, and maybe get him to give us some names. The police can't do anything until Stephen talks."

"So make him talk."

"It's not that simple. He's scared to death, and with good reason. When he does talk, he shouldn't be *here*. He should be gone, somewhere safe."

A frozen beat of silence. "Are you trying to tell me you want him to come *here*?"

"The thought occurred to me, yes. After all, you *are* his father."

"You don't have to remind me who I am. But that—Yes!" Vague noises followed, a hand over the phone, two male voices. A moment later the sounds cleared, Vic's words still distant. "Tell him I'll be there in a minute." A light thud. "Okay, I'm back. But I need to get to this meeting."

My fingers gripped the receiver, the sharpness of his tone snipping all threads of hope.

"Bottom line, Annie, you're going to have to deal with this. I can't take Stephen now. The kids can come for their week in August, like we've planned. But right now Sheryl and I are working, so what would he do here anyway but get into trouble?"

"He's already *in* trouble, Vic. Here."

"That's just my point."

"Yeah, well, he needs to get out of it. At least in Texas he doesn't know anybody."

"So what do you want him to do, sit around my house and watch TV all day?"

"It beats getting killed here!" From the corner of my eye, I saw Jenna make a face. I turned away, unable to watch her disgust, my own anger roiling like brew in a cauldron. "Besides, there's no reason why he couldn't get a job there. Summer's just started."

"Annie, no."

"Why, Vic? Don't you *care* what's happening to your son?"

"He's your son too, remember. You *are* his mother."

The cauldron boiled over, searing my chest, my limbs. My throat cinched so tight that for a moment, no words would come. "Please, this one time. We really need your help."

A huff, as if I'd asked the world of him. "You know I'd love to help, but really I can't. There's enough going on at our house right now, and Stephen would be just more than we could handle."

Oh, really? Were they worried about a serial killer there too? "What could possibly be going on that would make rescuing your son such an impossible task?"

The minute I'd blurted the question, I wanted it back. Somewhere in the depths of me, I knew the answer would not be pretty. Chalk it up to my decade of drawing faces in a courtroom. To the memory of my defense attorney father. I knew the one mantra of a lawyer in court: never ask a question you don't know the answer to.

"Annie, this is not the time."

"Oh, yes it is." What was I, some kind of masochist? Why couldn't I just let this go?

"I have to get to my meeting."

"What are you so afraid of, Vic?" For moral support, I looked over my shoulder at Jenna. She wrinkled her nose and punched the air. "I'm three states away and obviously have lost all ability to make you feel guilty years ago."

Oh, good. Now he'd bang down the phone for sure.

"All right, Annie, you want it? I'll tell you. Sheryl's three months pregnant and sick as a dog. She can hardly go to work. She'd never be able to handle Stephen."

The words fizzled through me, a hot iron slapped against skin. I felt my mouth drop open, the dampness of my fingers as they pressed the phone. Sheryl, pregnant. The woman who didn't want a thing to do with my kids. Vic, a father-to-be, again. Spawning some other child when he couldn't lift a finger to help the two he already had, the two who needed him so badly.

And Stephen, with all his self-destructive defiance. Wasn't it founded upon the betrayal from his father in the first place?

I breathed into the receiver, hearing the air moan over the line. My only solace, small indeed, was the pause on the other end. Apparently even Vic could entertain a modicum of shame.

"That meeting—gotta go now, Annie."

I stared at the wood grain of the table, for some reason caught by the unevenness of its lines, the mottle in its color. All wood looked like that—a metaphor for events in this world. Random in pattern, predictable unpredictability.

"Go *now*, Vic? You went years ago."

I clicked off our connection and slowly laid down the phone.

"What happened, what'd he say?" Jenna pushed herself to the table, fingers wrapping around the back of a chair.

I gazed at my sister for one frozen beat. "Sheryl's pregnant."

Her chin jerked, red creeping up the sides of her face. She flexed her jaw, then uttered a few choice words. I remained motionless, all emotional energy dissipated, while she set about the kitchen like a madwoman. Flinging open the dishwasher, clean plates clattering in her hand, throwing silverware in the drawer. She even kicked a cabinet. How I wished I could do that. What had happened to my own rage? Better a bonfire, however consuming, than the meltwater that puddled in my heart.

The phone rang. I stared at it for a disbelieving moment before picking it up. Surely Vic wasn't calling back.

The ID display read "private caller." Great, someone with a blocked number. Maybe some reporter. Should I ignore it? My finger hesitated over the *talk* button, then pushed. "Hello."

Jenna slowed, a couple of glasses held midair, watching me.

"Hi, I was wondering . . . would this be Annie Kingston?"

A female voice, too hesitant to be a reporter. "Yes."

"You don't know me. I'm Naomi, Jeff Waite's mom. He's a friend of Stephen's."

I raised my eyebrows at Jenna. We knew Jeff Waite, all right. The guy Stephen had been arrested with over a year ago. Jeff had faced a felony for the amount of marijuana he had stashed in his car, and further charges for driving under the influence.

"Hi, Naomi. I'm . . . sorry we haven't met."

She took a quick breath. "I feel kind of funny calling you but, you know, this raising kids stuff isn't easy. Anyway I wanted you to know that I heard about what happened to Stephen yesterday. And then Jeff, who usually doesn't talk to me, told me something I thought you should hear. Maybe he's told Stephen already, I don't know . . ."

What now, God? I can't deal with one more thing. Jenna pulled out the chair next to me and sank into it, studying my face.

"I haven't heard anything, Naomi. Please go ahead."

"Okay. Last night Jeff got a phone call from someone he and Stephen both know. Jeff wouldn't tell me the guy's name. But the guy wanted to know where Stephen was. Said Stephen's not answering his cell phone, and he didn't return to work yesterday afternoon. Jeff just said he didn't know. Then the guy pressured him, saying there's a five-hundred-dollar reward to anybody who'll tell how they can 'get to Stephen.'"

For the second time in minutes, I held the phone in shock. This time I didn't feel the flame of rage or the iciness of fear. This time I felt . . . nothing. A deadness. As if my heart had been flayed and vacuumed. When I spoke my voice sounded unnaturally light. "Thank you for the information. I'm grateful. Something I needed to know."

"You're welcome. And I'm really sorry. I hope Stephen will be okay."

"He'll be fine." The words sounded so distant. Had they come from my mouth? "We'll all be fine."

I pressed the *off* button and held the phone out to Jenna, as if her acceptance of it could somehow take from me the reality of what I'd just heard. In hollow tones I related the conversation. When I finished, we both sat staring at the table. My finger made little circular tracings against the wood. At some point, Jenna pushed back her chair to put away more dishes, her actions rote.

A door clicked. I raised my eyes to see Stephen shuffle out of the stairway into the great room. He wore a pair of black cotton pajama bottoms with his chest bare, his usually spiked hair matted from sleep. The bruises on his face had worsened. Our eyes met, and he frowned from me to his aunt's rigid back.

"What's going on?"

Jenna swung around, silverware clenched in both hands. "I'm flying you out of here today, that's what's going on."

I glanced at Jenna's flushed face, only half surprised.

Stephen's mouth opened, his eyes narrowing. "To where?"

"To the Bay Area, that's where. To my town house. Where I will babysit you, and you will sit and do *nothing* until you give us the name of every single person who's after you."

Stephen screwed up his face. "Man, what got into *you*?"

Jenna pointed a handful of forks and knives at him. "*Don't* get me started. *Don't even.* Just go pack your clothes."

My son shifted his eyes to me. We stared at each other, unspoken words sloshing between us like water over rocks.

He knows.

I could read my son. Stephen clearly wanted to fight against being spirited away from his friends, his job. Independence was his middle name, rebellion his knee-jerk reaction. But his lack of argument, the hunch of his shoulders, shouted to the heavens. Somehow last night, despite my admonitions, he'd probably managed a phone call to Jeff.

Stephen now knew he was in too much trouble to fight Jenna. All he could do was accept our protection.

Protection that his father would not give.

Without another word, Stephen turned, bare feet squeaking against the wood floor, and shuffled back toward the stairs.

Chapter 18

At nine forty-five, I dragged into my office and shut the door against my family, against life. More than anything, I needed to read the Bible and pray.

I was hardly an expert on the subject of devotions. I knew that as a Christian, I should take time every day to spend with God. Knew that this time strengthened me, prepared me for the challenges that lay ahead. Talking to God I'd found easy enough. It was the listening part that gave me trouble. How do you listen to the Almighty? To someone whose voice is not audible?

Yet there had been times when I felt I'd heard Him. Through an impression, a sense deep within me that I should do something, maybe pray for someone.

That morning, I experienced something altogether new.

The time began normally enough. I'd been reading through the New Testament, and was currently in the book of Ephesians. I began chapter six—the part about children obeying their parents—with a markedly less than reverent attitude. What a chapter to find myself in. As if God couldn't wait to remind me of what my household lacked. But then I read verse twelve: "For our struggle is not against flesh and blood, but against the rulers, against the authorities, against the powers of this dark world and against the spiritual forces of evil in the heavenly realms."

Those words punched air from my lungs.

I raised my eyes from the Bible and sat very still, feeling that tingle at the back of my neck. Immediately an oppression flowed into the room, a Dread with a capital *D*, as if deadly fog had seeped through the windows to hover above me. My nerves pinged and electricity buzzed through my limbs. Goose bumps popped down my arms. I absolutely could not move.

What *was* this?

Pray.

The command burst through my brain, a white firework against midnight. It sounded from a voice I had never heard, yet I knew it. Compelling, all-consuming, above every authority, yet somehow quietly spoken. Soul-shaking without effort.

I bowed my head, squeezed my eyes shut. Never did it occur to me to question the voice, to question my own sanity. The word screamed in my ear could not have jolted me more. Prayers came of their own accord, tumbling from my mouth. Pleas for my safety, the town's safety, pleas for God and His angels to act, to overcome, to fight against the powers of this dark world that had settled over us all. The more I prayed, the more vulnerable I felt, as if some wicked being paused its ethereal pursuits to twist toward the earth, turn demon eyes on me.

Time suspended itself as I huddled in my chair, pleading, pleading.

Then, slowly, the oppression eased. Still I prayed. The dark fog broke up . . . turned to mist . . . vapored away . . .

My eyes opened. I found myself staring at the same Bible verse, Ephesians 6:12. I'd never read that verse before, still wasn't sure of its entire meaning. Yet on a deeper level, I understood the message completely. I'd *experienced* it.

But why?

Instant fear seized me, the terror of having stared evil in the face and survived . . . and knowing it could come again. *Would* come again. "God, what?" I asked out loud. "Why me?" My eyes flicked about the office as if I would find a heavenly answer written upon its walls. "And it's not done yet, is it? I know, I *feel* it. When is this going to end?"

At that demand, I heard nothing. Still, I grasped His answer. I had to keep praying. All of God's people in the area had to keep praying. We were in a fight against a cunning, murderous person, yes. But he was led by forces far greater than his own sickened soul, forces that writhed and gnashed their teeth in glee over his acts. In answer to our continued petitions, God would trample that evil.

Good grief, wouldn't Gerri be proud of me. I was beginning to sound like a preacher.

Minutes ticked by. Jenna and Stephen would be flying out soon. I needed to pull myself together, see them off . . .

By the time I left the office, a new resolve—and a deeper sense of dread—wove complex patterns in my soul.

# # # #

Jenna and Stephen were ready to leave at eleven thirty.

I stood in our cul de sac, sun beating down on my head. The Cessna was pulled out of our hangar and loaded, Jenna's preflight check done. Stephen turned to climb into the plane, but I caught him by the shoulders.

"Not without a hug, you don't." The words came out pinched and worn. I put my arms around my son and drew him close. "Please do some thinking while you're gone. As soon as you're willing to give names, maybe your life can start again. I love you."

"Love you too."

His response sounded automatic. But at least he'd said the words.

My heart clutching, I stood back as Jenna fired up the engine, then watched them taxi down Barrister Court. A left, then a right, and they'd reach the private Grove Landing runway. The plane turned off our street. Loneliness swooped over me, a bird of prey sinking claws into my shoulders. I slumped, drooping beneath the beat of its wings.

Do you believe your own words to Stephen, Annie?

Who could say how true they were? If Stephen did give names, if the guys were arrested, if he testified against some top drug dealer in exchange for immunity . . . how safe would he be during that long, arduous process? And afterward, how safe then? What if this just didn't end?

God, I need You in this situation. Please do something. Give us wisdom. And open Stephen's heart to You.

With a sigh, I dragged myself back toward the hangar to close the door. But as I reached the threshold, a vague sound made me turn toward Dave's house. He was coming down the steps. Kelly and Erin were already together in his home. With Jenna gone, he'd agreed to keep Kelly for the day while I attended my meetings.

I watched him cross the street and draw near, his brows knit, tongue seeking his lower lip.

"Hey." He pulled up before me, studying my face. "Are you all right?"

One thing about Dave. No, about me. Regardless of the warmth he'd shown me on many occasions, regardless even of last night, I still couldn't help but keep my chin up in his presence. Why should I deserve his empathy for my problems, when they paled next to his? His wife had been *murdered*. In their own *home*.

"I'm fine."

"Annie. You don't look fine."

Déjà vu. Where did I have this conversation before?

Tears pricked my eyes. I swallowed and looked away at nothing. Folded my arms, hugging myself in the heat of the day.

"Annie." Dave laid a hand upon my shoulder. "You don't have to be strong all the time, you know."

Strong? Me? I nearly laughed. "When this is all over, I'm probably going to have myself a very good cry. Problem is, it never seems to be over. You know Stephen's one of the reasons I moved here in the first place, to get him away from his friends in the Bay Area. At first all he wanted to do was go back there. Now he's dragging his heels to leave here, because he's got this whole new set of friends. All, apparently, in the drug business." I slid my hands to my hips, staring without seeing at the forest beyond our street.

"I know." Dave's voice sounded gentle. "And I feel so bad for you. I wish I could just make it all disappear. I do want to help in any way I can. And you know I'm praying for you and for Stephen."

I shook my head. "You already are doing a lot. You keep Kelly every time I need you to. Thank goodness you work at home. Speaking of which, I'm probably taking you from work . . ."

He gave me a wan smile. "Can't think of anyone I'd rather have keep me from work."

We gazed at each other, a current rising between us. The sensation swirled around me. I searched for something to say and found myself absently fingering my necklace. I slid my hand away, feeling a flush in my cheeks. No doubt from the sun.

Man, were my emotions running high this morning.

I can't remember who spoke first. I think he did, saying something about how he'd better get back to work, his words with a forced casualness but rough at the edges. And I said, "Me too." Then blathered on about that afternoon's meeting with the task force, and the city council meeting that night, all of which he already knew, because that's why he was keeping Kelly in the first place.

Finally, we said our good-byes and I turned to go, thinking I'd already made a fool enough of myself. But something pulled me back.

"Wait, Dave? I need to tell you two things."

"Okay."

"First, I really have to thank you again for this necklace. It's just beautiful, and I still don't think I deserve it."

His eyes fell to the pendant, then back to my face. "You're welcome."

"And second . . ." I took a breath. What if he thought I'd really flipped out? "A strange thing happened while I was praying this morning. And I just wondered if anything like it has ever happened to you." Briefly, I told him, stumbling for words to describe the indescribable.

"Wow." He shifted his weight, taking time to form a response. "I haven't had anything that overpowering happen, but I understand it. I believe it was real. And I know others who've had similar experiences."

"What does it mean? No, wait, that's not the right question. What I mean is, you know how new I am as a Christian. So I'm wondering why this happened to me? Someone like you or Gerri could handle it so much better."

He shrugged. "Sounds like you handled it just fine."

"Yes, but I hardly knew what to pray."

"You said God helped you. *He* told you what to say."

"Yes, but . . . that was Him, not me."

Dave gave me a look mixing tenderness and amusement. *Oh, brother, Annie, how dumb can you be?* I bit my lip.

"Annie, God specifically chose *you* to pray like that. And He may be choosing others in this area to do the same. When He leads His people to pray, it's for a divine reason. He wants to bring them closer to Him, teach them the power of prayer like they've not yet known. Think about it—it's not like He *needs* our prayers to give Him strength. But He *uses* our prayers to give *us* strength. And we all need more strength in our relationship with Him, no matter how long we've been a Christian."

I nodded, focusing on the street. A stray pebble lay by my foot, and I pushed at it with the toe of my sandal. "Okay. I guess I understand that. Thanks."

He pulled in a long breath. "Well. I really should get back to work now. Call me this afternoon? Tell me how your meeting goes?"

"Yes, sure."

I entered our heat-infested hangar and punched the button to shut the automatic door. My footsteps echoed as I crossed to the garage. I passed Stephen's car, the vehicle looking forlorn and abandoned. The sight made my eyes water.

Wonderful, soothing air-conditioning greeted me as I stepped into the kitchen. And in the next second, the ring of the phone.

I checked the ID display. It was Chetterling. "Hi, Ralph."

"Hi." Poor man sounded even more tired than yesterday. Probably hadn't been to bed all night. "You coming to our meeting today?"

"Yes."

"Glad to hear it. Some things you'll want to know ahead of time. First, we got an ID on Jane Doe, thanks to your drawing. Her father came in a little while ago. 'Course we'll confirm with dental records, but you know how it is. He knows his own daughter."

I flinched, the news both relieving and terrible. "Who is she?"

"Her name's Celeste Weggin, from Sacramento. Twenty-three years old, lived by herself in an apartment. She was driving to see a friend in Oregon. Her parents didn't even realize she hadn't gotten there. We're still looking for her car."

Celeste. Something about naming a victim, even when I'd seen the body, made the murder all that more real, more personal. Celeste.

"Thanks for telling me, Ralph."

He grunted. "Now the bad news. Another woman is missing, reported by a couple of housemates. This one's only nineteen years old. Her car was found off Lake Boulevard, just south of the town of Shasta Lake. Close to where she lived."

My heart turned over at his clipped, flat words. I pulled out a kitchen chair and sank into it. Then the realization hit me. Last night? While so many people in Redding were *praying?*

"Annie, you there?"

"Yes."

"One more thing I need to warn you about. I think you might know this girl."

Chapter 19

Such lovely treasures.

You draw me.

You repulse me.

I look at you each in turn ... and remember the last moments of the one to whom you belonged. You, creamy-colored square of beaded blouse. I first saw you peeking from beneath her jacket; she, leaning over to inspect her flattened tire. Her gladness for help, a kind word. Her willingness to eat, drink, partake of the fare I carried.

The ghostly flailing inside me was new then. Sooted feathers brushing my soul. Blissfully stilled—for a time—by the sight of her tortuous death. And by the cutting away of you, my first treasure.

And you, blonde hair, now bound with a rubber band. What was the name of she who bleached and fluffed and sprayed you? She, with the stomach-chilling reminders of my own mother in younger days?

Here, you, my mother commanded, *fasten this necklace upon me, these bracelets around my arm. Help me get ready. The others are coming. Ah, they are here, child! Run, answer the door, lead them to me.*

No, Mama, I don't want to let them in, please ...

Next you, sinfully painted nail. Red, the color of blood. Red, the color of *her* lipstick, smeared upon the glass that the child must wash. And you, black-hardened piece of bone and flesh, sporting your crystal ring. Here, yet another, you glitter earring—

Wait. What is this agitation inside me?

No, go away, just let me look. Let me gaze and remember and stroke. Here is my latest from last night. I pick it up, hold it in my hand, trace its sky color with a fingertip.

She danced well for me, this one, she danced while they prayed . . .

What is it? What? This disturbing vibrancy playing my bones.

I set down my new treasure. Scrunch tight my eyes.

A blister forms within me, pushing, pushing against my ribs. It rises. Bulges . . .

Breaks.

I smack the dresser. Here I fondle my new treasure, and still they don't know! When will they find my latest? What are they waiting for? They are fools!

I should have helped them, as I did last time.

Do some still dare pray? Hoping for safe return? This cannot be. I will not stand for it! They must be shown; they must see the truth.

Yes, the truth. They will soon know. By my own hand, I will guide them.

Chapter 20

How indifferent and bleak the sunny afternoon seemed as I drove into Redding. Hot sun and endless blue sky while my thoughts stumbled and sweated through a labyrinthine tunnel. Some moments, all I could do was pray. In others, I found no more words to say to God. He knew all our crushing needs, yet He seemed to do nothing.

Karen Fogerty was missing. Karen, with her golden hair and bright smile. A young Christian with her whole life ahead of her. A caring person, someone who would never do others harm. Karen, who was so alive and happy just last night, when she'd served us at the restaurant. Was she dead now too?

Just . . . please, God, no. Not this one. Not this time.

I couldn't imagine what her parents were going through right now. The mere fraction of a thought about my own daughter disappearing froze the blood in my veins. I prayed for Karen's parents as much as for her own safety. Then, selfishly, my thoughts turned to Stephen, my own lost child. And to Kelly, who did not yet know about Karen. The news would devastate her. She'd been through enough in the last few days. I'd called Dave and told him, but we agreed to keep the information from the girls for now, hoping . . . praying . . . that Karen would be found alive and well.

Even as I drove to the task force meeting, search teams—both of law enforcement members and volunteers—were combing the woods around Redding, looking for Karen's body, hoping not to discover it. Hope, always hope. Chetterling almost postponed the meeting to enable task force members to help in the search and in making phone calls, running down information on who last saw Karen. I'd told Chetterling about seeing her at Dunnings', what time we'd left. She punched out of work only a half hour later, and never made it home to her two roommates.

A half hour.

I pulled into the parking lot at the Sheriff's Office a few minutes before three o'clock. The moment I stepped inside the building I felt a heaviness in the air. An aura of dogged determination and wearied responsibility. I could hardly summon a smile, not even for the deputies and workers I'd come to know so well, nor could they for me. We nodded to each other, solemn, silent.

Ruby Mays lingered in the lobby, talking to Beverly Whiting, the petite receptionist. Ruby stood almost six feet tall, a large-boned woman in perhaps her midsixties with unruly gray hair, a hooked nose, and bulging brown eyes. I exchanged greetings with the two women.

"Wow, Annie, what a gorgeous necklace." Beverly stared at my pendant. "I've never seen you wear that before."

Did I feel a flush in my cheeks? "It's new. I just got it for my birthday."

"Aah." She lifted her chin, giving me a knowing look. "A man?"

Okay, no denying the flush now. "Yes. No. Sort of."

The two women exchanged a look. Beverly raised a shoulder. "My, I'd say she's a little confused, wouldn't you, Ruby?"

"Guess so."

Oh, great. I should never have worn the thing. What if Chetterling said something, what would I say?

On the other hand, why did I care?

Beverly held out a sturdy large paper plate of oatmeal cookies to me. "Annie, you want to take these in to the meeting? Ruby just brought them by for her 'troops.'"

"I'll do that. Thank you, Ruby." I accepted the plate. "Can't tell you how far a kindness like this goes right now."

"Well, it's the least I can do." She sucked in her cheeks, giving her face a gaunt look. "I was sorry to read in the paper that they found a body near your house. I can't imagine what that feels like. It's awful enough for me to be miles away—"

The door opened and Ed Trumble entered, one of the detectives on the Poison Killer task force. Trumble was a wiry man with a trim mustache under a pug nose and the dark, beady eyes of a bird.

"Yes, I know what you mean, Ruby. Thanks." I glanced at Trumble, who gave me a nod. "I'd better go. The meeting's about to start."

"Go get him, Annie, and all the rest of you." Beverly shook her head at me. "We all just want this to be over."

"Yes." Ruby looked me in the eye, brows knit. "*Please* get him. Soon. Some days it feels like I can't take much more of this. I know I'm an old woman compared to the victims he's chosen. Still, you never know. I live by myself out in the country, north of town. I probably check my doors and windows ten times every night. And I won't go out after dark any more."

Her intensity unnerved me because it matched my own. "I don't doubt it. I'm sorry you're scared. We . . . everybody is." I tried to give her a reassuring smile, but it came out lopsided. "I know they're doing all they can."

She looked at the floor and nodded.

Carrying the cookies, I walked away from the two women, their anxiety flowing with my own. All over Redding, it was the same. Women of all ages afraid, their men afraid for them. With each step toward the meeting, I couldn't help extrapolating the numbers.

One person, God, just one person, and look what he's done to so many.

By the time I entered the room and placed Ruby's cookies in the center of the long table, I felt almost tremulous. My leg muscles fluttered, as if preparing me for some desperate dash in a race against time.

Chapter 21

Tension built as task force members arrived. No one needed to mention Karen Fogerty's disappearance for us all to know that we thought of her, pled silently for her return. I watched hands reach for the cookies, but they were eaten distractedly while grim-faced people took their seats.

Chetterling pulled out a chair at the head of the long table, lowering himself into it with a hefty sigh. On his right sat Ed Trumble, and on his left, Nathan Hallibander, also with the Sheriff's Department. Other homicide detectives and forensic investigators from both the Sheriff's and police departments were present, the two branches of law enforcement working in tandem. And Harry Fleck, the medical examiner. An attractive Hispanic woman I didn't recognize sat opposite me, dressed in a blue suit and carrying a small briefcase. Chairs squeaked and file folders flopped against wood as everyone settled themselves. Looking at them all, I wondered if I should have attended.

"Okay, let's get started." Chetterling ran a meaty hand down his face, then blinked a few times. "First, as I've already mentioned to most of you, I've asked Annie Kingston, our forensic artist, to join us, both because of her work on the case and due to the location of the most recent victim. That is, we *hope* the most recent victim." He paused. "Also, I'd like to introduce Rosalee Sanchez to you all." He indicated the Hispanic woman. "Rosalee is a criminal profiler, based in Sacramento, who's been generous enough to offer her help on this case. We've given her access to all the files and we'll hear her first report today."

Rosalee smiled briefly and glanced around the table.

Glad you're here, Rosalee. We were the only women in the room.

"Okay." Chetterling's bleary eyes landed on my necklace, paused, then blinked away. "We're going to go through everything we've got so far. Some of this will be repeated information in hopes that we see something we've missed before, and we'll also hear updates." He looked to the medical examiner. "Harry, I'd like to start with your findings on victim number six, Celeste Weggin."

Harry opened a manila envelope and withdrew a set of eight-by-ten photos to pass around the table. "These were taken at the crime scene. I include these as well as photos at autopsy because of the lingering contraction of the muscles at time of discovery. The crime-scene shots, folks, show the horror of these deaths."

To his left, police investigator Rod Haimes began shuffling through the pictures. At the first one, his jaw set, and a steeliness came over his face. I knew these men had seen a lot of things, but most had seen nothing like this.

Harry related details about the identification of Celeste and her autopsy, then compared them to those of the other victims. Some of the information, I already knew. Much of it, I didn't. I picked up a pen to take notes.

Celeste was twenty-three. All victims' ages ranged between twenty and twenty-six. If Karen Fogerty turned out to be victim number seven (I shuddered at the thought), she would bring the lowest age to nineteen.

The victims were all single and white, except for Alicia Mays, number four, an African American. No social connections could be found between any of the women. They all lived in the Redding area except Celeste, who lived not far to the south, near Red Bluff. They worked in different places, had different circles of friends. None were known to attend any church. Four of the six had a string of ex-boyfriends, while two had not dated as much. Investigations of all the men connected to the various victims had not led to a suspect.

Trace evidence from the crime scenes remained minimal. A few brown fibers had been found on two of the victims, fibers which the lab had determined to be from carpet in an automobile.

The killer took a trophy from each of the women. This information had not been given to the media. Although Harry didn't emphasize it, I and everyone else in the room knew that withheld points of information would be important when a possible suspect was questioned. The detectives would look to trip the man up, see if he mentioned one of these points he wasn't supposed to know. Withheld information could also help weed out false confessors to the crimes.

Harry continued his report. All victims had been killed by a lethal dose of strychnine. "Which, as you remember, doesn't take much." Harry turned back some pages in his notes. "Lethal dose for adults ranges from thirty to one hundred twenty milligrams. Subcutaneously administered, however, the dose can be much smaller.

"The first five of our victims appeared to have taken some strychnine by mouth, then were injected with more. The last victim, Celeste, appears only to have been injected. We found the needle entrance area on her right upper arm. Symptoms usually begin after about fifteen to thirty minutes, or can take up to an hour, depending upon the amount of food in the victim's stomach. As we've discussed before, these symptoms are very dramatic."

Harry glanced down the table toward the criminal profiler. "Rosalee has asked me to go over again in layman's terms what death from strychnine looks like. This method of choice for death, and the time and symptoms it entails, has become an important factor in her assessment of the perpetrator, as she will soon explain."

Even before Harry could begin, my personal projector hummed on, churning out vivid pictures of Celeste's twisted face, her body. I stared at the tip of my pen against paper, steeling myself against the medical descriptions to come, *willing* myself to remain clinical, focused.

"Okay." Harry tapped the empty manila folder lying before him. "Strychnine affects the central nervous system by interfering with the level of glycine, a chemical that inhibits motor neuron action. Beginning symptoms can start with a general restlessness, apprehension, and a hypersensitivity to stimuli. Sounds are louder, lights are brighter, any touch is enormously felt.

"The next stage is generalized violent convulsions, although sometimes a victim skips the initial symptoms and goes straight to this stage. Any little stimulus sets off a convulsion, which lasts from one to two minutes, and is very painful because of the strong muscle cramping. The body arches backwards, hyperextending itself. Facial muscles contract, twisting the mouth open and widening the eyes.

Between the convulsions, muscles relax, and the victim can even fall asleep from sheer exhaustion. Then, *bam*, another convulsion hits ten to fifteen minutes later. In the midst of this, the eyes protrude, pupils dilate, the throat dries. Dehydration can set in pretty fast.

"Also between convulsions, there's cold perspiration. Since, of course, our victims were untreated, they could have gone through this cycle up to ten times, with each convulsion lasting longer than the last, and less time in between. A lot," Harry locked eyes with me, "like the muscle spasms in labor. Each coming harder, faster, less rest in between. Only at the end of this event . . . death."

Harry ran a hand across his jaw. "Not the way any of us would want even our worst enemies to go."

Silence spread a chilled blanket over the table. I glanced around to see everyone's focus downward, their foreheads zigzagged and mouths askew in private imaginings of the victims' last hours on earth.

"This whole process," Harry's voice dropped, "takes one to three hours. Eventually the victim dies from asphyxia. The muscles are so worn out and the convulsions so violent, the lungs fail to work. Of course, we're talking about fatal doses here. There's certainly good prognosis for survival if the victim receives prompt medical attention, which focuses on keeping the convulsions to a minimum, both through administration of drugs and through providing a quiet, stimulus-free environment. Even with a fatal dose, if the patient is treated and lives from around six to twelve hours, chances of survival are good."

Harry pressed a palm against the table and straightened his back. "If only we could get to them fast enough."

If only. I kept my eyes on my notes, biting the inside of my lip. Was there any chance, any possible chance on this earth, that we could find Karen before it was too late? Before the killer gave her a fatal dose and sat back to watch her die?

The projector in my head switched on, spinning out a scene of

Karen, her mouth pulled open like Celeste's, eyes protruding, back arching. The killer hulks above her watching, screaming, knowing the noise shoots right through Karen, causing her to convulse all the more . . .

I clamped my teeth together, squeezed my eyes closed, willing, willing the horrible scene out of my head. *God, take away these thoughts; I can't stand them!*

Someone called my name, but it seemed distant. Not until I heard it a second time did the meaning register. My eyes opened. I looked up to see everyone at the table watching me.

"You all right?" Chetterling peered at me with concern.

Embarrassment flushed through me. "Yes. Sorry. I'm . . ." I felt a sick expression flutter across my face. "It's just that Karen Fogerty . . . I know her."

Nods and empathetic murmurs filtered around the table. Rosalee pressed her palms together and squeezed, almost as though to say she would be squeezing my hands if we weren't separated by space and the constraints of a professional meeting. I managed a wan smile. "Please, go ahead. I'm sorry."

Harry cleared his throat. "I'm done anyway."

"All right, thanks, Harry." Chetterling gestured toward Tim Blanche, a homicide detective with the Redding Police Department. "You ready to tell us about obtaining strychnine?"

"Ready."

Tim Blanche was the father of three boys, one of whom went to high school with Stephen. I didn't like the man very much. He had an arrogance that gave itself away through slightly raised brows over penetrating blue eyes, and an Elvis-like curl to one side of his mouth. Tim was middle-aged, with thick salt-and-pepper hair, and a large mole on his left cheek. He moved with the concise quickness of a soldier following drills.

Tim read through his notes in a clipped tone of self-confidence. If he'd reached only dead ends so far, let it be known, his demeanor said, that it was through no fault of his investigations.

Strychnine, he reminded the task force, is a white, odorless, bitter crystal-like powder made from the plant *Strychnos*, found mostly in South Asian countries such as India, Sri Lanka, and in Australia. Current use was mostly as a pesticide, but as a controlled substance in the United States, strychnine could only be purchased by certified buyers.

Tim tapped a pen against the table. "I wish I could tell you more than last time as far as finding a suspect who has the stuff. We've gone through every business in the northern half of the state that's remotely connected to any industry that might use strychnine. We've of course checked all certified buyers. Every one has been ruled out as a suspect. But then again, we're not talking about that many people. And none of them says any supply is missing. The other avenue we're continuing to check is local travelers who've visited countries that may use strychnine more liberally. Tourist groups going to Australia, for example, or India." He pushed back in his chair, tossing down his pen. "I'll tell you, we just

. . . we keep trying, but so far it feels like we're spinning our wheels."

The pictures of Celeste came to me. I passed them on, averting my eyes. I'd seen all I needed to see in person. Still, just resting in my hands, the photos burned.

Oh, God, don't let this fate happen to Karen. Please.

A sudden thought gripped me. My prayers in the morning—had God called me to pray like that *because* of Karen? Because one of His own had now been taken?

Tim Blanche's voice faded as I stared at my notes. Remembering my desperate prayers, that stomach-clenching sense of evil. I could almost feel it again now, like a cold hand settling at the base of my neck. Clammy palm, fingers squeezing, their hint of a force so great, so powerful, that any more pressure could snap my spine like a twig.

Again, my mental projector kicked out imagined scenes.

Gerri Carson, eyes closed and palms pressed together, mouthing silent prayers . . .

a poison-dripping needle piercing skin . . .

groups of faceless people praying, in a church, in their homes . . .

maniacal laughter echoing across a darkened stage . . .

I blinked, wrenching myself back to the present. *Get a grip, Annie, you want to bring this meeting to a halt a second time?*

Tim finished his report, and Chetterling called on Rosalee. She pushed aside one spiral notebook and placed another on top of it, giving a general nod to the task force members. I glued a stare upon her face, forced my ears to listen.

"I'd like to tell you my most recent thoughts after studying the information on Celeste Weggin." Rosalee paged through the spiral notebook. "But first let's start with some general information, which some of you probably know, but it bears repeating."

I glanced at Tim Blanche and found him staring at my necklace. His eyes raised, locked with mine for a split second, then glanced away.

Rosalee rested her forearm on the table. "Okay, what we know in general about serial killers. They are typically males who have problems relating to others. He may have been a victim of abuse in the past, either physical, emotional, or sexual. Or a combination. Could have been neglected or abandoned by his parents. He often—but not always—has a record of other offenses. He can look 'not normal' to others, but here's the sobering part—many times he looks completely normal, completely forgettable. Or maybe even charming. Think Ted Bundy. Good looks and charm, to boot. Or think the Green River killer—family man, well liked, polite. Everything you'd want in a neighbor.

"Often the killer hates women for one reason or another. I'd say we certainly have that factor going here. He may be a loner, feeling like he doesn't fit in. He often holds others to a high moral code while totally unable to see that *he's* breaking the code in the worst way. For whatever skewed reason, he views himself above judgment."

The photos returned to Harry Fleck. Rosalee glanced at him as he slid them in the manila envelope.

"Now, as Detective Chetterling said, I've looked at the photos from all the crime scenes and studied the files. I'll admit my science is not an exact one, but I have seen things that lead me to particular suspicions about this killer. The first is the method of the deaths, which, as you know, is unusual. Other than the administering of strychnine, let's remember that we see few marks on the bodies. We have seen some bruising on the arms, which leads me to think that some of these victims were held down until the strychnine took effect. But no sexual assault, no stab wounds or beatings. In other words, none of the better-known signs of uncontrolled rage. And yet, as we heard from Harry, death by strychnine is a horrible death, and one that doesn't happen in just a couple of minutes.

"As awful as it is to imagine this death," Rosalee glanced at me, empathy in her eyes, "I wanted you to hear it, because this chosen method is very important. Think about it—the perpetrator has to *wait* for this death. Has to stand back and watch it happen in a slow, torturous process. A process I believe this killer enjoys witnessing. This tells me the perpetrator *does* feel tremendous rage toward his victims and wants to see them suffer. I believe he is a true misogynist. And I would guess that his hatred of women stems from hatred toward his mother. These killings, in fact, may be symbolic killings of his own mother, which would explain the lack of sexual assault."

Ed Trumble looked up from his notes. "Do you think he knows the victims?"

"No, I don't, and I'll get to that in a minute. First I should say that I think we're looking for a male at least in his thirties, very possibly in his forties or beyond. For two reasons. One—my sense that these deaths are killings of judgment. Such judgment would build in a person who's lived awhile, as opposed to some twenty-year-old out on a rampage. Two—because of the way death is administered. There's a patience that's required for these types of deaths, however twisted that patience may be.

"I also believe we're dealing with someone who's fairly well educated. At least a couple years of college. And someone who lives or works in this area, probably the west side of Redding. Someone who's comfortable here. Someone who absolutely believes in his ability to remain unchallenged. The fact that he leaves his victims where they can be found tells me that he doesn't expect to be tied to these crimes.

"Now—" Rosalee rested an elbow on the table, bringing two fingers to her chin—"It appears this killer manages to lure his victims into a false sense of safety, at least for a short time. I say this because postmortems show that most of the victims ingested strychnine before receiving an injection. Somehow, he got them to trust him enough to ingest the poison. How I don't know, because it's very bitter. This point, along with the fact that the perpetrator has been so cunning, leads to the possibility—and I emphasize that's all it is—that he is a member of law enforcement."

A collective groan rattled among us. Chetterling leaned his head back and stared at the ceiling.

Rosalee held up a hand. "As I said, it's just a possibility. But it rests on a point we know to be true. As more women are killed, citizens in this area are understandably more frightened, and should be more cautious. Yet somehow this perpetrator continues to lure his victims. So we need to be looking for someone who's able to do that.

"Now the flip side, if we're not talking about a member of law enforcement. Perpetrators often insert themselves into the investigation of the crime." She looked to Chetterling. "I know you've had quite a few volunteers looking for various bodies. In fact, they're combing the woods right now, searching for the latest missing woman."

"Right."

"I would urge you to look very carefully at those people. Anyone who's volunteered for every search. Some face that keeps showing up."

Tim Blanche and Ed Trumble exchanged a long look, Trumble spreading his fingers as if to say *don't know*. Blanche made a note. "We'll look into it."

Rosalee nodded. "I know tonight you expect many citizens at your city council meeting. Take a good look at all who come. I'll be watching too. Because it's possible our perpetrator will be there."

That brush once more against my neck, the touch as unnerving as fingernails on a blackboard. I would attend that meeting, listening, watching. Would the killer be there? Gleaning and calculating? He could be leaning against the wall of the packed room, arms crossed, silent, unnoticeable. He could be seated right down front. Maybe he'd ask a question. Or even accuse the Sheriff's Department of not doing enough to find the killer.

Rosalee told us she did not think the killer knew his victims. I jotted her reasons in my notes. One, the lack of signs that pointed to rage at the familiar, such as beating or the overkill of multiple stab wounds. Two, the positions in which the victims were found. Each had been unceremoniously dumped, with no arranging of the body or covering of the face, which are known manifestations of remorse.

This perpetrator seemed to *want* his victims found, the profiler noted. He'd left them in wooded areas, but never far from a path. With each body, the perpetrator seemed to be saying, "Here's one more of my pronounced judgments against women."

The criminal profiler sat back in her seat. "One final thing. It appears this suspect may be increasing his activity. If this missing woman is found to be murdered in the same manner, that would make two victims just a few days apart. This is not uncommon. The strikes of serial killers over time can become more frequent, perhaps more frenzied. They can begin to get cocky, as if they're playing a fatal chess game with the law, daring someone to catch them in a checkmate. I would not be surprised if this perpetrator began reaching out to you through letters or perhaps notes left on the victims."

Rosalee raised her eyebrows at me. "Annie, I agree with Detective Chetterling that the placement of the last victim near your house was intentional."

Fear pressure-sprayed through me. I raised my pen from my notes and watched Rosalee's face.

"I visited that crime scene earlier this afternoon," she said. "The quickest way to access it is to park at the cul de sac at the end of Barrister Court and go through the woods near the side of your house and down into the back. As you know, your house is clearly visible from the crime scene. I think this location was a taunt, a way to say, 'See how close I got to one of your own.'"

"Why me?" I forced my voice to remain steady.

Empathy clicked across Rosalee's face. She shook her head. "My guess? Partly due to logistics. You live near a forest, which seems to be this killer's area of choice. But also, I think, because you're a woman."

"And," Ed Trumble leaned forward to look at me down the table, "you've had a high profile in this area due to past cases. Unfortunately, thanks to that publicity, your house can be located, even though you're no longer listed in the phone book. And it's *your* drawings that have helped identify some of these victims. It's almost like this killer is telling you personally, 'Okay, here's another one.'"

My eyes sought Chetterling's. His mouth firmed, and he gave a slight nod. As if to say, *I know, Annie. I know. I'll be watching out for you.*

Other reports followed, task force members going in turn around the table. After that came a general discussion, ideas tossed around, men assigned to look into certain details. Many times I noticed Chetterling checking his watch, his eyes wandering toward the door, as if he expected an interruption at any moment.

I knew what that interruption would be. The finding of Karen Fogerty's body.

Though no more was said about me, for the rest of that meeting I felt singled out, as if a ghostly spotlight had turned its bleary focus upon my form. I kept my head down, listening, taking notes, not wanting to make eye contact with anyone. When we were finally finished, my watch read almost five o'clock, a mere two hours before the city council meeting began. Not much time to rest once I got home. I needed to check in with the girls. And with Jenna. I hoped Stephen hadn't driven her crazy yet.

"Annie." Chetterling stopped me in the hallway before I could scurry off. "What's going on with your son?"

What was he, a mind reader? I told him about sending Stephen to the Bay Area.

He shifted his notebook from one huge hand to the other. "You did the right thing, getting him out of here. Besides, if anybody can get something out of him, it's that sister of yours."

We exchanged a brief smile. Chetterling knew all too well about Jenna's high-spiritedness. She'd even let *him* have it a couple of times.

He tilted his head in a gesture of apology. "Afraid I haven't been able to do much with that drawing you gave me. Just shown it to a few people. So far nobody knows the guy."

"Ralph, thank you. That's okay. It's not like you don't have anything else to do."

He dragged in a long breath. "Yeah." His eyes fell to my necklace. "Birthday present?"

"Uh-huh." My pen nearly slid from my hand, and I busied myself with sticking it in the sheath of my leather binder.

"Pretty." He shoved his lower lip upward, puckering his chin.

"Thank you."

Fortunately, he said nothing more.

For the fifteen minutes it took to drive home, I did my best to empty my cluttered mind. To not think about the meeting. Not dwell on the suspicion that the last victim's location near my own backyard had been intentional. Not think about Karen Fogerty. Or Stephen. Or Dave. I turned on the radio. Found an oldies station. I hummed along.

I turned down the radio and prayed.

As I neared Grove Landing, my cell phone rang. Ed Trumble was on the line.

"Annie, more bad news. We've found another body. And it's not Karen Fogerty. You'd better come out to the scene for this one."

Chapter 22

God, is this ever going to end?

I pulled into the house long enough to fetch my camera. New, fervent prayers chain-linked through my head as I drove back toward Redding, through town, and west on Placer Road. The Poison Killer had continued to spread his tentacles, this victim in a thicket of oak and manzanita near Powerline Road, not far from town limits. Numerous houses were built on Powerline, but they were spaced apart. The body lay for a number of days before being discovered by a man following the suspicious smell.

Decomposition was well under way. The odor slithered and kinked through my intestines. I raked in a breath, balanced on trembling legs, held my camera with trembling hands, and set about to work. The quivering birthed at my very core. And with it grew an anger I've never known—a righteous, finger-curling indignation that made me want to shout at God to *do something!* To *stop* this death and tragedy.

Missing from the body: a thick strand of her black hair, cut close to the roots, and a glitter-studded white sandal.

I aimed my lens at the victim's ravaged face only to see a blur. Lowering the camera, I wiped at my eyes, then tried again. This time, I did not even care if other professionals saw me cry.

Voices, actions, sights, and sounds blended around me. Yellow crime-scene tape rattling in a sudden breeze. Chetterling, Jim Cisneros, Matt Stanish, and others checking the body, taking notes. The stench that sent juices seeping down the back of my throat.

About halfway through my task, I became aware of a word whispering over and over through my head. *Jesus. Jesus. Jesus . . . Jesus . . . Jesus . . .*

Another prayer sent by God? Or merely my own plea that I, that we all, could take no more?

Six forty. I drove away, sickened, tormented, and sweating. If the victim was not quickly identified, the following morning I would have to visit the morgue—again—to take more photos after she'd been cleaned up. Everything within me recoiled at the thought of entering that room one more time. And no doubt this would be the most difficult drawing of the entire case. I'd never before had to reassemble the features of someone who'd been dead this long. Just thinking about the task overwhelmed me.

I cut back through town, intent only on heading home. The city council meeting would be starting, but after what I'd just been through, I no longer had the energy to attend. The atmosphere at that meeting would be charged with fear, exactly what I didn't need. Yet before I realized it I found myself pulling into the parking lot of the city government building.

The room was packed. I slipped into the crowd standing by the back wall, nerves already tingling. Council members could barely contain order. People shouted out questions, comments, accusations. Why weren't the Sheriff's Department and police doing more? How did they expect citizens to feel safe? What was this rumor about another victim? Or was that two more—wasn't someone else missing?

A man standing on my left wrote furiously on a notepad. No doubt a reporter. He glanced at me, then did a double take. "Annie Kingston?"

He looked about my age. Intense brown eyes, deep set. Square-faced, with thin, straight lips. Salt-and-pepper hair. I'd never seen him before. "Hi." I looked back toward the front, hoping to deter any further conversation. I never liked talking to reporters. Someone on the second row launched a question, catching the reporter's attention. His pen scratched paper once more.

I thought I spotted the back of Ruby's head; she was seated in the third row. And Beverly beside her. I searched the faces of people standing along the walls to my right, seeing many I recognized. Gerri Carson stood halfway down, but she didn't see me. Her usually open, warm countenance seemed guarded, worn. She clasped her hands at her waist, moving them slightly up and down as if emphasizing spoken words. I knew she was silently praying.

Frank Nelson, the young officer who'd questioned Stephen yesterday, lounged against the wall not far from Gerri, out of uniform. I felt my face harden. Yes, he'd promised to show my drawing of Blake to other officers, but I wondered if he'd kept his word. He'd been so quick to judge yesterday. To dismiss Stephen to the heartless lessons of the streets.

Rosalee Sanchez had positioned herself near the right front of the room. Her eyes roamed over the crowd as she took notes. The sight of that folder in her hand, the moving pen, made me uneasy, even though I'd known she would be there.

Was the killer here, among us? Someone with two lives. Someone no one would guess until he removed his mask.

"Where are the detectives who are working on the case?" a man down front demanded. "They're supposed to be here to answer our questions."

One of the council members explained that they were "needed elsewhere at the moment" but would soon be on their way. This only sparked more angry comments, more accusations.

The electrified atmosphere was understandable . . . and yet not. It felt as though the entire roomful of people were being manipulated, puppets on strings pulled by malevolent hands. At the thought, that sense of blackness lowered itself upon me once more. Immediate prayer against the oppression rose within me. I asked God for an end to all this—*soon*. For a calming right now, in that room. And I asked His help for Chetterling, whenever he managed to arrive.

I knew the detective would come as quickly as he could. Even with a new crime scene to process, he understood the importance of his attendance here. Citizens needed to see his face, hear his words of quiet efficiency. Chetterling had the kind of presence that comforted people, made them believe they were in good hands, even in such a difficult situation.

The mayor, David Greenbaum, a balding, stocky man in his fifties, spoke into the microphone. "While we're waiting, I have an announcement you'll be happy to hear. One of our most helpful citizens, Ryan Burns, has offered $50,000 of his own money as a reward for anyone who leads authorities to the Poison Killer. Ryan—"

Applause and shouts of approval erupted. Greenbaum waited until they died down. "Ryan's a humble guy and doesn't like the spotlight. He didn't want to make this announcement himself. But he is here tonight, and I'd like to point him out to you." He stretched out his arm toward the crowd. "Please stand up and let the folks see who you are."

Heads craned, mine as well. I'd never seen Ryan Burns, although I'd heard much about him. Not yet thirty years old, he was quite the legend. Five years ago, thanks to winning millions in the California state lottery, he'd shot from a clerk at a photocopy business to the wealthiest citizen in Redding. His legendary status was further fueled by his shying from the public, even as he donated generously to the police and Sheriff's departments, and to local schools.

At the end of the second row, Ryan Burns pushed to his feet. He looked to be average height and pudgy, clad in jeans and a black T-shirt. He turned momentarily and half-waved a white, flabby arm. I caught only a quick look at his nonde-script rounded face and brown hair before he resumed his seat.

As applause swelled again, then diminished, I saw Chet-terling walk in the door.

He made his way down front and stood behind a micro-phone, ready to field questions. Feet apart, hands low on his hips, he pointed to one person's raised hand at a time, sum-moning order without having to demand it. As people were recognized, they could come down front to another micro-phone and state their names and questions.

Charlie Durst, the host from Dunnings' Restaurant, was first, wanting to know the latest information on Karen Fogerty. Jeff Strang, the wiry, angular-jawed owner of a Shell gas station, was next. He asked how easy strychnine was to buy. Should people be watching out for who might own some? Jamie Irvine, a round-faced young mother carrying a baby, wondered if plainclothes detectives were watching the streets at night. Grocery store clerk Frank Delaney demanded details about the body just discovered.

Chetterling answered what he could, refusing to give certain pieces of information because of the ongoing investigation.

From the corner of my eye, I caught the reporter writing faster than ever. I slumped against the wall, watching, listening, flitting glances around the room, hating the suspicions that grew like poison ivy within me at the sight of each new person who spoke. My feet hurt, and my back. The beginning of that day seemed light-years ago.

Well before the meeting was over, I'd had enough. I maneuvered around bodies and out the door, longing to breathe fresh air. Not ten steps from the door, I heard my name called.

The reporter.

Oh, great.

I slowed, fighting with myself for a split second. I wanted to ignore him, keep walking. But reporters tend not to be easily ignored.

"Yes?" I brushed my tone with impatience.

"Luke Bremington, crime reporter from the *Record Searchlight*. I'd like to ask you a few questions."

Our local paper. "Oh. What happened to Adam?" Adam Bendershil and I had butted heads last year—and I'd pledged never to talk to him again.

Bremington waved a hand. "He's still around, but I got this assignment tonight, and I wondered what credence you give to the belief that Celeste Weggin's body was left near your backyard on purpose."

I blinked at his run-on. He'd not even taken a breath between thoughts. "On purpose? I don't know what you mean." I turned on my heel and started walking toward my car. He followed.

"Come on, Ms. Kingston, you know there's been talk that the killer left the body there, knowing you'd find it. To taunt the Sheriff's Department."

"I don't know anything about that."

"Well, now that you've heard, do you agree with it?"

I focused straight ahead. "How should I know what the killer's thinking?"

"What do you think about the prayer meeting held last night at Covenant Chapel?"

Huh? In spite of myself, my footsteps slowed. Why would he ask me that?

Bremington jumped at his chance. "You know Covenant Chapel held a prayer meeting to pray that the killer be found, right? You attend church yourself. Do you think prayer's going to matter in this situation?"

I halted, tipped my head back to look at the heavens. Surely this was some kind of setup. Since when did reporters ask about someone's personal beliefs?

But what was I supposed to do—deny my faith?

I turned toward Bremington. His eyes bored through me, a hawk watching a field mouse. "Of all the questions you could ask me, you focus on this. I'm curious why."

He regarded me for a moment. "You are a Christian, aren't you?"

I couldn't imagine how he would know that, except through assumption, since somehow he knew I attended church. "Yes."

"I'm writing a feature article for the Sunday paper about how various kinds of people in town are dealing with this crisis. I covered the prayer meeting last night as one aspect of the story. I just thought I'd ask your opinion on the prayer issue."

Oh. And exactly what would he say about the prayer meeting? Would he be evenhanded? Cynical? Would all those who prayed be held up to subtle ridicule?

What does it matter, Annie? You afraid to speak what you know just because someone might make fun of you? I swallowed at that. No. I would not be afraid. "I see. Well, yes. I think prayer works."

"Have you been praying for this killer to be found?"

Why was he pursuing this? If only my conscience would allow me to just walk away. I shrugged. "Hasn't everybody?"

Well, that was probably true. Dire circumstances could turn even hard-lined agnostics to prayer.

He frowned. "But the way they prayed last night. Like I said, I was there. People prayed with this . . . power. Like they were wielding a sword in some fight to the death."

I licked my lips, my tired brain rummaging for a response. Part of me still did not trust this reporter, not at all. But another part whispered that he may be a man seeking truth, and who was I to withhold it?

"Mr. Bremington. Prayer *is* a sword. And in this evil world, we *are* in a fight to the death. Now if you'll excuse me, it's been a long day."

With a nod that I hoped wasn't so curt it spoiled my testimony, I turned toward my car.

# # # #

On the way home I called Jenna on my cell phone, aching just to hear her voice. As much as I didn't want to talk about the day, I ended up relating all of its events. By the time I finished, my throat throbbed. I emitted a hard little laugh.

"So. Jenna. How was *your* day?"

She sighed. "Annie, I'm so sorry. I don't . . . man, I don't even know what to say. Forget my day; it was a cakewalk compared to yours."

"Has Stephen told you anything yet?"

"No. And frankly, I've stopped asking. I'm just going to let him cool his heels, get good and bored."

"Yeah. Okay." Even if he'd told her some spine-wrenching piece of information, did I really want to hear it right now?

I took the phone from my ear long enough to wipe a stray hair from my face. My body longed for bed, and my heart longed for comfort as it had not done since Vic left me.

"Annie?"

"Huh."

"I don't want to think about you at the house tonight all by yourself."

I sighed. "Yeah, well, can't be helped. I've got work to do. I can't do the drawing until I take final pictures at the morgue tomorrow, but I can at least download tonight's photos into the computer, print 'em out, and begin to think about the victim's features."

"You know good and well you're not going to do any of that tonight. You can hardly think straight."

"Then curvy will have to do."

"Annie. Listen to me. I *don't* want you sleeping in the house alone."

Dully, I gauged a bend in the road. With every minute that passed, weariness wrapped its blanket more tightly around me. "Sure, fine, Jenna. And just who would you like me to sleep with?"

"Hah, very funny. Just go sleep in Dave's guest room. Kelly's over there anyway. I'll bet he won't want you alone in our house either."

Dave's house. With Kelly and Erin. That sounded so . . . good. No work, not tonight. Not with energy seeping from me like water from a cracked pitcher. I'd do it tomorrow. After I had all the photos. There was always tomorrow . . .

"Okay. Whatever you say."

Jenna hesitated. "Wow, you're not even fighting me. You *are* tired."

You don't know the half of it.

I pulled into the garage and climbed out of the car. When I opened the kitchen door, the high whine of our burglar alarm screeched through the air. I nearly jumped out of my shoes. I dragged myself over and punched in our code to turn it off, then plunked my camera and notebook on the table.

Upstairs in my bedroom, I gathered what I would need for the night.

Crossing the street, my footsteps slapped against empty pavement as if I were the last person on earth. I rang the Willits' bell, the warmth of its chimes beckoning me. Dave opened the door.

His face broke into a smile. "Well, h—" His lips flattened, eyes searching my sagging face. "What's happened?"

I lifted my tote bag a few inches, a spent, wayfaring beggar. "Jenna said I'm supposed to sleep in your guest room."

"Oh. Okay. Absolutely." Without further question, he reached to pull me inside.

Chapter 23

They found you, black-haired one. Finally. Aren't they the quick-witted people.

And still they search for my most recent.

There is always tomorrow, with its new pleasures.

I hold your sparkle-sandal in my hand, watching it glitter under a soft-hued lamp. The sandal that adorned your foot, the foot that weaved your steps across the line of immorality. You didn't sense I watched, did you. Oh, yes, when you met that man on a darkened road and thought I would not see, would not know.

But though they've discovered you, there is no rejoicing for me. They are as blind as ever, cave dwellers groping through tunnels of their narrow existence. Those who sold sex still sell it. Those who consumed drugs still totter and roar.

Those who prayed still pray.

And all the women beautify, beautify, adorning their bodies, jingle-jangle, while their souls remain silent and bleak, ice-swept landscapes devoid of sun. Oh, yes, I saw many of them, even today.

I stroke your hair, black and silky, sheened despite the dross of your empty life. I took this from you, as I took from the others.

And I will take more.

The wretched story from yesterday's newspaper is burned. I held it flaming between my fingers until I could hold it no more, then watched it crinkle and turn to ash in my sink, black on white. They *bragged* about their intent to pray? Called for people to join them? For churches to gather, God's people to unite against the oppression, the darkness, the evil that launches my hand?

As if I did not spawn my actions myself!

You who prayed last night, are you sorry now, cowed, beaten? You who awoke on this new and delicious day to another disappearance, another mystery?

She prayed too. Do not doubt it. My mother lit candles and danced with the men and women at midnight. She prayed to the Hindu gods and to Buddha and Allah. Anything, anything to cleanse the char of her soul that would not be cleansed. *Dance, dance, child*, her raucous voice raised my heavy eyelids, *for soon you will be grown.*

Please, Mama, no. I don't want to dance. I don't want to be like them . . .

Already the energy rises inside me. Unfolds its wings, brushing, teasing my ribs. Soon it will increase its flapping. Then the shrieking will begin, the clawing, throwing itself against my chest, tearing holes, bigger, bigger, until it bursts from me with pulsing hunger.

I lay your hair on the dresser, smooth it with a finger. Stare at myself in the mirror, stare, stare into my own eyes, looking into my soul.

I see the tremble of black wings.

Friday, June 24

Chapter 24

Another day, another drawing.

Dave had not let me leave his house without eating a bacon and cheese omelet, complete with a side of toast. He'd made the concoction with the proficiency of a breakfast chef, even flipping the omelet in the pan. If he was trying to impress me, he succeeded.

So much for wanting to lose a few pounds, I thought as I sat across from him at the table. It was just past eight o'clock. The girls were still in bed. I'd been sure to wear my necklace again. Dave's gaze fell upon it briefly, and he smiled.

"I'll just keep Kelly here, all right?" He filled my coffee cup. "I know you'll have to be out today. I think you should sleep here again tonight too."

Tonight. I hadn't given it a single thought. At that moment, getting through the day provided enough challenge.

"Maybe. I'll see, okay? Thank you for asking."

"Sure. I'd really feel better if you came back. That's a big house to be in all alone."

And we both knew how unsafe a house could be. Even a locked one with an alarm.

The morning newspaper sat on the corner of the table, its headlines now turned facedown. Another body found last night. And Karen Fogerty, missing. Her picture had smiled at us from the page, so full of life and joy, as we'd seen her just two nights ago. The article included quotes from relatives and friends of what a wonderful person Karen "is," how much she "loves" others and "is loved" herself. I felt grateful for the present-tense verbs and could only pray they still held true. Her mother, the article said, remained in seclusion, awaiting word from the search teams. Chaplain Gerri Carson was in close contact with the mother. Karen's father, desperate to do something, chose to aid in the search.

Dave and I both read the story, feeling its sucking pull. I knew Dave couldn't help but think of Lisa's death as he mulled over it. I knew he prayed, as I did, that Karen would be found safe. Now as we ate, neither of us wanted to further discuss the article or her disappearance.

The brazen practicality of life. Amid tragedy, the living have to find ways to go on.

I was scheduled to be in the morgue at eleven. By nine thirty I sat in my office, doing what work I could in the meantime. The grandfather clock ticked loudly from the great room as I downloaded last night's photos into my computer. I printed them out, looking away as the machine vomited forth its gruesome colors.

Everything within me wanted to get up and walk away. Leave the office. Do something—*anything*—else. I just didn't think I could handle the detritus of one more killing. They were coming so quickly now, as if each new day could not dawn pure and right, was destined to contain only tragedy and pain.

Quickly, then, the cognition descended upon me. The sense that I should pray. Immediately. As the whir and spit of the printer ceased, I felt an overwhelming desire to slide from my chair, get down on my knees—

The phone rang.

I glared at it. When was the last time a phone call had brought good news? Leaning over my desk, I checked the caller ID. Gerri Carson, at her office number. Of all people to call just then. *Thank You, God.* I picked up the receiver. "Hi, Gerri."

Her voice flowed over the line, a calming stream. She was just checking on me, she said, after all that had happened. A little tug inside her—no doubt from God—had urged her to call.

"I'm so glad you did. And how are *you?* I read in the paper that you've been spending a lot of time with the Fogertys. It must be so difficult, being with them, seeing their pain."

"You're not kidding. I was with Martha a lot yesterday. Jim was out with the search team all day. And when I called over there this morning, Martha told me he'd already left for another round."

I just could not imagine what they were going through. "How's Martha doing?"

"Holding up, some moments better than others. She has a strong faith. Still, you know, it's hard. One minute she's praying and the next she's crying. Sometimes she's doing both."

Sounded achingly familiar. I went through the same cycles over Stephen. And my problems with him paled in comparison to this.

"So tell me how you're doing," Gerri urged.

"Oh, okay. Well, actually . . . it's really good you called right now."

I told her about the emotions I'd been experiencing when the phone rang. How I'd felt something similar the previous morning, and how I'd prayed. I told her of my sense of oppression, the darkness, the prayers tumbling from my mouth whose words even now, only twenty-four hours later, I could barely recall. Instead, I remembered the spirit of them, the driving urge that would not be denied. When I finished, I sat back, a little breathless. Half wondering if I sounded like an idiot.

"Well," Gerri said, "you too, huh. You are about the seventh person I've spoken to in the last two days who's had a similar experience."

"Really?"

Amazing what her response did for me. Suddenly, I wasn't alone. Gerri believed me, as would others. They'd *understand* me.

"Yes. And before that, in the past week, I've talked to other people who said the same thing. It's the very reason why we set up that prayer meeting two nights ago. With so many people being called to ask for God's intervention, His meaning seems clear. The evil is increasing. And He's summoning His people to fight back with our most effective weapon: prayer."

I swiveled my chair away from the printer, where the Jane Doe pictures lay pulsing in their silent agony. "But, Gerri, if it's so effective, why did Karen Fogerty disappear the very night of that prayer meeting? It's almost like Christians were being punished or something."

Gerri made a little sound in her throat. "Sounds awful, but who knows—maybe we were."

I focused out the window, eyes roaming toward Dave's house, seeking some distraction. Gerri couldn't mean that.

"Annie, I know this is new to you. But the longer you're a Christian, the more you'll understand that there is a spiritual battle going on in this world all the time. Satan and his demonic forces are real, just as real as they were in biblical times. But God is stronger. The thing is, evil forces know that. So as God's people pray for His power to be at work, those evil forces are going to fight all the harder. Things *can* get worse before they're better. But God has promised us that His Word will prevail."

"Gerri," my throat tightened, "I just want them to get better *now*. Every hour, almost, I feel that oppression grow. Like a giant hand is squeezing me."

"It is intensifying, I agree with you. That only tells me that the battle is heating up. We have to keep praying now more than ever."

"Do you think this killer is a Satan worshipper or something? I mean, somebody really controlled by evil?"

"No doubt he's being encouraged by evil. But that doesn't mean he actively worships it. Who knows, in his twisted mind, he could even believe he's doing the world a favor through these murders."

I heard a soft *whoosh* of paper behind me. One of the Jane Doe photos had slipped from my printer tray onto the floor. Almost as if it called to me. I stared at it, a shiver clutching its way up my spine. Forcing myself to bend toward the thing, I picked it up.

"You coming into town today?" Gerri asked.

"Yes. Have to be at the morgue at eleven." I laid the photo on my desk, still feeling unnerved.

"Oh, of course. Look, I'd like to give you a tape of a sermon by a guy named Paul Sheppard. He's a pastor down in the Bay Area. The sermon's on this very subject of evil and prayers, and I think it might help you. I could leave the tape with Beverly at the Sheriff's Office."

"Okay, Gerri, thanks. I'll pick it up."

"Good. By the way, how's Stephen?"

Another wonderful topic. Briefly, I told her.

"Whoa, Annie! No wonder you're feeling squeezed. This *is* a lot to deal with at once."

"Yeah." I tried to laugh but it came out shaky. "I thought becoming a Christian was supposed to make life easier."

"Doesn't always work that way, does it? In fact, sometimes, when we ally ourselves with God, that's when Satan *really* unleashes his forces. He doesn't want Annie Kingston on God's side. His job is to convince you to give it up."

I closed my eyes. "It's only making me want to cling all the harder."

"That's the spirit."

After Gerri's call, I couldn't decide whether I felt better or worse, given her final comments. But I knew what I needed to do. Pushing from my chair, I slid down to my knees. Yes, I was inexperienced at all this, and flailing and weak.

Still, one thing I knew. My prayers would be heard.

Chapter 25

I drove to the morgue feeling worn and off-balance, as though I'd been trapped in some cosmic, existential play. Hadn't this same scene happened just a day before? Driving back and forth, back and forth, from the tragedy-smeared town to my own crisis-stained home. My prayers that morning hadn't seemed to do much for me. I could swear they hit the ceiling and bounced back. I *knew* that wasn't true, but still . . .

I need to trust You, God. That You heard and understood.

Gerri's words haunted me: *"Things can get worse before they get better."* That one sentence slithered through my head, flicking its tongue. I could not ignore it any more than I could ignore a deadly snake in my path.

How can things possibly *get worse?*

My cell phone rang. I took my eyes off the road just long enough to check the ID. "Hi, Ralph."

"Morning." The detective's voice thickened with weariness. He cleared his throat once, twice. "Sorry."

Oh, Lord, please help him. Poor Chetterling. Here I was, worrying about myself, while he carried so much responsibility. "I'll bet you didn't get any sleep last night. Again."

"You lose. I caught a couple hours."

"Chetterling, that is not enough sleep! Do you think you're some automaton who can just go forever? What good will you be on this investigation if you go under? You *have* to get some rest."

"Yeah, I hear you. Thanks, Mom."

Mom? Okay, fine. I was just trying to take care of the guy a little, when he obviously couldn't do it himself. What was it about Chetterling, anyway? As much as I cared for him, he had this ability to tick me off at the most unexpected of times.

"Annie, look, I'm sorry I didn't catch you before you left home. Frankly, I forgot to call. We've got a tentative ID on our Jane Doe. We're checking dental records, so should know pretty soon."

"Oh." The news shamed away my petty thoughts. An ID. What a relief to hear I may not have to create this next drawing. But identification meant more people—family, relatives, friends—stricken with shock and grief. Meant the circle of those affected by the Poison Killer's heinous crimes grew ever wider.

"Really sorry I didn't call sooner."

"No, no, don't worry about it. I'm almost in town, and I've got something to pick up at the office anyway. So I'll just swing by there, maybe hang around town until you hear the news. If it turns out I'm needed at the morgue, I'll be ready to go."

"Okay."

"Ralph, wait. Who is she, do you think?"

He sighed. "Trenise Willoughby. Nineteen years old. She just graduated last year from Foothill High School."

Foothill High School. The news dropped a rock through my stomach. "That's where my kids go! Stephen may have known her."

"Could be. Although she apparently didn't hang around with the best of crowds."

How tactful of Chetterling. Stephen didn't hang around with the best of crowds either, and he knew it.

I hung up the phone, my jitters reinforced. Selfish though it may be to think of my own family's needs, I hoped Jane Doe turned out to be someone other than Trenise. I would even choose to face another round of photographs and drawing over discovering the victim may have been an acquaintance, even a friend, of Stephen's.

Whatever happened, I'd now be in town longer than expected. I considered turning around and going home, then decided against it. First, because I'd told Chetterling I'd remain near the office, and second, because I was curious to pick up Gerri's tape. All the same, a voice within me nagged that I was acting the terrible mother. How much time had I spent with Kelly in the past two days? I knew she was happy hanging out with Erin. All the same . . .

To assuage my guilt, I called her at Dave's, explaining that I'd be gone longer than anticipated. Hard-beat music wafted over the phone, no doubt from Erin's ever-going stereo. "Okay, Mom, no problem," Kelly practically sang amid background laughter from Erin.

So much for being missed.

At the front desk of the Sheriff's Office, Beverly handed me the tape with a ragged smile. She, too, bore the effects of this never-ending case. "Need something to eat?" She indicated a table near the corner, spread with food.

"Wow. Where's that coming from? You can't tell me Ruby's doing it all."

"No. That's a plate of her cookies over there. But evidently at that prayer meeting the other night, Gerri signed up some folks to bring in stuff. She's awesome, you know. Says they're praying, but she knows prayers aren't all that's needed when folks are hungry. And the way things are going around here, people *would* go hungry. Just not enough time to run out and get something to eat. The tension's unbelievable, Annie. I feel like I'm in a pressure cooker."

An apt description.

I talked to Beverly for a few minutes, trying my best to encourage. But the words sounded empty, as if spoken into a vacuum. Then—what else to do but leave her to her duties?

No word yet from Chetterling on the ID. I didn't want to hang around the lobby.

Pushing open the door, I plunged back into the heat-stricken parking lot and headed toward my car. I would drive around town, air-conditioning running on high, and listen to Gerri's tape while I waited for Chetterling's call.

I would also check in with Jenna, see how Stephen was doing.

That thought did not thrill me. The last thing I needed was to hear more bad news, and something told me Jenna would have little else to offer. I set my cell phone in one of the cup holders of my car console and pulled out the tape. I studied the sermon title on the cover: "Learning How to P.U.S.H." I started the engine, popped the cassette into my player, and pulled out onto the street as the pastor's voice resounded through the car.

P.U.S.H. turned out to be an acronym for *Pray Until Something Happens.* I managed a vague smile at that. No wonder Gerri gave me this tape. Sounded like something she would say.

Not thinking much of where I was headed, I turned north on Market Street.

I listened, attention perking when Pastor Paul Sheppard talked about the importance of praying aggressively in times of spiritual warfare, saying that prayer was never wasted. Instead, it was "a meaningful relationship between an all-powerful God and powerless people."

Never wasted. I could believe that. Prayer *did* make a difference. *Even when we feel like it's just hitting the ceiling, right, God?*

I passed Lake Boulevard. When Market Street emptied into Interstate 5, I kept going north.

The pastor told a story from Acts 19 about the sons of a priest named Sceva. Apparently they were fascinated by the apostle Paul's ability to call demons out of possessed people. These men tried to do the same by admonishing the spirits in the name of "Jesus, whom Paul preaches." According to the Bible, a demon spoke out of one man, saying, "Jesus I know, and I know about Paul, but who are *you*?"

I blinked at the tape player. This story was new to me.

The pastor went on to say every demon had met Christ face-to-face at His death on the cross. As for Paul, the demon knew him by reputation as a man of God. "That demon probably said something like—" the pastor's voice turned raspy— "'See, I never had a run-in with the guy myself. But one day I saw some a my boys zippin' past. I yelled, *Hey! Where y'all goin'?* They said, *We're leavin'! Paul told us to get outta here!*'"

I smiled at that. Laughter and a few joyous "amens" sounded on the tape.

Turning west off Interstate 5, I followed Wonderland Road, running parallel to the freeway. I passed dilapidated houses, thick manzanita bushes, and vine-covered oaks as the pastor noted that Christians like Paul who've "built a reputation in hell" can't expect a persecution-free life. In fact, they shouldn't be surprised to find themselves on Satan's "hit list," up against opposition that seems beyond all rational sense.

Beyond all rational sense. Boy, did that fit this situation.

Tully Road approached on my left, one I'd never followed before. I turned onto it. Shortly past the railroad tracks, the narrow road wound into forest, with only an occasional house dotting the terrain.

Sudden apprehension seized me. What was I doing out here, in this deserted area? I locked my doors and looked for a place to turn around.

The tape caught my attention again, and I focused on the pastor's soothing voice. In times of crisis, he said, Jesus' followers should learn how to P.U.S.H. Scripture was clear: prayer changed circumstances. The philosophy that "whatever is going to happen will happen" was false—

My cell phone rang.

I turned down the volume on my tape player and picked up the phone, expecting to see Chetterling's name. But the Caller ID listed my sister's number in Redwood Shores.

"Jenna, hi. How are things going?"

"Not good, I'm afraid." She sounded grim. "I hate to tell you this, but we've got trouble."

Chapter 26

Such a disappointment to me once more, these reporters' words. So why do I keep coming back to you? Thin and see-through as the paper on which you're printed. No eloquence, no introspection. Just facts. Never-ending half-truths, and the raising up of those who are grieving, as if they deserve our sympathy.

At least your timetable succumbed to the discovery. You newspaper writers, trapped in your deadlines, managed to pull away from your schedules in this time of crisis. Found last night, she becomes the darling of this morning's headline news. Even now your readers gasp over these latest revelations.

But ah, the insipidity of the story! I smack my hand against you, paper. And you dare rattle back at me with flimsy indignity.

Still, you have a saving grace, even though it is a day late.

Her face stares at me, pretty, pretty, from the front page. A face now missing, a face last seen leaving her place of employment two nights ago. A girl who is not one to simply up and disappear. A reliable girl, a good girl.

A *Christian* girl.

A girl who, had she not been at work, may even have been across town with the others in church. Praying.

So sad that she wasn't. Someone catch my crocodile tears in a bottle. For surely we know such a deed would have saved her.

This world's foolishness is as vast as the ocean.

Does this not prove, oh pray-ers, that those fated to fall into my hand will do so? Are you so blind as to not see the richness in irony? The night you prayed—one of your own was taken? Had I known this fact, I could not have planned it with more precision.

Go ahead, search for the girl. Hope abounds until she is found. And now, with my foresight of yesterday, that moment speeds upon you. I pace the floor, listening for news, on tiptoe with anticipation. How wretched the truth will make you.

How gleeful I will be.

Chapter 27

My foot lifted from the gas pedal. I couldn't handle driving a car while hearing one more piece of bad news.

"Okay, Jenna, just a minute." I sounded so calm, as if my sister and I had exchanged places. But inside, I shook.

I glanced side to side and in the rearview mirror. No other cars. A house lay a couple hundred feet ahead of me. In the front yard a woman weeded in her garden. I pulled over to the side of the road and put the car in park.

The cassette still played at low level. Suddenly, no matter the wisdom of the sermon, the noise grated my ears. I ejected the tape.

Deep breath, Annie. And a prayer. "All right. What's going on?"

"You're not going to believe this. I was in the shower when it happened. First, Stephen got the bright idea to check for messages remotely on his cell phone. Like he needs to be calling any of his so-called friends."

Terrific. I *knew* my son wouldn't be able to withstand the lure of his friends. Good thing I'd taken his phone away. It sat safely in the top drawer of my dresser.

Jenna hurried on. "So get this. You know to check messages like that, you have to dial your own number, right? So Stephen dials it—and *Blake answers the phone.*"

Huh? Distractedly, I stared through my windshield at the woman bent over weeds. "How could Blake answer Stephen's cell phone when it's sitting in my bedroom?"

"Because when Stephen was beaten up, remember they took his wallet? In his wallet he carried his social security card. Apparently, all someone needs to switch a cell number to a different phone is that number and the user's social security number."

My eyes closed. I leaned back against the headrest. Feebly, I tried to absorb, like an already satiated sponge. "So Blake stole Stephen's cell number?"

"This is what Stephen is telling me. He told me everything, and I have to believe him, because the kid's scared witless."

"But—"

"Let me finish. No doubt Blake took over the number so he could answer Stephen's calls, try to talk any friend who phoned into telling him where Stephen went. So as soon as Blake says hello, Stephen hangs up in a hurry. But when you call a cell phone, the number you're calling from shows up, right? So *my number, here*, displays on the phone. Now Blake's looking at this Bay Area number, wondering who would hang up like that. So he calls right back. Stephen's smart enough not to answer. About this time I get out of the shower, start getting dressed. When I'm almost ready, the phone rings. I answer it. This voice says, 'I need to talk to Stephen. Tell him it's Blake.' I swear I froze in my tracks! I didn't even know what to do. Then Blake says, 'I know he's there. And I know you're at'—and he proceeds to tell me my address. He's traced it through the phone number somehow. Probably using the Internet."

My mouth hung open. Jenna's news cycled me back to when I'd picked Stephen up—was it just two days ago?—to the feeling of helplessness, of disbelief. That imagined doorway yawed open again, the threshold to cold, black space. How had I gotten here? How had Stephen gotten here? This defied all logic. Even if Stephen *had* stolen two thousand dollars of drug money, was that worth this kind of attention from somebody "up the chain"? Beating him up, taking a cell phone number to track him down?

And here I sat, working with members of law enforcement on a regular basis, and *nothing* was being done?

"Annie? You there?"

"Yeah, sure. I'm here." I pressed two fingers to my forehead. "I'm trying to sort this out. I don't even know where to begin."

Words from the sermon whispered in my head. *Christians shouldn't be surprised to find themselves up against opposition that seems beyond all rational sense.*

And I'd thought I needed to hear that sermon only because of the murders. Was everything going on in my life the result of being on Satan's hit list?

Anger rolled through me, a rogue wave. If so, I wanted no part of that list. *I don't care what you say, Pastor, I don't want it! I just want to be left alone. I just want to . . .*

Rest.

Yes. I so badly wanted to rest.

"Well, one thing's clear," Jenna said. "We can't stay here. I mean, what's the point; we're not safe."

"Right. Guess so."

I still could not pull my thoughts together.

"So I vote we fly back to Grove Landing. Stop this ridiculous running business. Think about it, Annie, here we are, going out of our way to cater to Stephen, keep him safe, just because he refuses to talk. Oooh! When I think about it, I just want to strangle him. I say we come back to Grove Landing, then you and I march him back down to the police station and *make* him talk."

The trail of yesterday's logic half shimmered in my thoughts, like windswept footprints in sand. "I know he should talk, Jenna. But that won't make him any safer. Not for a long time, anyway. Not until all of these guys, everyone involved, is put away."

"What other choice do we—"

"Where is he right now?"

"He's here. Slouched across the room from me, listening to every word. Which, by the way, I've been very happy to let him hear."

Jenna had a right to be mad, but her attitude was wearing me down. "Put him on the phone."

Jostling, the sound of a receiver being passed. I pressed my teeth together, glaring at the woman working in her garden. How unfair that she could pull out the weeds of her life so efficiently.

"Hi, Mom." Stephen's voice sounded strained.

"Okay. I want to hear what happened. From *you*."

He told me the story—no differently than Jenna's recounting. By the time he finished, I gripped the phone, the dust storm of a hundred accusations kicking in my head. *Why* had he called his cell for messages? Why hadn't he just listened to us for once? Sat there, *safe*, and done nothing? Why had he hung around with these people in the first place? Why had he started drugs? Why couldn't he *just be a decent kid*?

I hit the steering wheel with a fist.

But still . . .

A part of me wondered how I could be so mad at Stephen right now. My son was in serious trouble. Yes, he'd made some bad choices. But these people chasing him were far worse. Accused him of taking money, when he said he didn't. Even if he had, it was illegal drug money in the first place. And look at all they were putting him through now.

My eyes smarted. A long moment passed before I allowed myself to speak.

"Okay, Stephen. You've made another mistake, and you know it. But we'll have to deal with your decision-making later. Right now we need to bring you back here. This thing has gone way too far. You *will* need to talk to the police when you return, tell them everything. I know it's not going to be easy. But we can't just be on the run all our lives."

No answer. Not that I needed—or expected—one.

A light *beep* in my ear. Someone else trying to phone me.

"Stephen, hold on a minute." I clicked over to the second call. "Annie Kingston."

"Hi." Chetterling sounded like he'd been run over by a truck. "We've got our ID. It's Trenise Willoughby." He gave a weary sigh. "I was just with her parents. Man, this thing. It's a nightmare. I'm beginning to wonder if it's ever going to end."

You and me both, Chetterling.

I tried to comfort him. Utter platitudes about how he and his team *would* find this killer, and how good he was at his job. In the end—all vain, useless words. Chetterling thanked me for them, but I knew he felt no better. I clicked back to Stephen, thinking of Gerri's admonitions, and the pastor's sermon. What

I needed to do now, more than anything—what all the Christians in the area needed to do—was keep praying.

"Stephen?"

"Yeah."

He sounded so defeated, so scared. Sudden grief stabbed me, then twisted its blade. I closed my eyes, brought a hand to my forehead.

"Do you know a Trenise Willoughby? I think she graduated from your high school last year."

A hesitation. Only for a split second, but something about it . . .

"Yeah. Why?"

Did I detect a hint of suspicion? As though he prepared himself for news he didn't want to hear?

"She . . . I'm sorry to tell you this. But I just heard that she's been killed. The latest victim in these murders."

"In Redding? No way. She's not even there anymore. She left town, I don't know, last weekend or something."

I sat up straighter. "You mean you knew her that well? You'd talked to her recently?"

"I didn't talk to her. I just heard, you know. Word gets around."

"Word about *what*, Stephen?"

"That she'd left."

"Okay, got that. Why did she supposedly leave?"

Silence.

"Stephen, answer me! This is important."

"Don't trip, Mom, it's no big deal. She just had a fight with her boyfriend."

A fight. Boyfriend. "And who might that be?"

"Why are you so interested all of a sudden?"

"Because, Stephen. She didn't leave town. She's *dead.* And a fight with a boyfriend would be critical information."

"Are you making this up? I mean, just to trip me up or something?"

"I'm not trying to trip you up. Really, Stephen, I'm sorry. But her body's been identified. She never left town. She was murdered."

"Whoa. That's . . . Oh, man."

"I know."

He said no more. I let the news sink in, waiting for him to break the silence.

"But are you telling me they think her boyfriend did this? 'Cause what if he did? I don't even want to *think* about it."

"No, I'm not telling you that. But no doubt they'll question him." I paused. "Who is he?"

Another hesitation. "Nobody needs to know I told you, right? I mean, it's not like half the town didn't know who Trenise hung out with. I just don't need any more bad stuff going down on *me.*"

The tightness in his words was beginning to scare me. "Stephen, if half the town knows, what difference does it make if you tell me? We'll find out soon enough anyway."

"Yeah, I guess. Okay then. Her boyfriend was Blake. The guy who's looking for me."

Chapter 28

Possibilities and fears roiled within me as I drove back toward town. I'd already phoned Chetterling to tell him the news. If he hadn't heard the information from me, he'd have heard it soon through questioning Trenise's family and friends. But now he and his team could move all the more quickly. Somewhere in his cluttered office, Chetterling told me, lay my drawing of Blake. He just needed to find it, circulate it among his colleagues, send it to newspapers. They would put word out that Blake was a "person of interest" in the death of his ex-girlfriend, Trenise Willoughby. They *would* find him, Chetterling insisted, and pick him up for questioning.

Thank You, God, for at least something. It was no coincidence that I'd been talking to Stephen when Chetterling called.

Could this Blake be involved in the killings?

He certainly seemed cold enough. And he'd shown up at our house the very day the body of Celeste Weggin lay near our backyard. Had that been a tactical move? If Celeste was placed there for my benefit, was Blake both looking for Stephen *and* checking me out?

On the other hand, Chetterling and his task force, including the criminal profiler, believed these killings were carried out by a stranger to the victims. I bit my lip, nagged by a thought so poisonous, so preposterous, I didn't want to consider it. What if Blake had planned Trenise's death long ago, killing all those other women just to cover his tracks in *her* murder?

No. Too far-fetched. Something that happened only in the movies.

Or did it?

I drove east on Oasis Road, intent on returning home. Jenna and Stephen would be flying into Grove Landing within the next two hours, and there was nothing I could accomplish at the Sheriff's Office now anyway. Nothing to do but wait to hear what happened with Blake. If Chetterling could find good reason, they could hold Blake for a while just to keep him off the streets. Even so, I couldn't trust that would ensure Stephen's safety. How many underlings did Blake have working for him? In fact, he hadn't even been present when those boys knocked Stephen around.

At twelve thirty I pulled onto Barrister Court. I parked in the garage, slipped the remote opener off the car visor, and picked up the P.U.S.H. sermon tape. Exiting through the garage, I used the remote to close the automatic door and headed across the street to Dave's.

Erin opened the door, her eyes overbright. She took one look at me and threw herself into my arms. I hugged her, heart sinking. *Oh, no, now what?* After a moment, she pulled back enough to allow me to step inside. Kelly appeared from the kitchen. Soon I stood in the entryway, hugging both girls.

"We heard about Karen." Kelly looked into my eyes with pleading, hope that the news was wrong etched upon her features.

Oh.

"Alicia called about an hour ago, you know, our friend from church?" Kelly sniffed. "She said Karen's missing. And that she's probably dead."

My throat hitched. "Now wait, we don't know that."

"But she *is* missing, right?" Erin placed her palms against her cheeks.

I pressed my lips together, gave a little nod. "Yes." Sometimes I wished I could lie to the girls. "Where's your dad?" I asked Erin.

"In the office. Want to see him?"

"In a minute."

I shepherded the girls back into the kitchen, from where the scent of grilled cheese sandwiches wafted. "You'd better check your lunch. Looks like the bread's getting brown."

Teenagers are such an enigma. Given bad, even horrible news, they can react with complete unpredictability. The girls were sad, I could see that. But somehow they managed to turn their attention back to the priorities of the moment—to cooking their sandwiches, sliding them onto plates, fetching drinks. Even as they pumped me for information about Karen—not all of which I could give—their demeanor settled like cellophane under heat, shrink-wrapping to fit this new reality.

Self-preservation. Young girls need to cling to security in their lives.

They made me promise to tell them as soon as I heard anything more.

By the time I walked down the hall toward Dave's closed office door, they were eating their sandwiches at the kitchen table.

I knocked lightly.

"Come in."

He sat behind his executive-size desk, papers strewn across it, one hand poised above a calculator and a pen in the other.

"Well, hi. I thought you were Erin." He started to rise.

"No, no, don't get up. I'm just here for a minute." I pulled up a chair to the other side of his desk and sank into it. In one corner of the office stood a huge, leafy ficus. I gazed at it, admiring its foliage. Ficus plants were hard to keep healthy. Had Lisa tended it before her death? Had the patient care it required been a forced learning process for Dave?

"The girls just told me they heard about Karen."

He sighed. "Yeah. I've been talking to them for the past hour. Just got back to work."

Maybe that's why they'd settled so quickly. Dave already helped with the most difficult moments.

"I should have been here to help you. They must have been quite upset."

"They were. They are. But . . ."

"But they're teenagers."

He gave me a sad smile. "Yes. And teenagers have a lot of hope. Probably way more than we do."

I nodded, looking at my lap. "It's easier that way."

"Agreed."

We sat in silence.

"Well. I have the latest news for you." I raised my eyes to his, thinking how bedraggled I must look.

"Okay." He leaned forward, arms on the desk.

In a voice almost devoid of emotion, I told him about Stephen's call . . . Trenise . . . Blake.

By the time I finished, Dave's jaw slacked. He stared at me, pen tapping against a stack of paper like a sodden metronome. Something about the way his gaze held mine, the worry-deepened crow's-feet at the corners of his eyes, made my throat tighten. *For heaven's sake, Annie, don't cry.*

He started to speak, but I cut him off. "Look, I need to get going." I pushed back my chair. "I want to do a few things before Jenna gets here, and then, well, I just don't know what then. Anyway, if you want the girls to come over, that's okay."

"No, just leave them here. I'll take care of them. And if they need more hand-holding right now, you've got enough to worry about." One side of his mouth lifted. "Annie, I just . . . I wish there was more I could do for you."

"Dave. You have no idea how much you're doing."

The words came out wrong. Sounded too . . . something. I stood, a flush warming my cheeks. "One more thing. I wondered if you'd listen to this sometime." I laid the tape on his desk, realizing I'd forgotten to slide it back into its cardboard cover. The plastic against wood made a slight *click.* "Gerri gave it to me. It's a really good sermon, and I think it's all true, and I thought maybe we could talk about it sometime."

"Sure, be happy to." He glanced at the tape, then back to me. "Keep in touch, okay? Let me know if you hear anything else."

"I will."

At the door of his office, I turned back. "Dave? If possible, don't wait too long to listen to that tape. I think . . . I just sense that more's coming. That is, *if* you can believe anything else could happen after all this. And I think we're going to need all the prayers we can get."

Slowly, he nodded. "You keep your doors locked over there. And that gun handy."

I promised I would.

# # # #

For a blessed hour I rested on my bed.

Jenna and Stephen arrived a little after two o'clock. My sister climbed out of the plane taut-faced, hugging me without a word. Her hard-cut glances at Stephen, the firm set of her lips, told me all I needed to know. She hadn't forgiven him for his latest failure to listen.

And Stephen. Part of the bruising on his cheek and jaw had tinged a greenish yellow. Red and black bloomed around his eye. His attitude matched the wounded ugliness of his face. Defensive stubbornness floated about him in a noxious cloud. Methodically, he put away his earphones. Shoved forward his plane seat to pull his duffel bag and CD case from the back. Frowning, he slouched toward the garage area, carrying his possessions.

I could only imagine these two tangling while they'd been alone. And not until I watched Stephen cross the threshold into the kitchen did the stomach-punch of his return hit. Bye-bye, quiet house. Everything about him—his negativity, his lack of trustworthiness—affected all of us. The truth was terrible to admit but too real to deny. I no longer wanted to be around my son.

I ran a hand through my hair, then hefted Jenna's flight bag off the hangar floor. The thing weighed a ton. I never could figure out why she needed all that paraphernalia, or how it added up to so many pounds.

My cell phone rang from a distance. I'd left it on the kitchen counter. Muttering under my breath, I lugged the flight bag with both hands through the garage. By the time I banged it onto the table, my phone was on its third ring. I snatched it up.

"Annie, is Stephen back yet?" Chetterling didn't even stop to say hello.

"Yes. Just."

"We need you to bring him in so we can question him about Blake and what happened the other day."

Welcome home, Stephen. "Have you picked Blake up already?"

"No. But at least we know who to look for, thanks to your drawing. I circulated it in a hurry and somebody recognized him. Real name's Blake Dalveeno. Manages construction crews and projects for his uncle, who's a developer. I ran him through the system, hoping to come up with something. An unpaid traffic ticket—anything to allow us to keep him in custody for a few days. Guy's clean. So we need to be prepared to question him about everything we can. That's where Stephen comes in. If we find no reason to hold Dalveeno for the killings, maybe we can at least hold him for some other charge."

I pulled out a kitchen chair, lowered myself into it. "So you're telling me Stephen *really* has no choice now."

"Look, we'll do all we can to protect him if he's worried about talking. But he's needed in this murder investigation. I'm sure I can get him to see that."

I could only hope so. "What about the police? Stephen went to them first. They'd have jurisdiction over his being beaten up, right? And the theft of his wallet and watch?"

"Yes, but I'm working closely with them. We'll have someone from the police department present at the questioning. Probably Frank Nelson, the officer you talked to."

Oh, joy.

"By the way," I said, "Blake wasn't there, you know, when Stephen was beaten up."

"Yeah, but apparently he's pulling the strings. Stephen gives us the names of who *was* there, then we'll lean on those guys to tell us more about Dalveeno."

Suddenly, heavy fatigue settled over me. If only I could sleep for a week. Drugs and murder. Now maybe my own son knew the man we'd sought for months. *God, please, I don't want Stephen tied to this killer.*

"Okay. I'll bring him in. It's not going to be easy."

"You want me to send somebody for him? I'll be more than happy to."

"No." In spite of everything, the answer came quickly. I still couldn't bear to see Stephen in a police car—for any reason. "I'll manage."

"All right. See you soon."

"Chetterling, wait." I wanted to hang on one more minute. I wanted him to tell me everything would be all right with my son. *Come on, Ralph, just say something.*

Silence.

I bit the inside of my cheek. "Do you think Blake *is* the Poison Killer?"

"Don't know. He's a little young, at least according to Rosalee. But he fits the profile in other ways. Has a college education, lives and works in Redding, knows the area well. Apparently has connections for obtaining illegal drugs. And for some reason today he's not at his place of employment or his residence. I'm wondering why."

Not at work. Where *was* Blake? On his way to the Bay Area, trying to track down Stephen?

Jenna came into the kitchen, carrying her suitcase. I shot her a stricken look, and she stopped in her tracks. *What?* She mouthed. I held up a hand.

"Okay. Anyway. I'm . . . coming, Ralph. Be there as soon as we can."

I punched off the line, focusing on a spot of dirt on the wall, a spot I should clean.

"What is it?" Jenna set down her bag.

Dully, I moved my gaze to her face. "I have to take Stephen in. They want information on Blake. And they're not taking no for an answer."

Chapter 29

These hands of judgment take up mortar and pestle.

White are the powder crystals. I shake a small amount out of the bottle. They have no smell. So unassuming in appearance. So benign. Without proper care, one might think them sugar. Drop them in coffee. Oh, but the taste. Bitter as gall.

Grind, grind. Hear the *click-rasp* of marble upon marble, see the substance turn more fine beneath my loving labor.

The beat of wings flutters in my chest.

Click-rasp. Click-rasp. A lovely sound. A soothing sound.

How fitting that my mother brought these death-sands to me, never guessing the use I would put them to. The vain pursuit of her travels late in life now renders the grown child recompense.

Click-rasp. Tap-tap-tap. Precious powder falls from my pestle to join the tiny snow hill.

Pray-ers, where are you now? Is no one talking to God? You who believe it makes such a difference. Does any cosmic force now stay my hand? Some bolt of lightning? Perhaps some shimmer-ghost of heavenly fingers will reach through the universe, scattering stars and planets, and plunge toward earth like the thrust of a hand into a fishbowl. Come now, fingers, snatch at me! Grasp and scrabble as I twitch away to hide in my painted castle under waving plastic fronds, safe!

I lay the pestle aside. Look up toward the ceiling. Waiting. Daring. Come on, then, come on, if You be the power they claim!

Nothing.

Ah. I curl my lip at You. And at all of them.

Some sit and pray. Others *do*. I look at my death powder and ask—which is more powerful?

But enough of this. Why even allow such thoughts? Why give their claims a second's worth of energy?

Flutter, flurry, tremulous wings. Brush rib cage and muscle, bone and sinews, making me shudder.

I know they seek me, yes I know. Now more than ever. *No more death*, they say, *we will find him before another is taken.*

How little you know.

Truth? It lies here, in this mortar.

Unassuming. Odorless.

The color of purity.

Chapter 30

The interview room at the Sheriff's Office. I knew it all too well. Now, with my own son about to be questioned, *interview* seemed far too benign a word. *Interrogation* room was more like it. More than once in the past, I'd stood outside it as I did now, watching through the one-way mirror, listening to the questioning. A camera mounted at the top corner of the small room recorded what transpired.

My legs shook. Just getting Stephen here had proved a terrible ordeal. A sudden shiver drew my arms across my chest. My body felt like thin porcelain, ready to shatter.

God, help me. I'm so tired of being his mother. I don't know what to do!

Chetterling sat at one end of the battered rectangular table, closest to the door. Across from him lounged Frank Nelson, my favorite police officer. Just seeing that man with my son again made me cringe. Stephen sat between them. Facing me. Not that he knew I watched, fortunately.

"How can you *do* that?" he'd raged when I told him I was taking him in for questioning. "See why I don't talk to you! First thing you do is turn around and tell some detective." He lashed an arm through the air. "You think I was in trouble before? Just wait 'til Blake hears I told cops stuff that makes him look like a killer!"

He slammed his bedroom door in my face, the lock clicking with cutting, tangible rage. It took me ten minutes to convince him to come out. Somehow, even as pain eddied in my heart, my words flowed calmly. "Stephen, you have to open the door. If you don't, I'll just call someone to come get you. You don't have a choice, don't you see that? People are *dying*. And I want to help you. I want to get Blake off the streets so you can be safe again."

Surely the only reason Stephen opened his door came from heaven itself. God had answered a mother's desperate prayer.

When we arrived at the Sheriff's Office, my narrow-eyed son was escorted into the darkened interview room. Once he entered and the lights were turned on, the room would become visible through the glass. Pulling myself together, I proceeded to Chetterling's office, feeling more supplicant than colleague. I wanted . . .

I didn't know what I wanted. To draw pleas from a mother's well of child-forgiveness that the detective go easy on my son. To urge he be as hard on my son as allowed, because my well had run dry.

Chetterling was seated at his desk. He took one look at me and pushed to his feet. "You had trouble getting him here." Not a question; a statement from someone who knew me well.

"You could say that. But he's here."

He regarded me. "You don't have to listen to the interview, you know. Maybe it's better if you just waited here."

Sure, Ralph, and then what? How do I take care of my son if I don't know everything that's going on? I focused on a haphazard stack of files on the desk, emotions grinding within me.

"Annie, I'm sorry. I know this is hard for you."

I dragged my gaze back to Chetterling's face—and felt my eyelids flicker at the tenderness I saw there. He'd stepped outside of Ralph Chetterling, the detective, and looked at me as Chetterling, the man. Someone who cared. Who agonized with me. Remorse at my sarcastic thoughts panged me.

Out in the hall, footsteps approached the office. I looked toward the sound, suddenly in dire need for something to break the moment. The footsteps plodded on—just a deputy walking by.

I could still feel Ralph's eyes on me. Self-consciousness curled my fingers around my purse. Turning back to him, I managed a little shrug. "I'm going to listen, Ralph. I *have* to. You understand that, don't you?"

He drew in a breath, let it out. "Yeah. I do." He cleared his throat, his demeanor returning to all business. "Let me just find my notebook and pen on this messy desk, and we'll get going."

Now, as I watched, Stephen hunched at the table, upper body rocking, no doubt from the shaking of one of his legs. He focused on his fingers, spread against the wood, as though they might morph into new creatures of fascination.

Chetterling eased back in his chair, everything about his manner casual. His mere bulk was enough to be intimidating. In the close quarters of the room, his frame seemed larger than ever. "That's some fine bruises you've got on your face, Stephen."

No response.

"You've met Officer Nelson before, I understand. We thank you for coming down."

Stephen made a disgusted sound. "Like I had a choice."

"Well, your cooperation's appreciated. I know you talked a little to Officer Nelson the other day. Now we need to hear everything that happened. In detail."

I tapped a fist against my chin as Stephen related the sordid tale. This time I heard full names. Kenny Wraight and Dwayne Moody. Al Hanks, Eddy Bocerelli. These four had taken him in Al's van to Eddy's house. Kenny and Dwayne knocked him around, demanding the two thousand dollars, stripping him of his wallet and watch. With four against one, Stephen could hardly fight back. Kenny and Dwayne finally left him in the care of the other two, promising—more like threatening—to return. With Blake. Stephen had to escape. An unfriendly encounter with Blake would likely land him in the hospital.

My vision blurred. I pressed my knuckles against my chin, blinking the tears back. Just hearing the story again left me quivering inside. How frightened Stephen must have been.

God, thank You for helping him get out of there.

The four guys had sold drugs for Blake for some time, Stephen said. They sold pot around town and they shipped meth to New Orleans. *Methamphetamine!* Chetterling and Nelson didn't seem surprised. But as my shock settled I had to wonder—why New Orleans?

Blake always managed to remove himself from the meth shipments, Stephen said. His helpers packaged up the stuff and sent it. Someone in New Orleans wired payment to one of the boys through Western Union. That person then turned the money over to Blake, keeping a small cut. Stephen played middleman a few times. But the last time, no money was wired. Blake was incensed enough to personally call the New Orleans connection—who insisted he *had* wired the money, and he had the receipt to prove it. That's when the accusations against Stephen had begun.

"Blake's crazy." Stephen scowled. "I *never* got that money." But his denials didn't matter; Blake was convinced Stephen was the liar.

"This guy Blake." Chetterling drummed the table. "Do you know his last name?"

"Nah. He never told me. I don't know if the other guys know it or not." Stephen tipped back in his chair, affecting nonchalance.

I knew the question was a test of Stephen's candor. Could Chetterling read whether or not he told the truth? I'd lost my ability long ago. My son lied so convincingly.

"Well, I happen to know it. Dalveeno." Chetterling watched Stephen's expression.

He shrugged. "Whatever."

Officer Nelson rested his arms against the table. "So tell us about him."

Stephen brought the front legs of his chair down with a rattle. Not much to tell, he replied, but as his description unfolded, shivers danced down my spine. Blake was around twenty-five and "real smart." Arrogant about it too. Liked to show off his vocabulary, his knowledge of world issues and philosophy.

No kidding he's arrogant. How well I remembered his condescending attitude.

He read all the time, especially the classics, Stephen said. My son could ask Blake any question about a book he had to read for English class, and Blake would know the answer. The guy worked some cushy job for his uncle, supposedly driving from one development site to another, managing crews. But he didn't punch a time clock and pretty much seemed to be on his own.

"Where does he live?" Nelson asked. Another question to which he and Chetterling knew the answer.

"In Avonshade Townhouses. Cool place with three bedrooms, right by the pool."

"Does he live with anyone?"

"Not that I know of."

"Do you know anything about his family? Parents, brothers, sisters?"

Stephen returned to examining his fingers. "No brothers or sisters. I've never heard him talk about a father. Maybe he never had one around." Stephen drew the corners of his mouth down in a "who-cares-anyway?" expression that singed my heart. My son cared, all right, that his own father had abandoned him. Cared more than he would ever admit to anyone, including himself. "And his mom's dead, but he hated her anyway."

Hated his mom. I stood very still, watching Chetterling's face. Though it remained deadpan, I could practically see the equations add up in his brain.

"Oh, yeah?" The detective sniffed. "What was so bad about her?"

"I don't know." Stephen hooked and unhooked his thumbs. "I think she was like a prostitute or something. Into weird stuff, you know, like crystals. And drugs."

"Did she live here in Redding?"

"I guess."

"When did she die?"

Stephen eyed Chetterling with an annoyed frown. "How'm *I* supposed to know?"

Chetterling held Stephen's gaze until my son looked away. "All right. Tell us about Blake's girlfriend, Trenise."

She'd been hanging out with Blake way back when Stephen met the guy, he said. Which was maybe last November. She took all kinds of drugs. Was a real snob about her looks. Blake got mad if anybody else so much as glanced at her.

My purse began to weight my shoulder. I set it on the floor—but felt no lighter. Unseen hands pressed at the base of my neck, weighing me down. Everything Stephen was saying about Blake Dalveeno fit. In quick succession my brain flashed real and imagined pictures of Blake,

hurling jealous accusations at Trenise, fist aimed at her cheek . . .

pointing a finger at me in my home—"You will give Stephen a message for me . . ."

sneering over the contorted body of Celeste Weggin . . .

luring Karen Fogerty into his car . . .

lugging Celeste's body into the woods behind my house . . .

hulking over my Kelly, cowering on the couch . . .

No. *No.*

This was too much. Yes, I wanted the killer found, wanted him off the streets. But to think he could be Stephen's "friend." That my son had hung out with him, been in a car with him, been in his house. That he had been in *my* house. Standing *over my daughter.* Chills stitched down my back.

Chetterling sat with arms crossed, nodding. "So . . . Blake and Trenise. They had a fight?"

"Yeah."

"Over what?"

A shrug. "Some guy, don't know who."

"What happened?"

Stephen scowled. "Look, I don't know! When can I get out of here? I'm getting tired of all these questions. You think I'm supposed to know everything that goes down?"

"Hey." Officer Nelson leaned toward Stephen, impatience tightening his voice. "Chill out, man. It's not like anybody's mistreating you. You want to spend some time sitting in a jail cell, thinking about those drugs you sold?"

Chetterling raised both hands. "Okay, let's just calm down." He aimed a heavy look at Officer Nelson, telling him without words to back off. I couldn't help but narrow my own eyes. I understood the "good cop, bad cop" routine, but couldn't help feeling smug at Chetterling's staged reproach.

"All right." Chetterling rubbed his jaw. "Stephen, all we want you to do is tell us what you *do* know. We're not expecting you to be on top of everything. Understand?"

"Yeah." Stephen folded his arms and tipped back his chair.

"Okay. So. You said Blake and Trenise had a fight. Do you remember when?"

Stephen rocked up and down, up and down in the chair. "I only heard about it, remember. So that's all I can tell you. I think I heard . . . it was last Saturday. That they'd had a big fight, and she was leaving town to go live with her sister in Sacramento." He shook his head. "I thought she did, too, you know. Move. I never thought she'd be somebody who ended up dead. That's . . . that's really messed up."

The detective grunted. "Did you happen to be with Blake two nights ago?"

Two nights ago. When Karen Fogerty disappeared.

"Me? No." Stephen touched his green-purple jaw. "Two days ago I got this. I didn't go anywhere the rest of that day."

"Did you talk to Blake that night? Or anybody who mentioned where he might be?"

"Nah. I wasn't talking to nobody. My mom even took my cell phone."

"All right." Chetterling shifted in his seat. "Let's cycle back to the drugs for a minute. I'm not clear how this operation works."

Chetterling's "for a minute" stretched over twenty as he wrought from my son the hierarchy of the drug-selling gang. Blake, second in command, worked under some businessman in town, whose name Stephen claimed not to know. The other four guys worked under Blake. He supplied the drugs; they sold. Whenever dirty business of any kind went down, Blake made sure he wasn't around. Always someone to do the dirt for him, while he kept his hands clean. He bragged about his lack of a criminal record and vowed to keep it that way.

"Then why do you suppose," Chetterling wondered, "he went, *himself*, to your house? Walked in the door without being invited, knowing he was bound to be confronted?"

"You're his mother, correct? The famous forensic artist." Blake's insolent words as he faced my gun as if it were a toy. *Had* Blake come as much to check me out as for Stephen? After he'd placed his latest victim near my backyard?

Stephen focused on the table. "I don't know. Except, ever since last week with the Trenise thing, he just went kinda crazy. Went all off about the money. Thing is, Blake doesn't like to not be in control, know what I mean? So he gets all ticked off over Trenise when she says she going to leave, and then he gets all ticked off at me. I don't know what's going on with him."

By the time Chetterling and Nelson were finished questioning Stephen, I could have predicted the detective's plans. He'd get right to work on finding exactly "what was going on" with Blake Dalveeno. Did Blake know any of the other victims? Did he have access to buying strychnine? Chetterling, with the help of other task force members, would pick up all four boys Stephen mentioned to question them separately. Lean on them to find out more about Dalveeno. Officer Nelson would be involved. He'd pursue the charges against the boys for what they'd done to Stephen.

Afterward, Chetterling and I stood in his office once more. Stephen was out near the front desk, waiting for me with the impatience of a chugging engine. "You'd better keep your son at home and out of sight for now." Ralph looked not at me but *through* me, his mind clearly on the tasks ahead. "His four so-called friends. We can hit 'em with a number of charges, hold 'em at least until arraignment. But Dalveeno— like Stephen said, he's a wily one."

I sagged against his desk, staring at the floor. "I can't believe Stephen was selling meth. I just can't believe it." I put a hand over my eyes. "Why would they ship it to New Orleans?"

"It's harder to get the stuff there, so they get more money for it."

Oh. Ever the businessman, Mr. Dalveeno.

"Ralph, *now* do you think Blake did these murders?"

He inhaled slowly. "I still don't know, but it's the best lead we've had yet. Guy sounds smart enough to be our man. If he did Trenise, he did the others. The MOs are the same, and

Trenise can't be a copycat, because the trophies haven't been made public." He blinked, and I could see his focus sharpen on me. "Just be extra careful, okay? I'll let you know as soon as we've located Dalveeno.

"But you'd better start praying we find a solid reason to hold him."

Chapter 31

I'd promised to call Jenna when Stephen and I headed home. *Good thing*, I thought as I picked up my cell. *Might as well talk to my sister, seeing as my son still refuses to utter a word to me.*

Her voice was a blessed relief. "How did it go?"

"Terrific."

"I'll bet." She sighed. "What would you like for dinner?"

Dear Jenna. Nag that she could be, she knew from just one word when I'd had all I could take. She'd save her pestering questions for later.

"I don't know. I don't care about dinner."

"Care or not, you need to eat. I'll bet you didn't have lunch."

Lunch? I couldn't remember back that far. "Look, Jenna, you really want to help me? Take Kelly and Erin out for dinner and a movie. They've been cooped up at Dave's house for a long time now, and I just don't have the energy to do it."

"That's what you want? Okay, on one condition. Promise me you'll eat something."

Oh, good grief. "Yes, Mother, I'll eat."

Half an hour later, I stood in the middle of the kitchen, my insides feeling like they'd been through a blender. Jenna and the girls had already taken off, and a stone-faced Stephen had headed straight down to his lair the minute we arrived home. I couldn't hear his music. He must be parked in front of the television.

Tiredness gripped me. I couldn't even think what to do next.

The grandfather clock bonged five thirty. I raked a hand through my hair, telling myself I really should listen to Jenna and eat. As for Stephen, I'd let him fend for himself. Sooner or later, hunger pangs would drive him up the stairs.

From the pantry, I grabbed the first can of soup I saw, poured it into a large bowl, and stuck it in the microwave. I ate automatically, spoon from bowl to mouth, bowl to mouth, the tick of the clock a mournful metronome in the surrounding silence. The more I tried to block out all thought, the more my projector brain threw out pictures in vivid color.

The gray-white, high-boned cheeks of Debbie Lille, victim number one . . .

Celeste Weggin's foot sticking out from behind the bush. Her wide-open, shocked eyes . . .

Stephen's bruised jaw . . .

Blake Dalveeno's pointing finger . . .

Chetterling's face, full of empathy . . .

Stephen rising from behind a dumpster, Officer Nelson's cynical expression, Kelly waiting as I followed the smell into the woods, my necklace in the box, Dave's eyes, Stephen pulling his bag from the plane, Stephen's scowl, his slammed door, his first baby picture, Vic on our wedding day, Sheryl pregnant—

"Stop!" I pushed aside my empty bowl and slapped a hand to each temple. How I wished I could just turn my brain off. Go to bed, sleep for a week. "God," my eyes slipped shut, "what do You want me to do? How much longer is all this going to go on? I can't take much more with Stephen."

Pray.

Odd, the way the unspoken word reverberated through my chest. I knew it came from the Lord, but it made no sense. I *was* praying.

Pray. P.U.S.H.

All right. Okay. Maybe this wasn't from God; maybe it sounded more like a nagging Gerri. Whatever it was, I'd heed it. What else could I do?

From nowhere, a rebellious part of me kicked in. *Sure, pray, Annie, but first you have things to do.* I needed to rinse my bowl and spoon, put them in the dishwasher. Which I did. When that was done, I needed to brush my teeth, so off to the bathroom I went. As I put away my toothbrush, I remembered seeing a stack of mail on the kitchen counter that needed opening. Before I knew it, I was back where I started, in the kitchen, reaching for the first envelope.

Suddenly, I came to my senses, my hand stilled midair. Wait a minute. Why was I bustling around like this?

Pray. Now.

The words came stronger, more intense. Like yesterday morning. I heard them one at a time, as though they were spoken through mental telepathy straight into my brain. The words were quiet, yet firm. With an absolute, undeniable authority.

I drew my hand back from the stack of mail, turned around and exited the kitchen. Through the great room, into my office. There, I closed the door, fell into my desk chair and sank my head into my hands.

And prayed.

Words tumbled from my mouth, words from deep within me, petitions I wouldn't have conceived on a conscious level. I heard myself pleading for Jesus to shatter the evil forces whispering thoughts to the killer. To break through the hardness in Stephen's heart, turning my son toward Christ. To protect me, hedge me in, secure and shield me. Over and over my tongue uttered the name Jesus, calling for His power, claiming victory in His authority. At times I fell silent, then more words would come. A sense of urgency pushed me on, focused my concentration.

Then, slowly, the intensity began to diminish. Still I prayed—until a peace wrapped around me, as if a prolonged noise to which I'd adapted had finally ceased.

Afterward, I sat staring at my desk, pondering. The prayer time had been another special call from God. Crazy as it might sound to half the world—even if it sounded crazy to the *whole* world—I couldn't deny I'd heard God's voice. Still, I appreciated the confirmation from Gerri. I wasn't alone in this. Others were being called to pray in the same way.

The prayer time left me with a new bit of understanding. Or perhaps the understanding rose from both my experience and the P.U.S.H. sermon. That as much as God might impress me like this in dire matters, I shouldn't wait for such a summons to pray just as fervently, with as much faith, in all matters of my life. *Time and time again*, the pastor had said, *the Bible shows us that prayer makes a tremendous difference.*

Boy. I'd better start praying about a lot of things.

I rose from my chair, left the office. Wandered through the great room, thinking I'd like something sweet to eat. A cookie, candy bar, whatever. And the mail did await me in the kitchen.

The phone rang. Instantly my mind set off running with all the possibilities of who it could be, and the news awaiting me. Surely nothing good. In the kitchen, I picked up the receiver.

"Annie, it's Dave."

A warmth spread over me, probably because I'd expected the worst. "Hi."

"Just checking on you. It's awful quiet over here with the girls gone."

I laughed. "Bet it is." Wandering over to the counter, I picked up the stack of mail and began to leaf through it.

"Annie, I just listened to that tape you gave me—the Pray Until Something Happens sermon? It's very good."

"Yes, I know." *A credit card bill. Water bill.* I laid them aside to open later. "I'm glad you heard it. Because just now I've . . . had another prayer experience like yesterday."

I told him what had happened, my eyes returning now and then to the mail. *An unwanted catalog. Toss it. Advertisement for a new mortgage. Don't need it.* "Seems like with everything going on right now, I could do nothing *but* pray all day long." *A small padded manila envelope, handwritten return address—the Sheriff's Department. What's this?*

"Any news on Karen Fogerty?" Dave asked.

"Nothing." I pictured the faces of Karen's parents. How terrible and long this day must have been for them. "And with every hour that goes by . . ."

"I know. This is so awful. The girls are still upset. Did you think to tell Jenna not to talk to them about it?"

Had I? For the life of me I couldn't remember. I gazed at the manila envelope in my hand. "She won't say anything. She's out to give them a good time, get their minds *off* things for a while." I lay the envelope down. Some small object inside caused the bottom to bulge.

"It was really nice of her to take them."

Such small talk, while the world roiled around us. Dave, in his house alone, and I in mine . . . well, I might as well be alone. If only I could invite Dave over, talk to him face-to-face, spill everything that had happened, everything I was thinking, feeling. But of course I couldn't. "Yes. I should have done it myself, but . . ."

I studied the envelope. Picked it up again.

"You've got enough going on. I imagine right now you could just use a good rest."

Dave was tactful enough not to ask about Stephen's sudden return. He must wonder. After all he'd done for me, hadn't he earned the right to know at least this much? "Speaking of rest, I obviously won't need to stay in your guest room tonight, now that Jenna and Stephen are here."

I gave the envelope an experimental wave, feeling the weight of it. What *was* that inside?

"Sure. Just didn't want you being alone."

"Thank you." I bent my head over to cradle the receiver between my shoulder and ear. "I want you to know something, Dave, even though I can't tell you everything." From the butcher block, I chose a paring knife and slit open the envelope. "Stephen had to come back to talk to a detective about what happened the other day." I pressed the top edges of the envelope, causing it to balloon open. Inside I saw a single piece of folded paper. I drew it out and laid it on the counter without reading it. "They kind of came down on him hard, told him he didn't have a choice." Turning over the envelope, I moved my hands toward its sides. Whatever lay in the bottom seemed stuck. I shook the envelope gently. "That's why I went back into town this afternoon." The object didn't move. I shook harder. I felt the object give way. "Stephen was so angry—"

A little finger rolled out. Plopped upon the counter. A real, cutoff finger, red-blackened at its base. Still wearing a light blue topaz ring.

I dropped the phone and screamed.

Chapter 32

Six thirty. Still I hear nothing.

Are you all this incompetent?

Maybe it did not arrive in the mail today. Or maybe the receiver is out of town.

No. You would not leave. Not now. I keep you here. I keep you all here, working, fearing, wondering.

You, Annie Kingston, are no better than the rest. You know that, don't you. You know it every time you fasten that pendant around your neck. Oh, yes, I've seen it. I know much more than you think I do.

She was your age once, too, turned from her flamboyant young motherhood into tiresome, flimsy woman. Always beauty, always in pursuit of charm, the outside scrubbed and painted while the inside caked with filth.

By that time she had long dragged me into the dust.

There will be a day when you all will thank me for what I've accomplished. While this world turns on and on, I have dared to make you all face the truth, caused you to look at your silly little lives and your silly little habits.

And your silly little faith.

I have faith too, more than you all. Faith that this earth is faithless. All I can do is make my mark, stamp it upon you, brand it into your skin to sizzle and itch. When I am no more, you will remember me . . . and mine.

They are all mine—those I have chosen.

I take who I will. I judge as I see fit. Wrenching away life and breath as actions demand. I live among you and am seen but unseen, the adult grown from the tortured child. Now nurturing whom I wish, nestling them under the shelter of my shivering and wretched wings.

Ah, but I am the poetic one.

Chapter 33

I bent over, hands clutching my head, rasping in air. Backing away, away from the horrid thing that lay on my counter. Vaguely I registered sound from two directions—sounds I should respond to but could not. Stephen's footsteps pounded up from the basement. Dave called my name, the distant tinniness coming from the phone receiver, now skidded away from my feet.

Stephen shouldn't see this. I should do something, hide it . . .

I couldn't move, couldn't do any more than breathe, and still the footsteps pounded. The door to the basement yanked open, Stephen trotting across the great room floor.

"Mom, what *is* it?"

Sanity kicked in. I whirled around, hands out, just as he neared the kitchen. "No, Stephen, don't! Just—"

"*What?* Why did you—?" His eyes fell on the counter.

"Annie, are you *there?*" Dave's disembodied voice, fear-filled now, desperate.

Stephen stilled. His mouth opened but no sound came at first. He tried again, sputtering the words. "Oh, man, what *is* that?"

He started to move around me. I caught his arm. "No. Don't."

No more sound from the phone.

My son's expression folded in on itself, then twisted. "Oh, Mom, tell me that's not what I think it is."

If only I could. I crossed my arms over my chest, casting about for any reason to convince myself the finger wasn't human. Some rubber appendage, that was all, designed to look gruesomely authentic. A sick, sick joke for some warped person to stick in someone's cake at a party, float in a glass of punch. My visual brain flashed the two pictures, substituting a fake sheen. Then they faded away, replaced with reality, the memory of

that finger, wearing that ring, wrapped around a glass as Karen serves me at the restaurant . . .

I moaned aloud, shoved the scene from my head.

"Stephen, look, just . . . back up. Okay? Stay away. I'm going to have to call—"

Distant footsteps pounding again, coming from our front porch. Someone hit the door, pressed the bell, once, twice. A fist pounded. "Annie? *Annie!*"

Dave. Oh, no, I've scared him to death. I turned toward the sound, swallowing. "I'm . . . I'm coming!"

I looked back to Stephen. "Don't touch it, you hear? Don't go near it. Or the envelope or anything. It's all evidence." Holding one hand up as a warning, I moved around him, then hurried toward Dave's frantic voice. I fumbled with the lock, breathing hard, and threw open the door.

"Annie!" Dave jumped over the threshold, his face white, and opened his arms for me. Without hesitation I pressed myself against his chest, and he hugged me tightly. I could hear the erratic thump of his heart. "What happened?"

My mind churned through responses. I didn't want to tell him. Didn't want to thrust more terror into his life. What was it about me that wooed tragedy and crises to ride my shoulders like some attacking beast? My fingers curled on Dave's shirt, balling up the fabric. Even as I hesitated, I knew Stephen watched us, could almost feel his vibrations of surprise and distaste at our intimacy.

Dave's hand cradled the back of my head. "Stephen, what happened?"

No, no, don't ask—

"Come look for yourself."

Did Stephen's curt reply arise from his fear or his disapproval of Dave holding me? Maybe both.

I pulled away, wanting to spare Dave the sight. "It's from Karen." Tears scratched my eyes. "I got something in the mail that was . . . cut from her body. Her little finger. I know because I recognize the ring on it."

Dave's mouth opened, horror seizing his features. His lips moved silently, as if he searched for adequate words and found none. "Are you sure?"

I nodded.

"How—?"

"I was opening the mail while I was talking to you, and it . . . fell out. I'm so sorry; I didn't mean to scare you, but I just reacted, and once I dropped the phone I couldn't move, couldn't pick it up . . ."

He laid his fingers on my lips. The spill of words stopped. "Okay. It's all right, Annie."

Something about his tone, the way it had firmed, bespoke a shocked man who'd regained his senses and taken charge. Everything was far from all right, but simply hearing him say those words helped settle my fluttering nerves. Dave eased me aside, and I didn't try to stop him as he walked toward the kitchen. He passed Stephen, who shuffled back a few feet, watching Dave's every move. I could sense when Dave reached the counter, although I no longer saw him. I stood, knuckles pressed to my cheek, and waited.

Dave reappeared, grim resolve on his face. "There's a handwritten note on the counter. It must have come with the package?"

A note? I stared at him blankly. "Oh, no. I mean—yes, I forgot." My legs moved, pulling me toward the kitchen. Dave headed back to the counter. "Don't touch it." As I hurried by Stephen, I reached out to reassure him with a touch. "Is the note face up?"

"Yes."

Dave's squeezed tone told me that he'd read it.

I slowed as I neared it, preparing myself. The single piece of common notebook paper lay askew, the knife with which I'd opened the package nearby. I picked up the knife, using the tip of its blade to straighten the paper. Dave moved close to me, looking at the note again, his hands fisted.

Annie Kingston:

I gave you Celeste. Now I lead you to Karen, for they are too slow to please me.

Take Tully Road heading west. The second left, into forest. Go about a mile. She is there, on the right.

See how clear are my directions.

See how unfailing is my hand.

Tell the pray-ers—perhaps they should take up a new sport.

My blood congealed, my stare stuck to the last line like wet fingers to ice. When I could tear myself away, I turned to Dave and saw in his eyes the revulsion that must mirror my own. I clasped my hands, my throat wrenching tight.

Then a realization gripped me. *Tully Road.* The very one I'd driven yesterday. Where I'd pulled over to the side to talk to Jenna. I'd seen a woman way down that road, working in her garden, as if all was right with the world. And somewhere near me, maybe only a mile or two, Karen had lain, sprawled and discarded, in the forest.

"Mom, what does it say?" Stephen's voice brought me up short. He stood only feet away, craning his head toward the counter. He began to move around me, but I grabbed his arm. "Don't touch it!"

"Okay, okay, I know."

He edged up to the counter and cocked his head, reading the note. I couldn't find the energy to stop him.

A wave of despair washed over me. What was the use of trying to stop *any* of this? No matter what we did, things only got worse.

Stephen turned to me, his face pinched. "This guy's *crazy.* What does he mean, he gave you Celeste?"

I blinked at him. "I've got to call Chetterling."

The phone still lay on the floor. I picked it up, held it to my ear. No dial tone.

"It may still be connected to my line," Dave said. "I think I just threw my phone down without hanging up."

"Oh." I hit the *off* button, waited a few seconds, then hit *talk.* When I heard the tone, like a flatlined heart, I punched in Chetterling's direct number. He answered on the first ring.

"Ralph, it's me."

In a deadened voice I told him everything, walking over to the counter to read the killer's chilling message aloud. The finger lay there, shrieking at me in mute agony. I couldn't look at it, and I couldn't help but see it. Chetterling listened without interruption, his frozen silence ringing in my ears. Through the phone line, I could sense the weight of the news upon him. "If you'll trust me to collect this evidence, I'll bring it to you. I'll put on gloves, put all the . . . everything in a bag."

"No, no, we can't do that." The utter weariness in his answer. Another loss of life, another murder to solve, when he'd already faced a Sisyphean task. "I'll send somebody out right away. You never know if some hair has fallen out of the envelope that you might miss."

"Okay. We'll wait."

I hung up the phone. The three of us looked at each other. "Stephen," I said, "when the girls get back, I don't want you saying a word about this, understand?"

"Yeah, sure. Whatever." For once, my son looked sufficiently cowed. "I'm just gonna watch TV up here for a while." Without another word, he exited the kitchen.

I didn't know what to do. I didn't want to look at what lay on my counter, but neither could I leave. It was almost as if the thing pleaded with me to stay and watch over it. Guard this piece of Karen's precious body.

"Come on." Dave laid a gentle hand against my back. "Let's go sit out there and wait."

"Okay." Robotlike, I let him lead me. We sank into a couch in the great room and stared at the fireplace. A sitcom's canned laughter filtered through the closed TV-room door. Dave put an arm around me, and I laid my head against his shoulder. Neither of us spoke.

Fifteen minutes later, Jim Cisneros arrived to collect the evidence. I led him into the kitchen. Dave and I stood back, watching, as he examined the counter for any tiny fiber or hair, as he picked up the envelope and note and finger with gloved hands. He placed them into a paper bag and gave me a grim nod. "Thanks, Annie. So sorry this had to happen to you."

I saw Jim to the front door, locked it behind him. When I turned to Dave, his eyes glittered. My heart cracked at the sight. I fought to keep myself from crumbling. No time to let my emotions loose. That would come later. Now, there was something I had to do.

"C–Could you stay here with Stephen until Jenna gets back?" I folded my arms and hugged myself hard, my voice brittle. "I have to go. I have to help them find Karen."

His forehead creased. "Annie, no you don't."

"Yes. Yes, I do." I couldn't tell him all the reasons why, because I didn't fully understand them myself. Certainly I wouldn't be needed. I only knew that I'd been one of the last people to see Karen alive, and now a part of her had been sent to me. Karen's soul already rejoiced in heaven; I clung to that. But the earthly Karen, the Karen I had loved, deserved my special attention, however hard that might be to give. When found in the way the killer had left her, stripped of human worth, thrown to the uncaring elements, Karen deserved for someone who knew her and cared for her to be present, a personal friend among the probing, prodding hands of strangers.

Somehow, Dave must have seen all of this on my face, because he made no more protests. "I'll take the girls back to my house for the night. I won't tell them why you had to leave."

"Okay. Thanks."

He ran a knuckle down my cheek. "While you're out there—I'll be praying for you."

I nearly lost it then. "Good." My voice trembled. "I'm going to need it."

Chapter 34

Chetterling's office was too cluttered for our little group to meet within its walls. Instead, we gathered in the conference room where the task force had met two days and eons ago. Ed Trumble, Nathan Hallibander, Jim Cisneros, and Tim Blanche from the police department hunched around one end of the long table as a gloved Chetterling carefully removed the contents of the bag and laid them down. I hung back, having no desire to see the items again. At sight of the little finger, Ed muttered an expletive. Quickly, then, they all recovered, pushing aside their emotions like unwanted files upon a desk. I could see their mouths firm and eyes narrow as thoughts shifted to observation and data gathering.

"You said it's Karen Fogerty's?" Nathan rubbed his stubbled jaw.

I told them about the ring. "I know we can't be absolutely sure without DNA testing, but . . ."

The four men crowded in to read the note. "Wow." Tim Blanche shook his head. "Guy's gone totally loony on us."

Jim pointed to some words on the paper. "Look how he makes a capital S. See, here it is one, two, three, four times. Kinda tilted the wrong way, not connected to the following letter."

Chetterling grunted. "You know, what strikes me is this guy's arrogance. He's waiting to get credit for another kill, and we don't find the body fast enough for him."

"Yeah, know what you mean." Tim shook his head. "Be interesting to see what Rosalee Sanchez thinks about all this."

Matt Stanish bounced into the doorway, grinning like a Cheshire cat. "Hey, gang, so here's the party!" Too late, he spotted me. The smile vanished. His jauntiness fell away, replaced with an appropriate sag to his shoulders as he approached the table. "Hi, Annie." At his almost apologetic tone, I nodded back. I didn't fault him for his demeanor. Gallows humor was necessary for those working homicide cases. Especially this time. As tension mounted and beds remained unslept in, morbid jokes became the comfort of the day, a means for emotional survival.

Chetterling waited while Matt looked over the items, then he placed them back in the bag. I knew this evidence would be logged in and taken as soon as possible to the lab in Sacramento. There, testing would be done for possible DNA from the killer through saliva on the envelope, for fingerprints on the notebook paper, eliminating my own. A handwriting expert would analyze the penmanship.

Chetterling did not protest when I announced I was going with them to the crime scene. One look at my expression, and he knew well enough not to try talking me out of it.

I rode with him to the site, the others following us in three cars.

Ten minutes after eight. The sun edged toward the hills, anxious to hide its head from this horrific day. I gazed out my window at passing streets, houses, people. Was the Poison Killer someone I saw? Did he live in a house that now slid by us?

Chetterling and I didn't speak until we were on the freeway heading north.

"Tully Road. Guess what, I was on it yesterday." I spoke toward my window.

"You were *there*? Why?"

I shrugged. "Just driving around. Listening to a sermon about prayer." *Forgive me, God, if my voice sounds bitter.*

A pause, Chetterling trying to read between the lines. "Oh."

"I was waiting to hear from you about Trenise. Gerri Carson had given me this tape, and I didn't want to go home . . ." A shiver grappled with my shoulders. "It's so . . . unsettling, thinking I was right *there*, maybe near where she is, not realizing. You know what I mean?" I turned to him, and he flicked me an empathetic glance. "Like you're right next to evil and you have no idea. It could swipe at you, and you wouldn't even see it coming until it was too late."

Air shuddered down my throat. Maybe I shouldn't have come. I wasn't even there yet, and already I felt shaky.

"What's happening with Blake Dalveeno, anyway?" I asked.

Chetterling shook his head. "We're looking for him. And we haven't had time yet to talk to the four boys, but you know we're on it. Good thing we had your drawing of Dalveeno. It's been faxed to all surrounding jurisdictions along with the make of his car and the license plate number. Interesting how the guy's suddenly disappeared."

Yes, it was.

Sighing, I leaned back against the headrest.

"Annie, maybe you need to get away for a while. Take the kids somewhere."

If anyone needed a rest it was Chetterling. His whole face drooped, and every few minutes I'd hear him take an extra deep breath, trying to fill his oxygen-craving lungs. I'd swear he even blinked slowly.

"I can't leave now, and you know it. What if you find another unidentified victim and need someone to draw her? Who'd do it? Like you, I'll take a vacation when this is all over. If it's ever over."

Chetterling laid his hand on my arm. "Annie, you're one of the strongest and best people I know. You'll make it through this. Through the murders, your son's mess—all of it."

His hand remained upon me, fingers gentle yet firm, and all I could do was stare at it. I didn't have the slightest clue what to say, how to react. This touch, so uncommon for Ralph. Why here? Why now? As for what he said . . . it was just plain crazy. How could *I* be one of the strongest people he knew? Unless he was surrounded by mushmelons.

"Well, I . . . thank you."

When in a quandary, change the subject.

"Ralph, what do you think about the last line of the killer's note? About prayer. Like he's making fun of those who pray."

Chetterling lifted his hand away. My skin felt cool where the warmth of his fingers had been.

"Sounds like that, doesn't it?"

I thought about my times of prayer—how strong, how all-encompassing they'd been. Part of me wished I could tell Chetterling, but I wasn't sure he'd understand. "Oh, that reminds me. Did you call Gerri and tell her what's happening? She'll want to be with the Fogertys. And do Karen's parents know about any of this?"

"The parents have been notified we have a possible discovery." Ralph winced. "Didn't think to call Gerri, though."

"I'll do it right now." I pulled out my cell, thankful to have something to keep me busy. As her phone rang, I saw the Wonderland exit up ahead. "You need to get off here for Tully Road."

"Yeah." Chetterling slowed, then took the exit.

Gerri's quiet greeting sounded in my ear.

"Hi, it's Annie." In a voice wrung of all emotion, I told her the barest details. As for the package I'd received, I mentioned only the note with directions to Karen's body.

I gazed ahead as Chetterling turned onto Tully Road. *The second left*, the note had said. *Then about a mile in.* We passed the area where I'd pulled off to the side yesterday. And the house where the woman had gardened.

We passed the first left turn.

"Gerri, I can't talk much now. We're on the way to the site. But I thought you might want to get over to the Fogerty's house."

"I'm here already. Someone from the department called me. That's why I'm speaking so quietly."

"Oh. Okay, then." Wonderful Gerri. I should have known she'd already be on this.

There, ahead. The second left.

Sudden panic seized me. I didn't want to go. I didn't want to see Karen. What had I been *thinking*? Why had I ever gotten into this car? My breathing hitched. Chetterling glanced at me.

"Annie, you all right?" Gerri's voice floated to me.

"Yes, I'm just . . . I have to go now."

"Okay. We'll be—"

"Gerri, wait, I have to tell you. That note he sent? He taunted the pray-ers. Told us we should 'take up a new sport.'"

She sucked in a breath.

Chetterling turned left. Only a mile to go. Dread eeled its way through my lungs.

"Well, now, did he?" Gerri's words pulsed with meaning. "Tells you a lot, doesn't it, that he would call it 'sport.' As if prayer's some game instead of the power line of our existence."

Power line of our existence. Odd, how the phrase struck me. I could almost feel its current through my body, my soul.

The narrow road churned beneath our wheels. I kept an eye on Chetterling's odometer, watching a tenth of a mile scroll by. *She's on the right.* I needed to get off the phone, look out my window for signs of a path trodden through brush. The dread in my chest swelled, and the only way to push it down was to reach for hope. Tell myself maybe this body would not be Karen at all. Maybe I'd gotten it all wrong. The ring on that finger only looked like Karen's. Maybe we wouldn't even find a body. The same killer who sneered at prayer was now sneering at us all, laughing insanely as he led us on a chase for nothing. Or—perhaps even as we searched here, he lurked somewhere else, reveling in our diverted attention as he snatched another victim off the streets.

Jenna, Kelly, Erin.

They were in town, at a movie. What if the killer was out there right now, watching them leave the theater, as he may have watched Karen?

Dear God, no! Please keep them safe!

"Gerri." My throat cinched so tightly I could hardly talk. "I have to go. We're just about there. I'll call you soon."

"Okay. I know this is hard for you, Annie. I'm praying."

"Thank you." I clicked off the phone, laid it on the seat.

Chetterling squeezed my shoulder. That almost did me in. Tears sprang up, clawing for release. I pressed my eyes shut and swallowed—hard. *Not now. Get hold of yourself.*

I focused out my window. Chetterling slowed the car to a crawl.

Chapter 35

Ralph, look. There."

Chetterling braked.

I pointed out my window, a little ahead of the car. "Somebody's broken through that brush."

He leaned my direction, peering intently. "Yeah. That may be it."

We drove a short distance before pulling over. The other cars passed, parking in front of us so the potential crime scene would remain clear. If we were in the right spot, somewhere back there the killer had stopped in his own car.

A telling scent hung in the air as Ralph and I climbed out, shut our doors. We exchanged a knowing glance. Other doors slammed, feet hitting worn asphalt, men's low voices. Now that we'd arrived, my fears had dissipated, replaced with the dead calm of saturated atmosphere awaiting the break of a storm.

"Ralph." I stopped him before he could go. "If it's Karen, I'd like to ask you a favor."

"Shoot."

"When you're all done processing evidence, can I have a few minutes with her? Alone?"

His eyes locked with mine, and I saw their compassion. He nodded once, then turned to head down the road.

I leaned against the car, arms crossed, gazing at my feet. Waiting. Behind me, the other five men passed, trailing Chetterling. I knew they would gather near the area of broken passage, allow him to go in alone for discovery. If he found something, he'd call Matt and Jim in, then perhaps the other two. The less traipsing around the crime scene, the better.

"You okay, Annie?" Harry called over the car as he passed.

"Yeah, fine."

I heard Ed Trumble remind Tim Blanche in a low voice that I had known the victim.

Had known. Past tense. My hope quivered, then puffed away, smoke in the wind.

Chetterling's call drifted out from the woods. "She's here."

I slumped, sank my head in my hands.

No. No, no, no. God, why? How could You let this happen?

For a long time all I could do was stand there, blaming God, demanding answers. Trying to assimilate this latest terrible news, feeling the drip-drip of its acid into my soul. Memories of Karen, alive and well, flung themselves through my head. Her smile. Her genuine caring for Kelly and Erin. The sound of her voice.

Oh, the grief her parents would endure. The shattering, savage grief.

God, I can't feel You now and I can't hear You. But I can't walk away from You, either. Where would I go? Please help me hang on, help us all!

When I raised my head, my neck ached.

Sounds of the men at work filtered into my consciousness. So much for them to do now; no time for the sadness they, too, must feel. All the search for evidence, starting at the perimeter of the crime scene and moving in. The notes jotted down, photographs taken. Someone would call for the "meat wagon"—that detestable term—to come for transport of the body, telling them to give the detectives around an hour's lead. All the activity now, the low buzz of voices, the crunch through forest filtering to my ears.

I couldn't stand to hear it.

I slid back into the car. Chetterling's keys hung in the ignition. I turned them halfway, opening my window just enough that I wouldn't swelter. Then waited, my mind settling out, dulling. I craved the release of tears, but they would not come. They pooled behind a wall deep within, seeking the slightest crack. But the bricks held firm.

Time passed. I picked up my phone, called Dave. Even as I related the news, even at his caring, broken voice, I couldn't cry. Nor could I think. He wondered what to do about telling the girls, and I had to force the processing of his question before saying he must wait. No one else should know before Karen's parents were notified.

Dusk colored itself into darkness. Blue lights flashed, reflecting off the rearview mirror. Memories clashed in my brain—Pastor Paul Sheppard's admonitions to P.U.S.H., the killer's hateful note, Gerri's response, my times of prayer . . .

Power line of our existence.

I wanted to phone Gerri again, but resisted. By now someone had probably told Karen's parents. Gerri would be busy supporting them.

When feeling returned to me, at first a mere trickle, then in rivulets, it flowed with a cold anger and righteous resolve that sucked at my very soul. When I'd become a Christian last year, my life changed. After all my floundering, I'd found purpose, hope. Now this killer, this *animal*, wanted to take that away. Wanted to strip me of my beliefs, my trust in God.

Hadn't he already taken enough?

You evil man. You monster. I'm not going to let you do it. You're not *taking my faith from me.*

That's right. I would *not* fall into bitterness against God because of this. I would not give this killer the satisfaction of winning. I *would* continue to pray, and so would all the other Christians. God *would* answer. No more deaths. This was *it*. Enough was *enough*.

If evil wanted a fight, it would get one.

And evil would not win.

My breathing quickened. I felt resolve firm my expression, raise my shoulders.

I almost began to anticipate the task that awaited me.

Past nine thirty. Should be time soon. On the road in front of me, the three vehicles hulked in the darkness, pulsing on and off in a wash of blue lights. I got out of Chetterling's car, walked back toward the crime-scene tape. Headlights from an auto on the other side of the road illuminated the area into a murky gray, flashing purple under the rotating lights. The stench in the air thickened.

Already, a small crowd of reporters milled, a deputy standing guard to keep them back from the site. How on earth did they hear news so quickly? As I drew near I recognized Adam Bendershil, whom I'd vowed after the Bill Bland case last year never to speak with again. And Luke Bremington, the reporter who'd asked me about praying—was it just last night? Vaguely, I wondered if his article would appear in tomorrow's paper.

At the sight of me, the reporters flurried like a flock of birds. Somebody's television camera swung up, a bright light in my eyes. I flinched. The group crowded around, pestering me for information. At this point, they knew few details. I stuttered that I was not the person to tell them.

"Ms. Kingston," Bremington lured me, "are you still praying?"

I froze in the garish light. They all watched me, vultures recording my reactions, hoping for some emotional reply. The TV camera's red *on* light glowed. I tried to ignore the question, but then, in that suspended moment, something happened. The rage of my faith bubbled up and clogged my throat.

I set my jaw, my chest burning.

Pens poised above paper, waiting.

"We have all had enough," I heard myself say. My voice was in a minor key but steady. "Contrary to what this despicable killer wants, the Christians in this town have only begun to pray. And all of you out there, regardless of your faith until now, I call on you, I *beg* you, to join with us, praying in the name of Jesus that this killer be found. Now. God *will* act."

The reporters blinked hooded eyes at me, pens dancing as they scribbled. I could almost feel the vibration of their glee. I didn't care. They thought they were using me for their stories. Oh, no. I was using *them*.

Adam Bendershil opened his mouth—and at that moment Jim Cisneros called my name. I gave the group a nod, then turned to follow Jim's beckoning hand. The camera still rolled.

"Ralph said to get you." Jim spoke in a low voice. "You wanted to see her for a few minutes?"

"Yes. Thank you."

Cisneros led the way with a powerful flashlight. Mindful of the crime scene even after its processing, I followed carefully, my footsteps planted in his. We soon reached the area. The detectives were just finishing their work, Matt Stanish shouldering his camera.

"Okay, everyone." Chetterling ran his large hand down his face. "I'll be out in a minute. I'll wait to walk Annie back."

The rest of the men looked at me but said nothing. Matt managed a ghost of a smile. Jim passed his flashlight to me, saying he'd follow the others back.

Wordlessly, they left.

I took a deep breath and allowed my gaze to fall on Karen.

She lay ten feet ahead near the trunk of a giant tree, our flashlights casting her in semidarkness. My eyes flicked over her legs, an arm, then lifted away.

Chetterling cleared his throat. "I'll hang back a little, okay?"

"Thanks."

"You know not to touch her."

"Yeah."

Flashlight cutting a large circle before my feet, I approached Karen, my footsteps shushing through ground cover and ferns. When I reached her side, I focused on the ground between my toes. Slowly, I bent over to set down the flashlight, aiming its beam away from her, into the brush. Then I knelt, eyes still averted, knees crunching against small twigs. I placed both hands in my lap, laced trembling fingers. Bowed my head.

Behind me, somewhere, Chetterling probably watched. I didn't care.

At first, no words came. None. Only the anger again, simmering, as I thought of Karen. Of her life, so promising, cut short.

No more of this, God. No more!

My lips began to move.

"Oh, God, here I am near one of Your children. And she's broken, God, so horribly broken. Look down on us here, in this forest, look down and see what's happened to Karen. God, my own heart is in pieces. I can't imagine how her parents feel. How can I even find words to pray for them? Lord, uphold them and comfort them in this terrible loss. May they feel Your arms around them even when they cry—*especially* when they cry. Give them some comfort in remembering the wonderful times they had with Karen. Give them comfort in hearing about the joy she brought to others, like Kelly and Erin, and many of their friends at church." I swallowed hard. "Oh, Jesus, still . . . I know these comforts will be so small when they think of their beautiful daughter and what happened to her. Only *You* can get them through this, only You. I just don't know how I'd make it, if it were me."

I prayed more for Karen's parents, then found myself thanking God for Karen's life. For the fact that she was now in heaven and would never again face pain or sadness. And I thanked Him for all she'd meant to so many people, including me and Kelly. But even as I praised Him, my rage began to pop like oil droplets in a pan. And so I called on Jesus for justice.

"Please, *please* protect us all. Help us find who's doing this before anyone else is killed. Help them find Blake Dalveeno soon. If he's not the killer, help Ralph and the others know that. And if he *is* the right one, help them find evidence against him quickly so they can keep him off the streets. Please, Jesus," my voice rose, strengthened, "unleash *Your* power and strike down the evil that's urging this killer's hand! Hear the prayers of Your people, Lord; we're all *crying* to You. Act—*now* . . ."

My prayers flowed on, the kinds of petitions that, until this week, I had never prayed before, and even now did not entirely understand. I found myself rocking, rocking, my fingers tightening and fisted together, pressing against my legs as the words poured forth. Finally, the prayers abated . . . trickled away until I only rocked, my eyes squeezed shut and body trembling. How much time had passed, I couldn't say. My eyes were dry, yet I'd cried inside with every fiber of my being.

Everyone was waiting for me. I needed to go. I pushed from the ground, my calf muscles half asleep and tingling. Chetterling materialized behind me, and I leaned on his arm, willing strength back into my legs.

"Thank you, Ralph, so much, for letting me do this."

"Sure." His voice sounded hoarse.

He escorted me back to the road, our flashlights orbing the oppressive darkness.

By the time Karen's body was loaded into the back of the waiting van and we drove away, it was almost eleven. Chetterling and I didn't speak until we reached the Sheriff's Office parking lot.

"Annie, hope you get some sleep." He tried to smile, but only one side of his mouth worked.

"You're the one who needs sleep. And you probably won't get it now, will you?"

He sighed, pressed two fingers between his eyes. "Maybe I'll catch a few hours."

I picked my purse up from the floor. "When you find Blake Dalveeno, call me, okay?"

"Yeah. You want to watch the interview?"

"Absolutely."

He nodded.

As I drove home, I called Jenna to tell her I was on my way. She said the girls were over at Dave's. I phoned him next. We discussed how and when to tell the girls. We couldn't wait long; the news would be out tomorrow. "How about if you come over in the morning," Dave suggested, and I agreed. I could find neither the heart nor the energy to do it tonight.

When I reached the house, Jenna waited. We talked awhile, Jenna giving me hugs and fussing over how terrible I looked. Only a dear sister could be so blatantly honest. Once the girls had left, she told me, she'd talked to Stephen about what had happened. "He's pretty subdued. The whole thing really rattled him."

I could only nod, my eyelids weighting. Jenna pushed my arm and told me to go to bed.

Under the covers I huddled, shivering, even as our air conditioner fought to keep ahead of the heat. My brain would not shut off, its projector flashing pictures of Karen as I remembered her, interspersed with her sprawled and dirtied limbs against the forest floor. My final thought, before blessed sleep came, was of Blake Dalveeno, and where he might be hiding.

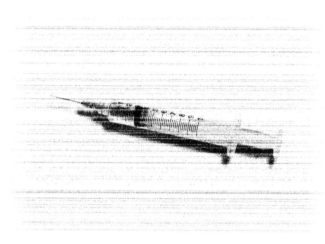

Saturday, June 25

Chapter 36

Dear, precious Karen Fogerty. How relieved I am that you've been found. Out there all alone in the forest, no one to care for you, no one to tend you. Now you will be tended oh, so carefully. And dressed, and made-up, and mourned.

How satisfying to see the night's news on the front page of the morning paper. Once again they have stopped their presses, just for me. The reporters gathered around, and all the official cars, with their flashing lights. All those people flocking at the mere beckon of my hand—

What is this?

"The Christians in this town have only begun to pray."

What?

How *dare* you.

This quote, pulled out from the article and boxed. How dare you wave this in my face! Surely, oh, newspaperman, you have bolded these words just to anger me. More of this prayer-mongering, more babble about God's work, when whose work, indeed, did you witness last night?

Hateful words! Inflaming words! Who is this reporter who would be so taken in? So Annie Kingston believes God will act. What will He do, zap me from the heavens? Where is He, then?

And where was He when I was a child and that fateful day rolled toward me unseen, unstoppable?

Of all people. Annie Kingston. How surprising. How ironic. That she be one of *them*.

Chapter 37

In my office Saturday morning, my prayer time was anything but energetic. I had expected, especially after last night, that the prayers would flow. I believed in the power of God. So why did the words block in my throat?

Head sunk in my hands, I tried to form petitions for safety. But only one word would come—*Jesus*. Over and over I repeated it, sometimes aloud, sometimes so softly I could barely hear it. Frustrated, I pushed back from my desk and stared at nothing.

I reached for the phone, dialed Gerri's cell number.

I told her of my inability to pray. Of all times, when I *knew* prayer was needed most. Gerri sounded as firm in her convictions as I'd ever heard her. She talked for a long time, pumping me up like a coach to a beleaguered player at half-time. "You *did* pray. In fact, you were doing exactly what it talks about in Romans 8:26 and 27. Promise me you'll read those verses when we get off the phone."

Gerri was a force to be reckoned with this morning. I assured her I'd look up the verses.

"And while we're on the subject," Gerri went on, "let me tell you what's been happening since last night. With the news that Karen's body was found, we've really gone on the warpath. A prayer list is being set up right now through my church. People across this town are signing up for half-hour slots of prayer, twenty-four hours a day, every day, until this killer is found. We've already got the next two days filled. I'm telling you, Annie, I can feel it in my spirit—something's going to break soon. And your repeating Jesus' name is a part of it. You were speaking such deep prayers that you couldn't even put them into words. But God knows." Her voice raised. "God *knows*. So you just keep at it!" She whooshed out air. "Boy, I'm telling you, I'm in a preachin' mood this morning."

That, she was.

I hung up the phone and hunched over my Bible to read the verses in Romans.

In the same way, the Spirit helps us in our weakness. We do not know what we ought to pray for, but the Spirit himself intercedes for us with groans that words cannot express. And he who searches our hearts knows the mind of the Spirit, because the Spirit intercedes for the saints in accordance with God's will.

The words battered at the door of my soul. I read the verses a second time, then a third. *He who searches our hearts* had to mean Jesus.

Wow.

I swiveled around in my chair and stared out the window. Gerri was right. Those verses spoke about what had happened to me. I hadn't known what to say, hadn't been able to form a single word. Yet my prayers had gone deeper than if I'd said a million. The Holy Spirit had prayed through me. *For* me.

I sought to wrap my mind around those verses. Here again I'd prayed in a new way—a way that had come straight from God. And a new truth struck me. Whether my prayers were filled with emotion or not, it didn't matter. God heard them.

Period.

# # # #

A half hour later, Jenna hustled about the kitchen making omelets and bacon with her efficient grace—a blend of talent that, apparently, our mother had hoarded until my sister's birth. Jenna was dressed in a pair of silky blue shorts and cream formfitting top that showed off her tan, her gorgeously thick hair still half wet from the shower. No makeup—yet. But she was a knockout without it.

"You want to go get the paper?" she asked.

"No. I'll pick it up when I come back from Dave's."

After breakfast he and I needed to tell the girls about Karen. I did not look forward to that. The paper would be full of the story.

"Okay, so I have an idea." Jenna broke an egg into a bowl. "Let's talk about something fun for a change."

That, I could definitely use. "Go for it."

She threw the shells into the sink and reached for a second egg. "Well. We went to a movie last night, as you know."

"Uh-huh." I watched her reach for a third egg. "Is that omelet mine? Two eggs are plenty for me."

She broke the third. "Yes, it's for you. And you're eating three."

"Jenna, I don't want three."

"Don't care what you want; you need 'em. You're getting too skinny."

"Too skinny? I *want* to lose weight. Maybe then I'd look half like you."

She threw me a withering glance as she picked up the milk carton. "Losing weight is one thing, Annie, but you don't have to do it in three days."

"I'm not trying to do it in three days."

"But you *are*. What have you eaten this week? Hardly anything."

I glowered at my coffee. Come to think of it, I couldn't remember eating much. I had to admit the bacon cooking in our microwave smelled terrific.

"I had a bowl of soup last night around five o'clock, so there."

"Oh, yippee for you, a bowl of soup." Jenna poured milk into the egg mixture and began beating it with a fork. "Anyway, are you going to let me tell my story or not?"

"Sure, you can tell it, if you can find the time around nagging me."

"I'm not nagging *you*; you're nagging *me*."

"Jenna, that would be the day pigs fly."

She huffed to herself. *Thwap, thwap, thwap* went her fork through the eggs. She set the bowl down, turned to check the melting butter in a small skillet on the stove. "So anyway, we were buying tickets at this movie, and I saw this most *gorgeous* man."

Oh, a man. I should have known. Jenna never went very long without a male in her life. But then, they tumbled after her like puppies.

"Who was he?"

"Wait a minute, you're pushing me ahead of my story."

"Sorry."

"Anyway, this guy really is something. Thick black hair, tanned skin. *Blue* eyes. I mean, can you imagine that combination—black hair and blue eyes? And he's built like . . ." she spread her hands, fingers curved around imagined biceps, "wow." She picked up the bowl of egg mixture, poured it into the pan. "And get this—he's with a boy around Kelly and Erin's age. Turns out the kid's his son. Named Curt. The boy, that is. He's in the same school with the girls, in tenth grade. Really cute. So he says hi to the girls, and they say hi back, and Kelly and Erin are making eyes at each other and whispering about how 'hot' he is. I'm thinking, 'you want hot, look at his dad.'"

She picked up a bag of grated cheddar cheese and shook some out over the omelet, then covered the pan with a lid. "Of course I'd already checked his left hand—no wedding ring. So, you know, we start talking, 'cause after all, the kids are talking, and it's the polite thing to do, right? His name's Eric. I always liked the name Eric." She wagged her head. "Ends up we're seeing the same movie. And the girls are dying to have Curt sit with them, so they ask him, and he says fine, and of course his dad's along for the ride, so . . ." Jenna raised her eyebrows.

I swear, sometimes she sounded like a teenager herself. "So naturally you end up sitting by each other."

"Yup." She lifted the lid, checked the omelet. Our microwave dinged that the bacon was done.

"And?"

"Well, let's see. He's thirty-seven. Divorced. His wife left ten years ago, when Curt was only five. She lives across the country now and rarely sees her son."

"You're kidding me." A *woman*, leaving her child, the way Vic had left his children? I couldn't imagine it. "Curt must have some issues."

"Yeah." Jenna's tone turned serious. "Imagine so." She raised a shoulder. "But he seems a level enough kid. And his dad—I'm telling you, Annie, this guy is *awesome*."

"What's he do?"

"Owns the Ford dealership in town, of all things."

"A *car salesman*? Good grief, Jenna, they're all a bunch of fast-talkers."

"No, not this one, huh-uh, I'm telling you." She lifted the pan lid, then set it on the counter. "Omelet's done."

Opening a cupboard, I took down two plates and handed her one.

She slid the omelet onto it, pointing with her chin to the microwave. "Bacon's in there; you can get your own. Put it on some paper towels to get off the grease. Mine too."

I couldn't resist a mock salute. She ignored me.

"My, my, who'd have thought there'd be someone attractive in Redding." I used paper towels to degrease our bacon. "Remember how you mourned when you moved up here, as if the area wasn't even civilized?"

Jenna just sniffed. She put more butter in the pan to melt, then returned to the counter and began to make her own omelet. "We talked until the movie started, and then afterward too. The kids wanted to go get ice cream, so we walked over to Baskin-Robbins. By the time we all left to go home, Eric had asked me out. Wants to take me to dinner sometime this week. Wanted to do it tonight, but I told him you'd need me. I told him who you are, and with everything that's going on, he understood. We talked about you for quite a while, in fact."

Asked her out *already*? Slowly, I removed the paper towels from the bacon, threw them in the trash. Turned on the faucet to wash my greasy hand—and stood staring at the stream of water.

"Well, aren't you going to say something?" Jenna threw shells into the sink.

"Why do you have to go out with him so soon?"

She looked at me askance. "A guy like that? Why wouldn't I?"

"Because . . . because you don't know him."

"I do know him. I mean, enough to see I want to have dinner with him."

"But you don't *know* him."

"Annie." She made an impatient sound in her throat. "Are you going to wash your hands or just stare at the water?"

I reached for the soap, moved my fingers under the faucet.

She returned to her omelet. "So why are you trying to spoil this for me?"

"I'm not trying to spoil anything. It's just . . . like you said, there's a lot going on right now. Namely, somebody's out there killing women. And it could be anybody."

Jenna put down her *thwapping* fork. Faced me squarely, a hand on her hip. "Are you trying to tell me," she spread the words like hardened butter, "I should be suspicious of *him*?"

"Right now we need to be suspicious of everybody." I took extra time washing my hands. I didn't want to look at her.

"That's ridiculous."

I turned off the water, reached for a paper towel. "No it isn't, Jenna. Really it's not. If you'd seen everything that I've seen . . . If you'd heard the detectives and criminal profiler talk. About how *normal* the killer probably looks. What a charmer he must be." I threw the paper towel in the trash and turned to meet her eyes. "Look. This guy Eric is probably terrific. Probably wouldn't hurt a flea. But right now, you just *don't know*. I mean, I drive down the streets and find myself looking at *everybody* suspiciously."

The scene of Karen's body flashed in my head.

I gestured toward the window. "He's out there right now, walking among us. Maybe even meeting women at the movies." My throat tightened, surprising me. I shook my head, looked away. "And that's why I want you to be careful. That's all. Just . . . be careful."

Jenna leaned against the counter. Crossed her arms. "I know you're right." She spoke toward the floor. "Really, I get it. I just . . . it's hard to think that way when you meet somebody, you know? I mean I can't imagine . . ."

I gave her a lopsided smile. "I know."

She sighed. Picked up her egg mixture and poured it into the pan. "Your omelet's getting cold."

"Yeah, well, so's your bacon."

We spread our mouths, Kermit-like, at each other.

"Mommie?" My sister said plaintively a few minutes later as I ate my omelet.

Oh, good grief. "What is it, Jenna?"

"Are you gonna let me go out with Eric?"

I sighed toward the ceiling. "I don't know. Maybe we should have him over here first. Let me look him over. And give him the Mother speech."

"Mother speech?"

"Yeah, you know—all right, sir, exactly what are your intentions? And by the way, while you're out with my sister, don't you dare try anything." I paused a beat. "Like slipping her some poison."

Jenna laughed through her nose. I started giggling and nearly choked on a mouthful of omelet.

"Annie, you're terrible."

I clapped a hand over my lips. Suddenly, I understood the homicide detectives' need for morbid humor. By the time Jenna and I stopped chortling, my eyes watered.

She set her plateful of food on the table. Pulled out a chair and sat down. We talked more about it as we ate, but the laughter had spritzed away, perfume on a wayward wind. My sister was determined to go out with Eric. Stubborn Jenna. Bossed me around, but *she'd* do as she pleased. I loved her dearly—and sometimes I could just strangle her.

Finished with my breakfast, I pushed back from the table with reluctance. "I need to get over to Dave's now."

"Yeah, I know." She peered at me. "I know you don't want to go, but . . . you look different somehow."

"What do you mean?"

"I don't know. Stronger or something. Not so like a willow in the wind."

I pondered that, then nodded once. "Hm. Maybe I am."

"Well, that's good." Jenna raised her shoulders. "Why?"

"Because—" I looked at her straight on—"I've been praying a lot. And prayer works."

"Oh." She leaned back, nonplussed.

"Really. You ought to try it sometime, Jenna."

She regarded the table, then looked up, mischief in her eyes. "If I do, will you let me go out with Eric?"

I threw my napkin at her face.

Chapter 38

The girls were still in bed.

Dave and I stood in his kitchen, not wanting to wake them up. I'd laid my cell phone on the counter. He smiled at my necklace, worn today over a scoop-necked blue knit shirt. "Nice to see you wearing it again."

He stood close enough that I caught the scent of lime shaving lotion. I looked up into his eyes and saw hidden meaning: he interpreted my wearing the necklace as a symbol of a connection between us. I smiled at him, a warmth I'd not felt in a very long time sliding through my veins.

He reached out and ran a knuckle lightly down my cheek. Whoa—hadn't expected that. The touch left a tingle in its wake. My heart did an awkward two-step as our gazes locked, his hand lingering on my skin. The air turned light and heady, like a rush of oxygen into a suffocating room. I tumbled into the sensation . . .

And then nearly panicked.

How could this be happening *now*, with all the tragedy around us?

How could it be happening at all?

I felt my face flush crimson, heart knocking against my ribs. Dave started to say something, and in that very second,

Erin's bedroom stereo kicked on. My eyes jerked toward the hall, and Dave pulled his hand away. He took a step back.

We both focused on the kitchen entrance like two teenagers caught amiss. If the girls appeared now, our expressions would give us away.

No girls.

"Well." I laughed nervously. "Sounds like they're up."

"Guess so."

We looked at each other, a *whoosh-whoosh* pulsing through my body. Dave's mouth lifted in a way that told me he'd felt what I had, and that he by no means considered this subject closed. I pressed my lips together in acquiescence.

Okay, Annie. Feet back on the ground.

A somber task awaited us. Together, we walked down the hall to knock on Erin's door.

The girls lolled on Erin's bed, pajama-clad, half sleepy-eyed. They took one look at us and stilled, expressions flickering as their brains processed our unlikely pairing at their threshold on a Saturday morning.

Kelly's head drew back, her cheeks slacking. "Is it Karen?"

I nodded.

My daughter flung herself off the bed and into my arms. Erin collapsed where she sat, sobbing. Dave strode over to sit down and pull her close. His eyes met mine over the tops of our mourning daughters' heads.

It took some time for them to cry themselves out. Then they lobbed questions. How? Was it the same killer? When? Where was she found? I answered as I could, withholding details. In the end, Kelly and Erin turned from us and toward each other. They needed to grieve alone, in their teenage way.

Dave and I slipped from the room, shutting the door behind us.

Back in the kitchen we faced each other once again. We were both shaken.

I drew my arms across my chest. "We need to get the girls out of here, get them doing something fun. This is all too much."

"Agreed." Dave leaned back against the counter and sighed. "I could fly them somewhere until tomorrow. I've got appointments Monday."

Dave's Piper was sitting in the hangar built into his home. I hadn't seen it out all week. He was probably itching to fly. Private pilots never wanted to be away from their planes for too long. But an overnight stay wasn't time enough for the girls.

"No, you know what? Maybe Jenna will do it. She promised to take them to Disneyland sometime. If she doesn't have any projects coming up, she should just take them and go." My gaze wandered out the front window. "Maybe Stephen should go too." I focused on my house, thinking about the idea.

"Sure."

I turned back to Dave. "Not that he deserves it. But it's just . . . he needs to get out of here too. He can't go back to work right now, can't hang around with friends. Can't even leave the house, really. He's going to go stir-crazy on me, I know it. And when he does, he'll do something *really* stupid."

"Annie, it's okay. You don't have to convince me."

I shook my head. "I'm trying to convince myself."

"Why do you need to do that?"

"Because . . . it's more than one thing. First, I'm not sure he should leave town. What if the detectives need to talk to him again? They've already gotten the information they need out of him but still . . ." I shrugged. "And second . . ." I bit my lip, unsure whether I had the right to speak so candidly about my sister. "Jenna won't want to take him. She doesn't like Stephen. Can't say I blame her; he's not exactly the nicest person to be around. And come to think of it, the girls probably wouldn't choose to have him along, either."

He gave me a look. "The girls would hardly have reason to complain, would they. Flown in a private plane to Disneyland?"

I smiled ruefully. "Guess not."

A realization sped through me. If Jenna took the kids, that would leave me alone at home—and I certainly didn't want to sleep in that big house all by myself right now, even with a burglar alarm and gun. Knowing Jenna, she'd insist that I wouldn't. But I couldn't stay in Dave's guest room again, not with the girls gone. And especially not after that moment in this very kitchen. Without a word spoken, we'd crossed a line, and we both knew it. Sleeping in the same house, even on different floors, would be too awkward, too . . .

No. Huh-uh. I wouldn't do it.

I'd have to go into town, stay with Gerri or maybe someone from church.

"Annie?" Dave's voice snapped me back to the present. "What are you thinking?"

"Oh. Nothing. Silly thoughts, when we have so much else to worry about. Okay, I'm going to go talk to my sister. I'll call you—"

My cell phone rang, and I jumped. *Oh, great. What now?*

I crossed to the counter where my phone lay, picked it up. A familiar number showed on the gray-tinged screen. "It's Chetterling." I shot Dave an anxious look, then clicked on the line. "Hi, Ralph."

"Morning." His voice grated with tiredness, but I detected a tinge of satisfaction. "We picked up our man."

"Dalveeno?"

"Yeah. Thanks to your drawing. Did you see it? Page two of this morning's paper. We got calls right away, and one tip led us to him."

I let out a breath and leaned against the counter. *Oh, thank You, God.*

"You want to come down and watch the interview?"

My mind whirled. So much for the next hour's plans. "Yes. Yes, of course, I'll be there." I turned toward Dave, creasing my forehead in apology. He gave a little nod, watching me intently. "Where'd you find him?"

"On I–5, below Red Bluff. Heading south. He tried to run. It was quite the chase, I hear. Took five highway patrol cars to stop him."

Dalveeno, running for it. The news pulsed with myriad possibilities. Blake sounded too smart to run unless he had very good reason. All this time he'd blended into society, his drug connections underground . . .

"This means you can keep him in custody for now, doesn't it?" I said. "You can charge him for trying to flee."

"You got it. But he won't stay locked up long for that. Let's just hope we hear some good stuff during the interview. What we really want is a good reason to obtain a search warrant in relation to the murders, not just the drug connection."

Please, Lord, yes. Do this for us.

Dave edged toward me as I clicked off the line. "Good news?"

I told him. Already I felt adrenaline tumbling through my veins. I ran a hand through my hair, feeling the pull to be gone, to hurry to the Sheriff's Office and witness the confrontation. "Look, I'll talk to Jenna quickly before I leave, okay? About taking the kids."

"Sure."

My gaze cut toward the entryway. I started to go, clutching my cell phone, then realized my selfishness. A single call, and here I stood, perched to scurry away for the umpteenth time, my daughter once again left in his care. "Dave." Turning back, without a second thought I hugged him. His arms slid around me as if it was the most natural thing in the world. One of his hands curved to fit the back of my head.

"Annie," he whispered.

I felt a tremble in his arms. Pressing my head against his neck, I hung there for a moment, just *feeling* him. When we pulled back, his eyes were overbright. "Be careful."

I creased my brow, wondering at the admonition. "I will."

He smoothed his hand down my cheek, a tender smile on his lips. Then, reluctantly, he let me go.

Chapter 39

The Sheriff's Office hummed with activity.

I knew all the deputies didn't need to be there, that they must soon return to their vehicles and the streets. But word had flashed through the department like sparks on tinder— a possible Poison Killer suspect had been picked up. A suspect who'd fled at first sight of the flashing lights behind him. Curious deputies, apparently hoping for a good look at Blake Dalveeno, now found excuses to walk the office halls. They passed each other in the lobby, speaking in low tones, comparing what they knew of the chase, the man.

Huddling at the front desk to whisper with Liz Keltz, the heavyset young woman who replaced Beverly on weekends, was Ruby Mays. Along the side of one wall stood the long table that held food brought by townspeople, now loaded with sandwiches, salads, and desserts. I spotted a signature Ruby plate of chocolate chip cookies.

"Hi, Annie," Liz said.

Ruby jerked around to spear me with a look, clutching her arms. "Hello, Annie." Her gaze bounced across my face, to the floor, and up again. She puckered her mouth, watching three deputies cluster in low conversation across the lobby.

She seemed nervous—not typical for Ruby. "Hello." I smiled, hoping to put her at ease. "I see you brought cookies."

She gave a quick nod. "Oh, yes, well, it's been a couple days, you know, and it was time." Her gaze wandered back to the deputies. I looked at Liz, raising my eyebrows. Liz pulled down one side of her heavily lipsticked mouth and shrugged.

"How are you?" Liz blinked at me with feigned cheeriness.

"Fine." I couldn't take my eyes from Ruby, who was rubbing her arms as if she stood in a freezer.

"Um. So what are you doing here? Come to eat?" Liz again, covering the awkward moment with more chatter. She tilted her bleached blonde head toward the table of food.

"Oh, I . . ." Vaguely, I gestured toward the hall. I didn't want to make public the fact that I would witness Blake Dalveeno's questioning. "Just some business." With another smile at Liz that I hoped didn't seem too forced, and another glance at Ruby, I turned to go.

"I need to be leaving too." Ruby whisked her purse off Liz's desk. She straightened her shoulders and whirled around, nearly colliding with me as she headed toward the door. Frowning, I watched her scurry away. *What's going on with her?* When she reached the door, something nudged me to follow.

"Ruby." I stopped her just outside the building. "I'm sorry if I shouldn't push, but it seems like something's wrong. Anything I can do to help?"

She gazed down at me, indecision flicking across her wide face. Her mouth opened, then closed. Opened again. "No. I'm fine, thank you. I'm just anxious. I read in the paper that they found another victim last night—that Karen girl. Do you know they found her off Tully Road? I *live* on Tully Road. Right across from the left turnoff to that little lane. *Right there.* I heard all the sirens go by." She drew in her shoulders. "He's never left anyone that close to me; he's always stayed south." She tilted her head toward the building. "Then I hear all the hubbub. That they found that man they were looking for, the one you drew for this morning's paper. And I'm just . . ." Her voice trailed away, gaze sliding to her sturdy-heeled shoes.

I squeezed her arm. "You're hoping it's him?"

Ruby looked up at me, paused, then nodded. But something in her hesitation called out to me, a silent plea for help.

She knows something. The thought pinballed through my brain. *"I live on Tully Road . . ."*

"Ruby. Did you . . . see something? Maybe on that road near your house?"

Her eyelids flickered. She drew back, then tried to cover her reaction with a tiny smile. "Of course not, nothing like that."

I pulled my top lip between my teeth, still gazing at her. She was lying.

Ruby took a breath, brightened her expression. "Well. I really must be going."

She turned.

"Wait. Here." I dug in my purse for a card. Held it out to her. "Just take this, okay? It has my cell phone number on it. If you . . . if there's any reason you want to call me, please do."

Slowly, she raised a hand, as if she was about to accept a tempting but fatal morsel of food. Her fingers closed around the card, and I let go. I started to leave, afraid if I lingered at all, she would shove it right back at me. But Ruby moved even faster.

"Thank you," she whispered, then fled to her car.

I reentered the building to watch the Dalveeno show, praying that she would call.

Chapter 40

So you've caught me, have you?

Here he sits like a rat in a cage, you boast, *bound for the snapping jaws of justice.*

Do you think you can stop me so easily?

Fools.

Do you not see that now I scheme more than ever? Goaded by your pious pray-ers, your driveling detectives and artless arrogance. Do you not know that four walls can't hold me? That there is more to me than meets your eye, more power, more *will*, in my right hand than in all of you put together? My childhood taught me strength, and you will not take it from me now.

Come, come, my mother wheedled. *Come now, it is time.*

No, Mama, don't make me. Please, no . . .

So question your prize catch. Bring on your intimidation, your abuse and torture. They will not stop me.

How taken aback you all will be, how amazed at the havoc I'll wreak. You all will suffer. I will bring down every last one of the pray-ers, every last one of the wives and daughters of you who sought me. Day after day, night after night, I will take and take and take. Even now I plan death and destruction.

The black wings have risen inside me, hatching virulent off-spring. So call to your God, all of you, grovel and moan before

Him. Seek to trap me within four walls, see if I don't fly away, up and out and over, and spread my deeds across this town like seeds dropped in the wind.

When your backs are turned, I will strike. Ever at your back I will be.

Chapter 41

In the claustrophobic room behind a one-way mirror, Blake Dalveeno sat with well-oiled poise, eased back in his chair, one arm on the table. His fingers drummed the wood with profound boredom. The only sign of anger was the half scowl on his face. It pinched the sides of his wide nose, narrowed his eyes, and smirked his lips. The dreadlocks looked perfect in their wildness. Blake wore a tight T-shirt, and every now and then his biceps jumped.

Flanking Dalveeno were Chetterling at one end of the table and Ed Trumble at the other. Ed hunched forward, beady eyes glaring at Dalveeno as if he'd like to take the man's head off. Chetterling sat with arms crossed, head tilted to one side. The expression on Ralph's face said he'd seen it all—and nothing surprised him.

I stood outside the one-way mirror, sure those around me could hear my heart thumping. Tim Blanche had hustled over from the police department to watch. He stood on my left, whispering to Nathan Hallibander. On my right lingered two deputies, neither of whom needed to witness the questioning, as far as I knew, but who couldn't pull themselves away from the show.

Perhaps they thought the same of me.

Just seeing Dalveeno sent pinpricks down my arms. We were mere feet apart, closer than we'd been when he defied me in my home. My brain shot out pictures of him hulking over Kelly, and I shuddered. Then I thought of Stephen. *This* was the kind of person my son hung out with in the life he kept apart from me. *This* was the man who held my son's life in his hands, who'd tracked Stephen all the way to the Bay Area.

Was he also the man who'd killed Karen Fogerty and the other women?

As much as I wanted the killer caught, even now, ambivalence coiled itself through my chest. To think this creature had been in my home, so close to my daughter. Worse, to think the Poison Killer worked the strings that made my son jump like a puppet.

But if Dalveeno *was* guilty, if he never walked the streets again, his drug ring would fall apart, wouldn't it? Stephen's life could return to normal. He could leave our house without fear.

God, after all this tragedy, could the answer be that simple? One man's arrest, solving all our problems?

Maybe. Gerri wouldn't be surprised, would she? I could hear her now, saying God works in amazing ways. That the prayers of the town had been heard, and my mother's prayers for Stephen as well.

How could I not wish for this?

Chetterling started the interview with the usual declarations for the video camera mounted in the top corner of the room—those present, date, Miranda rights read to Dalveeno.

"Yes, I understand my rights," Dalveeno said with plagued weariness.

The detective started with easy questions: where did Blake work? Hours? Who were his friends? Where did he hang out? If they were meant to get him talking, they failed. A wariness shimmered beneath Blake's facade, his eyes swinging back and forth between the two detectives. His answers were terse, as if he'd been instructed by a wily attorney. Speaking of which, where was Dalveeno's lawyer? He was certainly entitled to one, and if he was as cunning as we thought, why wouldn't he protect himself?

I whispered the question to Nathan. He shrugged. "We see it all the time. Guy thinks he's smart enough to beat the system, and a lawyer'll just make him look suspicious. The old downfall. Don't worry, we'll nail him."

If he's guilty, I wanted to add.

Chetterling skipped over information about Dalveeno's drug dealings, moving straight to the subject of Trenise.

"So when's the last time you saw her?" he asked.

Dalveeno frowned at the table. "Saturday."

"When Saturday?"

"Morning."

"Did she stay at your place Friday night?"

"Yes." Blake looked indignant, as if it was none of the detective's business.

Chetterling seemed unruffled. "Tell us what happened when you last saw her."

Blake drew in a breath, his nostrils flaring. "We had a fight, the last of many. I was growing tired of her immaturity. She wanted to leave town, go to Sacramento and live with her sister. I said, 'Fine, go, and take all your trash with you.' She packed her things and left."

"What time was this?" Chetterling watched Dalveeno under furrowed brows.

"I don't know. Eleven o'clock, twelve."

"And you never saw or heard from her again?"

"No."

"And you didn't wonder about that? Didn't even occur to you to call her, make sure she's all right?"

Dalveeno flicked a look at the ceiling. "Like I said, I was tired of her. She said she was leaving, and she did. What's to worry about?"

Ed Trumble snorted. "Not much, except young women around here are winding up dead."

Dalveeno lifted a shoulder. "Never occurred to me she'd be one of them."

Beside me, Tim Blanche made a little *tsking* sound. "Man, he's a cold one."

Trumble rested an elbow on the arm of his chair, thumb and forefinger smoothing his mustache as he stared daggers at Dalveeno. "Well, guess what, we've got witnesses—friends of yours, in fact—who saw Trenise in town as late as 6:00 p.m."

Dalveeno's mouth pulled as if to say *so what?*

"Word from these witnesses is that you were fire-breathing mad at Trenise. That you didn't want her to leave. That you felt you *owned* her."

"Oh, sure." Dalveeno's dreadlocked head wagged.

"So you agree with that."

His jaw flexed. He looked at Trumble with the superior air of a master teacher unswayed by a conniving pupil. "No, it's not true. You know you're making that up."

"Are they?" I asked Nathan in a low voice. Law enforcement wasn't bound to the truth while questioning a suspect.

If Chetterling and Trumble needed false information to trip up Dalveeno, they wouldn't hesitate.

Nathan kept his eyes on Dalveeno. "Nope, that's true." He layered the words with meaning. The detectives had caught their suspect in a lie.

"You didn't see Trenise past eleven or twelve o'clock?" Ed pressed.

"No."

Trumble and Chetterling exchanged a glance.

"All right." Chetterling uncrossed his arms, leaned against the table. "What were you doing Saturday afternoon and evening?"

Dalveeno evaded. He'd stayed in his apartment for a while, then hung out with some friends. After dinner at a local restaurant he felt sick to his stomach—maybe something he ate. He'd gone home, alone. Went to bed early.

In other words, no alibi.

I bit the inside of my cheek. This didn't have to mean anything. No one could be entirely sure when Trenise had been killed. Still, if no one saw her past six o'clock on that day . . .

Trumble's mouth worked as if he wanted to spit. "Where were you between the hours of ten o'clock and midnight three days ago, Wednesday the twenty-second?"

Dalveeno couldn't remember.

"Maybe you'd better try a little harder," Trumble retorted. "Could be worth your while."

Silence. Dalveeno stared toward the corner of the room. Finally, he raised a shoulder. "You don't see me rubbing my hands, do you?"

Trumble blinked. "Huh?"

A lengthy sigh. "Surely you've read Shakespeare. Lady Macbeth, rubbing her hands, trying to rid herself of the invisible blood staining them from murder? Her demeanor and protestations?" Blake looked from one detective to the other. Another sigh. "Clearly, such knowledge is beyond you."

Chetterling ran his tongue under his upper lip, surveying Dalveeno with obvious disdain.

"'Methinks the gentleman doth protest too much.'" Trumble sniffed. "Or is my rewrite of the quote beyond you?"

"Get him, Ed," Nathan muttered.

Dalveeno sneered. "Why did you bring me down here? You've got nothing on me, and you know it. You just need the proverbial scapegoat, or in the vernacular, a fall guy. After all, everybody's wondering why you haven't solved the case after six months and who knows how many murders. Well, hear this. I . . . won't . . . play . . . the part." He sat back, raised his eyebrows.

Ed shoved to his feet and leaned across the table. "Fall guy? Man, you're falling so fast—"

"Wait, whoa." Chetterling shot up his hand.

"I'm not waiting for nothin'!" Trumble turned on him. "He's—"

"Okay, okay." Chetterling's voice rose. "I got you, Ed." He lowered his eyes meaningfully to Ed's chair. Slowly, Ed sat back down, breathing malevolence at Blake, who sat watching the spectacle with detached amusement.

"Now." Chetterling cut a look of distaste at Dalveeno. "Let's try this again. Where were you the night of Wednesday, June twenty-second?"

"I'll answer again." Blake's words mocked in singsong. "I don't remember."

"Where were you the night of Monday, June twentieth?"

Monday. The night Celeste was killed. The night she was left near my backyard.

Dalveeno pursed his lips. "Don't remember."

"How about Tuesday afternoon?"

"Come on, what is this? I was working."

"Really. You didn't take off an hour or so to pay the Kingston home a visit?"

Dalveeno blinked.

"You know, the home of Stephen Kingston? His mother, Annie? The house whose backyard is right near where the body of Celeste Weggin was found that very same day?"

I focused straight ahead, knowing the two Sheriff's deputies at my side were looking me over, surprised at the information about Blake's visit. Tim and Nathan didn't react. Maybe Chetterling had told them of Stephen's tie to Blake.

Fear flicked across Dalveeno's face, then was gone so quickly I almost wondered if I'd seen it at all. He shook his head. "You guys are too much, the way you link things. All right, fine, I forgot. I did go to Stephen's house to see if he was home. But I certainly didn't know anything about a body in the backyard."

Chetterling began pumping out questions, hip-hopping from this subject to that. I knew he'd seen the expression on Blake's face and wanted to put another crack in that veneer. He covered all the victims—had Dalveeno known this woman, that one? He jumped from night to night of when all were found, going all the way back to January. Dalveeno couldn't remember his whereabouts on any of those days. Chetterling circled around to Karen again, to the restaurant where she worked. Had Blake ever eaten there? Was he in that area the night of Wednesday the twenty-second? How could he explain the fact that someone had *seen* him there?

"That's a lie!" Dalveeno pointed a finger at the detective. I could see the rise and fall of his chest. "I wasn't anywhere *near* that place Wednesday night!"

"Oh, really?" Chetterling arched his brows. "Thought you couldn't remember where you were."

On and on the detective pounded while Ed Trumble rocked back in his chair with a smirk of vengeance. Chetterling asked more about Trenise. *Why* hadn't Blake called her cell phone since she left? Is that the way he treated women— threw them away when he tired of them? No? Then how *did* he treat women? Did he hate all females? How did his mother treat him? What kind of relationship did they have?

The questions came, harder, faster. Dalveeno's posture began to slump, a sheen of sweat glistening on his face.

"What color's the carpet in your car?" Chetterling switched gears so fast Blake screwed up his face.

"Huh?"

"You heard me. What color's the carpet?"

Dalveeno's lips worked. "What difference does it make?"

Chetterling shrugged. "I *know* what color it is."

"Then why'd you ask?"

"Because it's the same color as fibers from a vehicle carpet that were found on two of the victims' bodies."

Blake's face flattened. "Oh, come on, so *what*? How many people in this town have brown carpet in their car? A thousand? Five thousand? Ten?"

"I'm wondering," Chetterling spoke slowly, "how many people *dated* one of the victims, *can't* tell us where they were the night any of the women were killed, *and* have the right color vehicle carpet."

"I don't know, maybe you ought to find out instead of wasting all your time with me."

Chetterling pushed his large face close to Dalveeno's. "Why'd you choose Karen Fogerty?"

"Choose her for what?"

"You waited outside that restaurant, didn't you? Waited for her to get off work."

"I don't know what you're talking about. I never even met the girl!"

"You followed her on her way home. Managed to stop her before she got there."

"No. I did not." Dalveeno's voice rose.

"You watched her die, didn't you? You like making women suffer."

Dalveeno's face flushed. "Stop right now or this conversation's over."

Chetterling spread his hands. "It can be over any time, you just say the word. But don't think you've cleared yourself. All you've done is dug a deeper pit."

"Look, I don't know anything about these murders!" Dalveeno pushed back his chair. "I'm a law-abiding citizen. I've got no record whatsoever, and you know it!"

"Law abiding? Let's talk about shipping meth to New Orleans."

Dalveeno stared. "What?"

"Let's talk about some of your helpers. Kenny Wraight, Dwayne Moody, Al Hanks, Eddy Bocerelli. These names ring a bell with you?"

"I don't—"

"These are the guys you had pick up Stephen Kingston last Wednesday afternoon and knock him around, demanding two thousand dollars."

"I wasn't anywhere near Stephen Kingston on Wednesday afternoon."

"Oh, you remember what you were doing then, huh? Unlike that evening, when Karen Fogerty disappeared?"

Dalveeno drew a hand across his perspiring forehead and shot a pleading look at Trumble. Ed only glared at him. Blake's suave demeanor was crumbling. The more he lied about the drugs—which the detectives clearly knew about in detail—the less they believed his denials of the killings. Chetterling kept at him, hopscotching his queries and accusations, Ed throwing in some of his own. I couldn't understand what the detectives were doing. Yes, they were wearing Blake down, but any minute now he'd refuse to answer any more questions. Then where would they be?

God, don't let them do the wrong thing—

My cell phone rang. I jumped.

Pulling it from my purse, I walked some distance away, out of earshot from the four men around me. I checked the number but didn't recognize it.

"Hello?"

Silence.

I bent over the phone. "Hello?"

"Oh. Hello. Annie?"

"Yes?"

"This is Ruby." Her voice sounded breathless.

My head came up. I glanced back at Tim and Nathan, and the other two men watching the questioning. I could no longer see through the glass into the interrogation room. "Ruby. Hi."

"I hope I'm not bothering you."

"Of course not."

"You said to call if I needed to."

"Yes. Absolutely. What can I do for you?"

Another long pause, filled with an ambivalence I could almost feel. I felt the tenuous connection between us, knew she could break it any moment. "Ruby?"

"Yes, I'm here. I thought maybe after all I should tell you. Since somehow you seemed to know. It's just that I'm so frightened, and I don't want to be pulled into this. I live all alone, you know, out in the country. I never asked for this."

"You're right, you didn't. Are you trying to tell me that you saw something?"

"Yes."

"What, Ruby? What did you see?"

She hesitated. "Car lights coming down the road out front—" Her voice hitched, and the words stopped.

"Yes, car lights?"

Sudden commotion from the four men made me look over my shoulder. Tim and Nathan faced each other, Nathan's mouth in an O. Tim brought up his hand with three fingers bent inward and forefinger sticking out, mocking a revolver. He pointed the make-believe gun at his own head and pulled the trigger.

Dalveeno must have just said something highly incriminating. I wanted to go back, hear what had happened. Ruby's voice fought for my attention.

"I'm sorry, Ruby, what did you say?"

"He's the right man, you know. The one whose picture was in the paper. Don't let him go. Don't let him escape."

I watched the four men, the two deputies not in the task force loop whispering to each other, apparently exchanging ideas about what had just happened. Suddenly, I wondered why Tim and Nathan had allowed them to stay. They could be hearing information known only to task force members.

"How do you know he's the right man?"

"Because . . ." Her breathing blew through the line.

"Ruby?"

"No." Fear tinged her voice. "No, I don't want to talk about this. I'm not sure I can trust you."

I frowned. "Of course you can trust me."

"But I don't want anyone else to know it came from me. Is there a way I can tell you this, but you don't have to tell anyone else where you heard it?"

"Well, I—"

"Otherwise, I just . . . can't."

The four men faced the window again, looking through it with intensity. Tim had his chin cupped in one hand. One of the deputies pressed fists against his hips.

What am I supposed to do? Make promises I can't keep, just so she'll talk to me?

"Annie?"

"Yes, okay. I won't tell anyone the information came from you."

"There's a reason, you know, that I'm being like this. It's not because I want to cause you trouble."

"It's okay, you're not."

"All right. Could you . . . perhaps come see me?"

"See you? You mean at your house?"

"Yes. I can tell you everything. But *don't* let anyone from the Sheriff's Department know you're coming."

I licked my lips, looking back to the men. No way did I want to leave now. But something told me this was very important. "Okay. I'll come."

"You understand where I live?"

"Yes."

"I'll watch for you. I'll come out on the porch so you'll see me. And even though it's daylight and you've got that man there, be very careful, all right?"

Maybe she didn't mean to, but she was scaring me. Blake Dalveeno was the killer, she said, and he was here, in custody. But I should still be careful? A chill burrowed its way to the hollows of my bones.

"I will. I'll even lock my doors."

"Good. I'll wait for you."

I clicked off my phone, a skeletal finger drawing on the back of my neck.

Blake in jail, but she's still scared. Why?

Then again, why not? How sure had I been of Stephen's safety, even with the prospect of Blake being locked up? There were too many others out there whom Blake had under his thumb—

The realization swirled through my veins, then settled like muddy sediment.

That's what Ruby was trying to say. Blake had not acted alone.

Then another thought hit me—harder.

Don't let anyone from the Sheriff's Department know you're coming . . .

Rosalee Sanchez's warning at the task force meeting kicked through my head. *The perpetrator could be a member of law enforcement.* My breath hitched. Oh, no. Not that. Was Ruby so frightened because whoever she'd seen on the road that night . . . she'd seen *here*?

Please, God, tell me it can't be.

Wait. No. If Ruby was scared of someone in the department, why did she come here today?

Maybe she was hoping to see him. Thinking another good look at him up close might convince herself that she'd been wrong. And instead she realized she'd been right.

Oh, God, help.

My legs would hardly move. What to do? *Annie, think!*

Somehow I pulled myself together. Walked back toward the four men, now looking at them differently. Wondering if I should trust them.

Keep your voice steady. Don't let them know.

I licked my lips. "What happened in there?"

Nathan stuck out his chin. "Dalveeno said he could never cut off some woman's little finger."

My eyes widened. Ruby was right! If Blake was innocent, no way would he know that information.

Nathan *tsked*. "You should have seen it. Chetterling wore him down, then played him like a fiddle."

I studied Nathan's eyes, wondering . . . "Does Dalveeno realize he's slipped?"

"Come on, you know Chetterling. Poker faced all the way."

I bit my lower lip, looking through the window at Dalveeno and the detectives. Trumble was pounding the suspect with questions. Blake looked worn to a frazzle.

"You think they're going to be in there awhile?"

"Yeah." Nathan answered, distracted, watching Trumble.

"Then they'll hold him?"

"Of course they'll hold him." Nathan gave me a quizzical look. Tim frowned at our whispering. "Next thing will be scrounging up a search warrant for the drugs and the murders—on a Saturday. When we get it we'll search his car and house."

I watched through the one-way mirror, barely hearing the sounds from the little room. Indecision and worry turned like rusted gears in my head. But if there was one person in the department I would always trust, it was Chetterling.

I had to tell him about Ruby's call. And my suspicions. Now.

Before I lost my courage, I walked around the corner and knocked on the door. The surprised reactions of the four men drifted toward me.

"Annie, what are you *doing?*"

I ignored Nathan, stepping away from the door as it opened. I did not want Blake to see me.

Chetterling poked his head out. One look at my face and he stilled. "What is it?"

I motioned for him to follow me a few feet down the hall. When I turned to him, I was shaking.

Chetterling took a breath. "What's happened?"

I told him about Ruby's call. No need to remind him of Rosalee Sanchez's words; Chetterling put it all together right away. He lowered his head, staring at the floor. Emotions rippled across his face—disbelief . . . fear . . . hope.

He looked up at me. "We're probably wrong about this. Ruby has to mean something else."

I nodded, wanted to believe that as much as he did.

He ran a hand down his face. "I have to think about this. I don't want to believe it, but I can't . . ." He closed his eyes. "Okay. We'll move Dalveeno to another room, where nobody can stand outside and watch. I'll work around to asking about an accomplice. I'm going to have to trust Trumble." His head shook. "Man, listen to me! How could I *not* trust Trumble? How could I not trust *everyone* here?"

My heart squeezed. Finding a traitor among his own people would be the absolute worst for him. "Ralph. Like you said, we're just guessing right now. Let me go out to Ruby's and talk to her. I'll find out. I'll keep my cell phone on, and as soon as I hear, I'll call you. Nobody else here needs to know I'm going."

His pain-filled gaze fell back to his feet. "Yeah." His voice was gruff. "That's what you should do."

I touched his arm. "Okay. I'm going. I'll call you as soon as I can. If it takes awhile, just know that I'm working on her. Like you're working on Dalveeno." I tried to smile.

Chetterling's mouth softened. "Thanks, Annie. You're . . . incredible. Be careful."

As I crossed the heat-drenched parking lot toward my car, a terrible thought came to me. It was Chetterling, amongst his own colleagues, who needed to be careful.

Chapter 42

I tried not to think too much as I drove to Ruby's house. My emotions only went in circles. I should be excited and relieved that God had heard our prayers. The case was about to break wide open, and Blake Dalveeno was off the streets.

Now this.

God, even though the truth might be horrible, help me get the information from Ruby. Give me the words to persuade her to talk.

I so wanted to hear Jenna's voice right now. And Dave's. I needed my sister's support, and I needed Dave's prayers. But under the circumstances, wouldn't it be crazy to tell them what I was doing over a cell phone? All those airwaves. All those Sheriff's deputies with radios . . .

Still, I should check in with them. I knew they awaited any news.

I speed-dialed my house. Jenna answered.

"Annie! What's happening?"

"Everything's fine. The case is moving right along."

"Blake?"

"Looks like it's him, Jenna."

She sucked in a breath. "Oh, *Annie*."

"I know." I could feel her thoughts whirling. The man had been in *our* house. *Right next to Kelly.*

"So are you on your way home?"

Oh, boy. "In a little while. I've . . . got some stuff to do here."

"Wait, what's going on? You don't sound right."

Jenna, this is not the time to read me like a book! "No, everything's fine. I just can't talk on the phone."

"Oh. I get it."

If she only did. "Um, I'll call you again when I can. Shouldn't be too long. How about if you start looking into Disneyland hotels? I was thinking maybe you could take the kids even today. I'll be home in time to see you off."

"Right-o, private pilot at your service."

"Jenna, you're wonderful for being willing to do this."

"I know."

I managed a smile as I clicked off the line. Next I called Dave.

"Annie, how *are* you?"

What those words did to me. Not *what's going on with the case?* Just how are *you?* The concern in his tone seeped right into my heart.

"Dave, I need your prayers right now. I can't tell you what's happening over the phone, but I need all the prayers I can get. Maybe you could call Gerri Carson too?"

"I've already been praying. About ten minutes before the phone rang, this heaviness came over me. I had to stop what I was doing and pray immediately."

Oh.

I slowed to turn off Wonderland onto Tully Road. Ruby's house lay just a couple miles away. Something about that turn . . . As soon as my wheels churned the narrow road, I felt a fibrillation in the air. And Dave's words, meant to soothe, only rubbed my nerves. He'd *known*, even before I called.

But that was a good thing, right? God was calling him to pray.

Maybe, maybe not. One thing I'd learned during this past week. God didn't send people that strong urge to pray without a very good reason. And lately that reason had spelled danger.

"Well, keep at it, Dave." I fought to keep my voice light, but the words quavered.

"Annie, are you okay?"

"Yes, I just . . . want this to be over. I want to get on with my *life*, Dave."

I'd almost said *our lives*.

"I know. And we will. Soon."

We. Had I spoken my thoughts? Had I said what I didn't mean to say?

The questions upset my balance, threw me off kilter. The last thing I needed right now was to doubt my ability to say the right words.

Sudden fear twittered up my spine. Maybe I shouldn't be doing this. Why was *I* out here? Ruby held a secret so soul-shaking that it had frightened her to the core. Who was I to extract it from her? What if I couldn't bear the truth any more than she?

There, ahead. The second left turn off Tully Road. The turn that had led to the crumpled body of Karen Fogerty. And across from that turn, Ruby's house. White wood, with green shutters. A small porch, yellow and red flowers lining the front walk.

And Ruby, standing soldier-like, one hand wrapped around the support of a porch pillar.

"Dave, I'm . . . I have to go. Just keep praying, okay? I'll call you as soon as I can."

"Okay. I'll be waiting."

I punched the *off* button, slid the phone into my purse, and turned into Ruby's driveway.

Chapter 43

Thank you for coming."

Ruby Mays looked down her hooked nose at me with a falsely brave smile. Even as she welcomed me, her eyes darted left, right, up, and down the barren road, as if ectoplasm would morph from the asphalt and smother us both.

She led me inside and locked the door.

The house was compact, remarkably clean, and color-chaotic.

We walked over the small hardwood floor entryway and turned left into a living room. Large yellow flowers spattered the couch and chairs, which were stuffed with multihued pillows of green, purple, and red. The seat pad on a rocking chair fought for attention with hues of bright blue. Dolls in all shapes and sizes, clothed in lace and ruffles and silk, populated small tables and the white brick mantle over a narrow fireplace.

"Please. Sit anywhere." Ruby lifted her arm in a distracted wave.

"Thank you." I chose one end of the sofa, pushing aside a pillow, another at my back. Dozens of painted doll eyes fixed upon me, like the glassy stare of a cadaver. *Oh, great.* That thought was all my brain needed to spin out pictures of

Celeste Weggin's twisted face in the forest. I dropped my gaze to the carpet.

Ruby sank into an armchair, ignoring the pillows that vied with her body for room. She laced, then unlaced her fingers, her shifting focus snagging on my necklace, then springing up to my face.

For a moment neither of us spoke.

I cleared my throat. "Please. Tell me what's on your mind."

Her gaze drifted out the window. "I saw them that night." She spoke toward the road, as if the scene replayed before her eyes.

"Who did you see?"

"*Them.* That man whose picture was in the paper. And the girl. And somebody else, I don't know who."

I don't know who.

Oh, God, thank You. I tried to keep the relief from my face.

"I have these binoculars." Ruby's bulging eyes clouded with wariness. "I bought them after the first three murders. They've sat on my dresser these few months, where I could pick them up if I heard anything at night. But this was the first time I needed them. One wall of my bedroom faces the road, you see . . ."

Her words filtered away. I waited, afraid that anything I said would block them for good.

"I'd just gone to bed, all lights off. And I heard a noise out front—a car door slam. Now, a car going by wouldn't have bothered me so much. But one stopping, someone getting out . . ." She raised her eyebrows. "So I slid out of bed and went to get the binoculars."

She looked out the window again, her pause stretching so long that I feared she'd lost her willingness to talk. "Tell me exactly what you saw," I prodded.

Ruby drew in a breath. "The car was pulled over to the side of the road. This side. That man—the paper said his first name is Blake—got out of the driver's seat. I *know* it was him. I got a good, long look at him through the binoculars—the face and that hair—and the moon gave a fair amount of light. Then when he opened the rear passenger door, more light from the car spilled on him."

A doll across the room watched me with wide, porcelain eyes, as if shocked at what she heard.

"He spoke to someone in that backseat. Then the right front door opened, and another person got out. A male. He walked around the car and stood next to the Blake character. That's when I got a good look at *him*."

I longed to ask what he looked like, but knew I shouldn't. Not now. Not yet. *Just let her talk, Annie.*

The doll stared and stared at me. As did all the others lining the mantel. If I got up, walked around, their eyes would surely follow my every move.

"Blake said something to him, then stood back. The other male talked to the person in the car. He looked mad, as if he was giving commands, and the person wouldn't obey. Then he reached into the car—and he yanked a woman out by her arm." Ruby pressed her palms together. "I have to admit I never got a good look at her, because her back was always to me. But she seemed young, just by the way she moved. And she also seemed very afraid. She cowered against the car as the male said things to her. I couldn't hear, of course, but I would swear they were evil things from the way his lip curled and from his gestures."

Oh, Karen. I could hardly bear to imagine the girl's fear, the threats she must have endured. Surely, she'd *known* what was coming.

"Then it happened." Ruby glanced right and left, as if unseen malevolence watched us. "I made a bad mistake. I have this touch lamp on my dresser, you see, with a three-way bulb. If you touch any part of it, the lamp goes on to lowest power. Another touch, and it goes up to second power, and then to the third. There I stood in the dark, looking so intently through the binoculars, thinking I couldn't be seen. But then Blake looked toward my window—and stared, as if he *could* see me. He caught the other young man by the arm, and they both glared at me. Why, it scared me to death!" Ruby brought a hand to the side of her neck. "I lowered the binoculars, and that's when I saw that my lamp was on. I must have touched the shade—three times to turn it to full power. I tell you, I smacked the thing to turn it off, my heart galloping. But it was too late. They'd *seen* me. With binoculars. Watching them . . ."

Ruby blinked double-time and focused on her lap, her mouth working.

I let out a breath. No wonder she was so frightened. She was the only witness—someone who, in Blake's eyes, would need to be silenced. Look what he'd done to my own son when he thought Stephen acted against him.

Ruby wiped her palms against her skirt. Her fear permeated the air. The dolls watched, piercing me with their cold, hard stares. How did she stand living with them? The faces, their pupils, were anything but calming and warm. They looked as though they might come to life any minute and hiss at me. I suppressed a shiver. The very walls of this house, filled with knickknacks and riotous colors, seemed to be sliding inward, an inch at a time.

For heaven's sake, Annie, what's wrong with you? They're just dolls.

"Ruby, I can understand why you're so afraid. You think they'll come back to hurt you somehow."

She wagged her head. "I didn't know, though, you see. I suppose I didn't *want* to know. I kept telling myself what I witnessed was just some argument, nothing more. It couldn't have anything to do with the murders, it just couldn't, because then, I would be . . ." She moistened her lips. "Then last night came all the lights and sirens, and I wondered. This morning for some reason I didn't get my newspaper. I planned to take more cookies to the Sheriff's Department anyway, so I went into town, and there I read all the news. About that other girl, Karen Fogerty, found *right here*. And I saw a picture of the black-haired woman who was identified. Trenise something? And your drawing of that man, Blake. That's when I *knew*." Her face pinched. "I'm sorry I acted so out of sorts, but by the time I got to the Sheriff's Department, it was all beginning to sink in. And I simply didn't know what to do."

The sound of a passing car filtered through the closed windows. Ruby balked, then shot from her seat to peek through the gauze curtains. I tensed and leaned forward, trying to see.

Ruby didn't move a muscle. I heard the car tires singing upon road, closer. Long seconds passed.

"*Oh!*" Ruby breathed. She straightened, turned back to me. "It went on by. Sorry. I'm just so jumpy."

"That's okay." I gave her a quivery smile, wishing I could phone Chetterling, tell him the second man wasn't someone Ruby recognized from the department—

Wait.

Ruby's words filtered through my head. *Other girl. Karen.* I frowned as I watched Ruby sink into her chair. *Other girl . . .*

"What is it, Annie? You look deep in thought."

I blinked. "Yes, I . . . What you saw, Ruby. It was Wednesday night, right?"

She flicked her eyes away, stared at the carpet. Her arms folded—an action I'd never seen her do before. I waited.

Silence.

"Ruby?"

She took a deep breath. When she looked at me again, it was with the guilt of a child caught in a horrible deed. "No. Not Wednesday. Last Saturday."

Saturday?

I held her gaze, my thoughts grinding, changing gears. *Saturday.* She hadn't seen Karen, then . . .

"What color was the girl's hair?"

"Black. Long, black hair."

My fingers curled against the arm of the sofa. I could not believe what I was hearing. "So you saw Trenise . . . a *week* ago. And you didn't say anything?"

She bit her lip and nodded.

I swallowed, trying to keep the sick accusation from my face. How *could* she? Ruby may not have realized everything last Saturday, but with all the killings, she must have had her suspicions. And as much as she'd hung around the Sheriff's Department? She should know the detectives would want to hear anything like this. But what had she done instead, to ease her conscience? She'd baked *cookies*.

And Karen had *died*.

Oh, God! Why? With all those prayers going up to You? If she'd just said something, if You'd led her to do that, Karen might still be alive!

No wonder Ruby was so reluctant to talk. Half out of fear, sure. But the other half? Pure shame. She knew she might have saved Karen's life. She *knew* it.

Ruby laced her fingers tightly and sat very still, as if awaiting judgment. I felt it rise within me. I wanted to give it to her, oh, yes I did. Wanted to fling into her face what her selfishness had done. How her actions had cost a life. A precious, dear *life*. So *what* if she'd been scared? I'd been scared too in the past few days. Did that keep me from doing whatever needed to be done?

God, why? You could have changed this!

The anger rose, flushed my face, but I forced it back down. Pressed it into a hidden part of me, a dark barrel of a place, and clamped on the lid. I couldn't let Ruby know that my insides shook, that I wondered where my God was right now. I couldn't do anything to lose my connection with her. One wrong move, and it might vaporize before my eyes. The only thing I could do now was save the *next* life. Ruby had to go with me to the Sheriff's Office and give her statement. I *had* to convince her.

The dolls watched with salacious smiles, waiting to hear what I would say.

I searched the corners of my mind for the right words.

"Ruby, I'm . . . sorry this has been so difficult for you. I can imagine your fear. Even with Blake Dalveeno in custody, you must be worried about him being let go. And about the other man who was with him that night."

Relief planed across her face. "Yes." Her voice was low. "Especially with the drawing of that Blake in the paper. I'm afraid he'll think *I* was the witness behind that, you see? He will think because of *me*, he's been arrested. So I worry that, even now in the daytime, the other man . . ." Her eyes drifted back toward the window.

Drawing. Of course. She'd just given me the opening I needed.

I leaned toward her, gentling my words. "Now that I'm here, I could interview you about that other person you saw. I can draw his face, take it back to the Sheriff's Office. They'll find him, too, and bring him in soon. Then you won't have to worry. Then you can tell your story to the authorities and know that *no one* will be after you. You'll be a hero, Ruby; you'll be the one to crack this case."

She gazed at me, fingers working in her lap. "Yes, that's what I thought. About you drawing the picture, I mean. And maybe . . . maybe if you take the drawing back, and they find the other person, then they won't blame me so much for . . ."

"They won't blame you, Ruby." I hoped she believed that. Maybe someday I'd manage to forgive her myself. "Let's see. I don't have my materials with me."

"That's all right." She pushed from her chair with resolve. "I do a little drawing myself, you know. Nothing like what you can do. But at least I have a sketch pad and some soft-leaded pencils. Will that work?"

"Yes, sure. Thank you." I rose, waiting as she left the room. Dozens of doll eyes followed my every move, their smiles turned to sneers—as if they knew whose form would soon appear on my paper and could not wait to see my shock.

I turned away . . . and felt their lingering stares on my back.

Chapter 44

Ruby led me from the living room into the kitchen, which looked out to her backyard. I saw tended green grass, with a few spots of brown. Fruit trees dotted the perimeter. A rotating sprinkler sat in the middle of the yard, attached to a long hose. I pictured Ruby in the heat, moving that sprinkler around until the whole yard was watered. It would be a long, hard job. One that needed doing every day in the rainless summer.

Beyond the yard lay open field, then forest. I couldn't help but skim those trees. The view would be pretty—on any other day. Now it seemed menacing. What if someone lurked in those trees, watching us?

What if he'd been sent by Blake to quiet Ruby?

The skin on my arms prickled.

I almost wished we'd stayed in the living room with the dolls and the walls closing in. Here, the windows were too large, that field of high grass and those trees too—

Annie. Stop it.

Ruby bristled, nervousness in her every movement. I scanned the forest, pretending not to notice, as she bustled about, pouring us both a glass of lemonade, piling cookies on a plate. She set the drink and cookies before me with fluttering hands. "The lemons come off my own tree." She twitched her head toward the backyard. "They're very tangy.

I put in extra sugar. But, oh." She blinked at the cookies. "If you eat them and then take a drink, the lemonade will be all that more tart."

I smiled at her. "It's okay, Ruby, thank you."

We sat at the table. I chose a seat where I could look out to the yard through the window in the top half of Ruby's back door. I didn't want that field, that forest, behind me. Ruby started to pull out the chair opposite me, but I stopped her. "No, please. Sit here, on my right. And while you tell me what the man looked like, I want you to look at the wall, okay? Not at me."

If Ruby focused on *my* face, her memories could subconsciously be steered toward my own features. And, God knew, we *had* to get this right.

Please, Lord, let this picture lead us to the second person—before anyone else dies.

"All right." Hands trembling, Ruby obeyed.

I settled myself, picked up the pencil. Tilted the pad of paper so she couldn't see what I drew.

The back of my neck began to tingle.

I tried to tell myself the feeling meant nothing. Ruby's anxiety was rubbing off on me, that was all. But I'd denied a similar feeling just before I discovered Celeste's body. This time I should pay attention.

Somehow, I sensed that the face I'd soon draw would have a terrible effect on me.

For a second, I almost didn't want to know.

I took a drink of the lemonade. *Whoo.* Ruby was right. Sweet, but with an aftertaste that pursed my mouth.

"Oh, dear." Ruby placed fingers on her lips. "Is that too strong for you? Would you rather just have water?"

"No, no, it's great. Thanks."

She leaned back in her chair, clearly unconvinced.

"Okay." My heart picked up its pace. "First, tell me about him in general."

She couldn't be sure of his hair color. Blond maybe? Light brown? He was young, she said, but when I asked her to qualify that, she couldn't. "Most people look young to me." She shrugged an apology.

Great. For all that meant, he could be *my* age.

I asked Ruby questions, let her think before she answered. Minutes dragged by, my eyes skimming the field, the forest, for any unusual movement; hers closed while she pictured the face and tried to describe it. She drank her lemonade, I drank mine. Painstakingly, little by little, she talked, and I sketched the facial contours. I willed myself to think of nothing except the task at hand. But my overactive brain would not listen. It mocked me with flashes of horrifying scenes, both imagined and real. I followed Ruby's descriptions to draw the man's eyes and saw

Celeste's, wide open and flat-glazed, staring with shock toward the heavens . . .

I shook my head, took a sip of lemonade.

"Oh, dear." Ruby winced. "I'm not doing this well, am I?"

"You're fine, Ruby, you're fine. I'm just . . ." My gaze nailed itself once more through the back door window.

She peered at me, then followed my line of vision toward the forest. Air seeped from her throat. "I know."

We looked at each other, fear swirling between us. Why did I feel like we'd started a countdown—and the minutes were running out?

"Let's do this." I hunched over my paper.

We finished the eyes, moved to the brows. They were flat, Ruby said, sort of straight across. And the cheeks. Were they a little rounded? she wondered aloud. Perhaps yes, just a bit. A squared jaw. And the lips. They were . . . how could she describe them? She looked away, thinking, and I saw

a close-up of Karen's mouth, twisted in that strychnine-produced rictus . . .

I clutched my pencil and waited, anxiousness mounting. *Come on, Ruby, come on. Who is this man? Who is he?*

She described his lips. I drew, frowning, trying to concentrate, thoughts rattling. My brain spun out the embodied face

emerging from the trees behind Ruby's house. He stalks us, mouth leering, eyes demon-red with hatred. Ruby and I can't move in our panic. I wrench myself toward the phone, but too late! He shatters the window with a large piece of wood and squeezes through the glass shards, uncut, unstoppable . . .

Ruby sat back, looking drained. "Would you show me now, before we do any more?"

I focused on the roughened sketch, and one thought knocked around my head. *I don't know this face!* For a second time, relief flooded me, then dammed up in my chest. Wait. We weren't done here yet. Not yet.

I showed Ruby the drawing.

She stared at it, unblinking, for what seemed like a long time. Finally she looked at me, her lips pulled inward, fingers lacing, unlacing . . .

I steeled myself. "It doesn't look like him, does it?"

She shook her head like a disappointing child before a parent.

Oh, no. She'd cost us time, and wasn't our time running out? I could *feel* it. He was coming.

I lay my hand over hers, my heart flip-flopping. "It's okay, Ruby. We'll fix it." The words sputtered.

Come on, Annie, pull yourself together.

"Yes," she said firmly, as if trying to convince herself. "We will."

Whoosh-whoosh-whoosh, surged the blood in my veins. I tried to focus on my paper, but my eyes jerked up to scrutinize the backyard, the field, the forest. The hair on my arms rose. Was he coming closer? Stealthy, unseen. Riding on the wind. He would pump us both with poison, laugh maniacally over our convulsing bodies as we died—

Annie, concentrate!

"Okay, Ruby. I'm ready. Let's—" My breath backfired. "Start with . . . the eyes."

"Are you all right?" Worry bent Ruby's voice. "Maybe we should stop."

"No, no. Let's go."

The forest . . . the field . . . the front yard. Where was he? How long did we have?

The pencil in my hand trembled. I reached for my glass of lemonade, took a long drink.

"I'll hurry, Annie, all right? You obviously need to get home and rest."

"Yes. Good."

She threw her hand out, startling me, and flipped to a new page in the drawing pad. "Let's just start over."

Normally, I would remain in control, would never have followed such a suggestion. But now, if that's what Ruby wanted, fine. Anything to be done with this.

I searched the trees at the edge of the forest. Something— a breeze?—fluttered and tossed their leaves.

Ruby scrunched her eyes shut, forehead creasing. "All right. I can picture him better now. His cheeks are . . ."

And she began to describe him. Differently than the first time. She spoke . . . I drew. And my heart thump-thump-thumped against my ribs. I opened my mouth to breathe, nerves agitating, ghosted fingers of air wisping across my arms. My eyes bounced up to forest, down to paper, up to forest, down to paper. My fingers shook as they pushed the pencil. *Hiss, hiss, hiss* scratched the lead, the man's cheeks slowly forming . . . and the chin . . .

And the eyes.

I can't say when I knew. Understanding birthed in the murky waters of my brain, poked out a malformed head, then yanked away to lurk in the denial depths of my soul. No, this couldn't be right. The face burned into my memory and the emerging one on paper only resembled each other, that was all. The drawing would turn out different. Ruby would veer in her description; my hand would follow her lead. They were not, not, *not* the same.

My legs weighted to the chair. My chest hurt. Even the bottoms of my feet prickled. The trees out there in the woods—I could swear they were moving, trunks bent aside by some entity, some supernatural force that floated across the field, death-breathing over the grasses . . .

"And his nose." Ruby focused on the wall, certainty now in her voice. She described it, *his* nose—the angular lines, the narrow nostrils. I drew, and I saw, and I wouldn't see, and my pulse thwack-thwack-thwacked, air rappelling down my throat.

A sound.

I jerked. "What was that? Did you hear it? Out front?"

Ruby's face blanked. She pulled from her concentration to ogle me. "Hear something? No." Fear etched her face. She rose. Left the kitchen. Left me sitting *alone*, with the window, and the backyard, and the field and forest. *Tup-tup* went her feet across the linoleum. I waited, squirmed in my chair, nerves squiggling, feeling the twist of my torso.

Ruby reappeared, one hand on her chest. "There's nothing, dear. But, oh, you scared me."

"So sorry."

She sat down. Air shooshed out of her seat cushion. Her eyes closed. She resumed her description.

I drew.

My body zinged.

The features emerged with more detail. In the muddied waters of my brain, the knowledge of who he was poked its head up once more, then surfaced. *No. Please, God, no.* My stunned gaze leaped to the forest, now wanting, *begging*, for my imagined predator to be real, to ride out of the trees and over field grasses, smash his wooden club through the window. To be anyone, any *thing*, but the face Ruby's memory and my hand had wrought.

My limbs shuddered, and still I told myself *no.* Hope still lingered. His hair would be different. Surely. That one aspect alone would change his appearance. Lies, I knew, but I clung to them, a drowning woman clinging to a lifeline.

Ruby described his hair.

No, no, no.

My hand sketched. It was no longer a part of my body. Some appendage, removed, with a mind of its own, creating what I did not want it to create. Ridiculing, tormenting me.

My throat cinched, lungs billowing to pull in air. With an unsteady hand, I lifted my glass of lemonade, took a drink.

Ruby peered at me. "You poor dear. I've pushed you too much. I'm finished. Let me see."

Yes, let her see. Let her tell me that I've drawn him all wrong, that I've forgotten all I learned in the past two years, cycled back to when I first interviewed Erin Willit after her mother's death and did not know what I was doing . . .

I lifted the sketch pad. Turned it toward her.

Ruby's buggy eyes widened. "Yes! Yes, that's him. Oh, my, he *is* young, isn't he? I should have known. But you got it. Oh, yes, Annie, thank you!"

My head nodded, up and down, up and down. Lips moving, no sound coming. Shock picked up my banging heart and squeezed. Turned it over and shook it dry. With a victorious smile, Ruby tossed the drawing pad on the table. The click of its metal spiral against wood reverberated in my ears.

My eyes pulled to the drawing.

My own son's face stared back at me.

Chapter 45

Annie, what *is* it? You look so peaked."

I couldn't answer. I could only reach for my lemonade, drain what was left of it, the bitter-metal-sweet tang pursing my lips, filling my senses. I held it in my mouth, reveling in its bite, wanting it to snap all the way down my throat, command my attention away from the truth that loomed before me.

My hand set the glass down with a *clunk*. "Excuse me." I pushed away from the table. "I just need to . . . use your bathroom."

"Of course, sure." Ruby stood, hovering. "It's that direction." She pointed down a hall, away from the living room. "Do you need help?"

"No." The word wheezed, my pulse thudding. "I'm fine."

I tottered out of the kitchen, one hand slipping along the counter edges for support. Over the threshold into the hallway. There, I floundered. *Where did she say? Right? Left?* I looked right. Living room. Mean-eyed dolls. *No. No dolls.* I turned left.

Thunk, thunk, my feet on the hardwood floor, fingers trailing the rough-textured wall. I reached a door. Looked in. *Bathroom.* I moved inside. Tried to shut the door, but my body stood in its way. Stepped back. Closed the door. The sound of its latch echoed in my head.

What to do, what to do?

I couldn't take that drawing to the Sheriff's Department. Couldn't give it to Chetterling. Maybe I should just pack up my family and run. Flee. Never come back.

I gripped the edges of the sink, its porcelain brittle-cold against my palms. My ankles shook.

Maybe the drawing wasn't right. Ruby was just misguided. Wanting to please me so much that she claimed it was accurate.

Where was Stephen last Saturday night, anyway? I hung on to the sink, racking my thrumming brain. He couldn't have been with Blake, just couldn't have. *Think, Annie, think. Remember something, anything!* I stared down into the silver drain, wishing I could spill down it like liquid, through pipes and out to sea. *Saturday, Saturday . . .*

The memory hammered me. Stephen had gone out with friends. Had come back late, past his curfew . . .

No. That didn't mean anything. Just a coincidence. What about Wednesday, when Karen disappeared?

My knees turned to gelatin. I pushed away from the sink, sat down hard on the closed lid of the toilet. *Think, think.* My head sunk in my hands.

Yes! Wednesday! My head rose up. I focused blearily on a blue towel hung over a wall rack. Stephen wasn't even here that night; he was with Jenna in the Bay Area! Relief tumbled and somersaulted and skidded through my chest. I dragged in air, breathed a silent prayer of thanks to God—

No.

Wait.

Thoughts, memories, pinged through my head. No. Stephen and Jenna returned to Grove Landing just yesterday,

Friday. So they left Thursday. Wednesday Stephen was home. Down in his lair. He'd been beaten up that day.

He could have sneaked out the back sliding glass door. He'd done it before.

And run to Blake Dalveeno, the very day the man had him beaten up?

Maybe Stephen helped kill Trenise last Saturday, but not Karen.

Nausea roiled through my stomach. Maybe Stephen's story about the drug money was all a lie. Maybe he'd been beaten up as a warning not to tell about the murders. To keep him in line.

I brought my hands to my face. This still could not be right. Stephen wouldn't kill anyone. He *couldn't*. Maybe he'd been forced to be there. Never, ever could he have done these terrible, horrible things.

But who would believe that? Ruby had seen him—with Blake and Trenise. Ruby, the witness I'd so wanted to cajole into telling her story.

Oh, God, what should I do? What can I do?

I pulled myself up, feeling light-headed and weak. My eyes flicked around the bathroom, unable to focus. I grasped the sink, staring at my own reflection. At sunken eyes and a face cast in the blue-white of death. My brain waves undulated, warped. Sheer duty pulled at me, my mother's heart already ceased in its beating. I found myself back out in the hallway, ready to turn toward the kitchen, pick up the hated drawing to take it to authorities. Maybe I would falter once I reached the table. Maybe I would take the sketch and rip it into a hundred pieces. Tell Ruby she was *wrong*. I would drive away and go home, and nothing would come of this. Ruby wouldn't tell anyone. I would pray, beg God to erase this afternoon, turn back the world to when I got out of bed, to Jenna cooking breakfast in our kitchen. Everything would be all right. Somehow. Someway.

The fantasies tripped through my mind as I steadied myself in the hallway, hand against the wall, ready to turn toward Ruby's kitchen, toward my fate. Every breath I took resounded through my chest. I could hear the pump of blood through my veins. I raised watery eyes, my blurry vision scudding the length of the hall, across an open bedroom doorway at its end. There, it hooked on something.

Blue. Dancing. Half transparent. On the wall of the bedroom. Tiny flecks of blue. Sprays and sprays of blue, shimmering and shining.

I frowned at it, blinking. *What is it?* Flickering, shimmying, spangling the Sheetrock. The sight tugged me, pulling hand over hand on an invisible rope attached to my chest. My legs moved forward, and the blue coruscation pranced. My hand trailed the hallway wall, so very, very rough. Surely it would cause my fingertips to bleed.

I reached the room's threshold.

Ruby's bedroom.

I shouldn't do this. She awaited me in the kitchen, worried. What was I doing, sneaking into her bedroom, poking where I didn't belong?

Blue, glimmering blue. Tiny fairy lights across the wall. Beckoning me to follow, follow. Perhaps I'd sprout my own wings, fly with them, across the wall, out the window, and away.

My head cocked, listening. No sound from the kitchen.

I stepped across the bedroom threshold. Trod across thinned carpet. Reaching my hand up, arm out, reaching for the cerulean twinkle, mesmerized.

A shaft of sunlight shone through the front window, illuminating dust particles in the air. My outstretched arm passed through that cone of light—and the waltzing blue flecks poofed away. *No, no, where did they go?* I ogled my arm. How had I done that? I withdrew my arm. The speckles glimmered anew.

My gaze followed the beam of sunlight, riding down, down, spilling at the bottom on a dresser I hadn't seen from the hallway. There sat the source of the dancing color. Something glared under the heat of the sun, shooting light into my eyes, right through my head. I winced. What was it?

I reached out to lift it, move it away from the light. It nestled, hot, in my palm.

An earring. Large blue stone. Surrounded by smaller white ones. Fake jewelry.

I had seen this earring before.

Thoughts bouncy-bounced. My body shivered. My head started to wag.

Memory ice-picked my chest.

I dropped the earring.

Both my hands came up with fingers spread, shaking, shaking. *No. No, no, no, no, no.* I started to back away, and my eyes fell on something else. *Oh, God. Oh, dear Lord, help me!* A tip of a finger, with a dirtied long red nail. My jaw sagged open, flexed . . .

And then I saw them.

A white sandal with silvery stones.

And there. A square piece of beaded fabric.

A lock of black hair. And one of blonde.

A blackened, shriveled little toe.

My intestines crimped.

I backed away, back, back, my feet losing traction, my thoughts a horror movie in reverse. *Think, Annie!* Rewind the tape, shift the world on its axis, back to the beginning, all my fears, all the wrong assumptions, the misunderstandings shriveling . . . dying . . . mutating . . .

Rebirthing.

My heart revved, slammed against my chest—*Let me out, let me out, let me out!* I raised a hand before my face, watched it tremble.

She'd given me her poison, hadn't she. In the lemonade. That sweet metallic drink. It had hit my stomach, its absorption only slowed by whatever might remain of the large breakfast Jenna made me eat.

I was going to die.

I listed to one side, trying, despairing to *think*, to process . . .

No. It couldn't be a fatal dose. The lemonade would have been too bitter.

But it didn't matter. She only sought to torture me, draw out my fall. She would soon be on me with her needle. Surely even now she waited in the kitchen, eyes murderous. Did she wonder why I was taking so long? Was she preparing the deadly solution even now, laughing to herself, chuckling how she'd fooled me, played me to the very end, mocking me with suspicions of my own son?

How had she known what he looked like? How had she *done* this?

Ruby. Ruby, Ruby, Ruby.

I teeter-tottered over her bedroom threshold, into the hall. How long did I have before she came looking for me? How long had I taken? I couldn't measure. A minute? Five? Ten?

My cell phone. My gun. Both in my purse, in the living room at the other end of the hall. I must get there, snatch the purse up. Sneak outside to my car, lock the doors.

How much time did I have before I started to spasm?

My knees knocked, the mere knowledge of the death drink within me now hastening the dreaded symptoms. My legs jellied. I would never make it down the hall. I would never make it out of this house. I was going to die here. Ruby would take my body to the woods. My brain flashed a scene of my own

mouth twisted, glassy eyes open, limbs hooked and warped. Chetterling stoops beside me in the forest, fighting to maintain his professionalism as he studies my ravaged and dirty body . . .

A low moan escaped me. *Oh, God, remember all the prayers.*

From the kitchen, a sound tumble-pranced. My ears pricked.

Ruby was singing.

Chapter 46

The time has come, all you self-righteous ones. Your moment draws near. I hold in my capable hands a double prize, do I not? Annie Kingston, one of you pray-ers. Annie Kingston, friend and colleague of detectives.

Didn't I say you couldn't hold me? As you swagger in your offices, boasting, *We have our man!* Fools. We will see how you brag, how you swell your chests, when you find this next victim. And you, pray-ers, who will you turn to when you learn how your God has utterly forsaken you?

Oh, to see your faces when you hear that she has disappeared! Did she dare tell someone she was coming here? No matter. You will still look into my eyes and not see. "Alas," I will cry, "she was coming, yes, but she never arrived! Where can she be? I am so afraid for her; please find her, well and whole!"

And I will soothe your greedy mouths and stomachs with my gentle-baked cookies.

Yes, consume what I make. And wallow in the havoc I wreak. Roar and scream and weep and wail. You are no more than indignant ants beneath the paw of a lion.

No one shall stay my hand! I will remain among you, seen but unseen, the weak and neglected child grown into the warrior of vengeance.

Mama, no, don't make me!

Be quiet! Your time has come. You are grown now, eleven years old. My pendants I've put on your neck, my bracelets on your wrist. You will dance and be with the men now. You will join our ceremonies.

There was no one to save me. And no one will save you, Annie Kingston.

I will torture them. Make them wait days to discover what happened to you. I will hide you deep, deep in the dead of night, and you will not be found until I decree it. But they will not find all of you, oh, no. I will start with that unsightly, sparkling necklace. It will be mine. You cringe now, don't you, Annie. In my bathroom, crying over your son's iniquities, as my liquid ambrosia spills into your veins. Yes, you suffer, as I have led you to do. The glee in my soul as I read your thoughts! Poor girl, you questioned your God about Karen's death. The beauty of that pain upon your face! See how I have taken even your faith away from you.

Suffer and moan, oh, pious Annie, abandoned and alone.

And I will prepare your magic wand.

Chapter 47

How long was the hallway?

I would have to pass the kitchen to reach the living room.

Ruby hummed and chortled to herself. Enjoying my misery. The noise seemed loud, so *loud*, lights and sensations rushing me, playing with my head.

I pressed a palm against the thorny wall for support, took one cautious step. *Thud!* My heel thundered against the wood. I bit my lip and slipped out of one shoe. Then the second. Barefoot, I stood, the floor hot and roiling beneath my soles. I opened my mouth, hitched a breath. Picked up my foot, took a second step. The wood turned to quicksand, pulling my feet right through the floor, into a dark abyss.

A clink from the kitchen. Ruby was moving around.

The hallway spiraled, then compressed into a dim tunnel, a vacuum that would suck the air out of my lungs. Spiders hatched and crawled down my legs, my back. My jaw creaked open, seeking oxygen.

Move, Annie. Move!

Shuffling feet, the wall piercing my hand. My chest burst into flame. My head shook . . . wagged . . . palsied, my vision jumping. At the end of the tunnel, down and down, the living room colors pulsed. Somewhere there, drowning in the sea of yellow and blue and green, floated my purse, my passage to freedom.

The sound of running water in the kitchen, a waterfall that rushed and pounded my ears. Ruby, washing my glass?

My ankles wavered, then tightened. I tried to lift a leg. It would not budge. Could I slide it forward? The skin on my foot turned to glue, stuck to the floor.

Jesus, Jesus, Jesus.

The door to the bathroom drew near. I clawed my fingers around the threshold and pulled, *pulled*, until my body moved forward. One step, and another, and suddenly I could not stop. My leg muscles stiffened and gaited me down the hall, zombielike. The kitchen door approached on my right, Ruby somewhere in there, and I screamed at myself to stop, *stop* before she heard me, before she saw me. I must sneak by on cat's feet, and instead my heels hammered, hammered, *hammered* against the floor—

My body jerked to a halt. In the sudden stillness my heart clattered and rattled. Surely Ruby would hear. The kitchen door was just steps away. I leaned forward, peeking through the entry, seeing only the sides of cabinets. Where was she? What was she doing?

Maybe she stood there, right *there* out of my vision,

huddling with a syringe in her fingers, a sneer on her lips, waiting until I materialize before her, and she leaps at me, plunging her needle into my arm. I collapse to the floor, writhing, twisting . . .

Somebody turned off the camera in my head. The scene vanished.

The living room, Annie. Go.

I hugged the left wall, took another step. More of the kitchen moved into view. A few linoleum tiles. The far side of the kitchen, the edge of a hung picture frame. Where was Ruby?

Her singing stopped.

Air tore through my throat, blood rushing through my veins, filling my ears with thunder. The back of my neck yanked tight, and my mouth contorted. Pain spurted through my face, around my head. Pain . . . Awful pain . . .

Until the muscles relaxed.

Dear God. I was running out of time.

How long would it take for an ambulance to get there once I called? Five minutes? Ten? Ten. Whole. Minutes.

I didn't have that long. Already my body and face betrayed me, twisting, arching, my muscles and sinews taking on a brutal life of their own. I would not be able to fight Ruby.

Tears raked my eyes. *God, at least let my death be the last. And take care of my children.*

From the kitchen, the giant whir of a drawer opening, the raucous shuffle of utensils. *Bam!* The drawer shut. I scrunched my eyes closed, willing myself to remember the room's layout, where the drawers were located.

Yes! On the other side of the kitchen. Ruby would be facing the yard, the forest, her back to me . . .

Somehow I moved forward. My throbbing heart, the house, the world, fell silent as I slunk by, drawing up my shoulders, turning my head to eagle-watch Ruby's hunched back, her busy arms doing something at the sink.

She did not turn around.

I reached the other side of the door. Her figure vaporized away.

I peered ahead. The hall-tunnel unscrewed, widened. The living room rose up like tidewaters, all splashing colors and sunlight. I reached both arms out, shuffled toward the glaring, and the dolls leaped into view, on the mantel, on tables, lasering me with their glittering, obsidian eyes. At the doorway, I wavered, then waded into the room, my feet leaving hardwood floor, sloshing across carpet, the dolls scowling, sending silent shrieks to Ruby to *come, come quick and stop her!*

I stumbled into the back of the couch. A gasp roared out of my mouth. I froze. Surely Ruby heard. Surely she came for me; she would reach me right here, and here I would fall . . .

My body jerked. I slithered around the couch. Around, around a table, swimming upstream, looking for my purse. Where was my purse, where *was* it?

There. Against the leg of the couch.

Sounds in the kitchen. Footfalls. Ruby was coming. Coming to kill me.

My arms thickened, hardened. And my legs. I listed toward my purse. It lay feet away. So very, very far away. I lifted a wooden arm, straining for it. My fingers brushed leather, clamped around the top of the purse, struggled to raise its leaden weight.

My leg muscles fizzled. I dropped the purse. Leather smacked against carpet, contents clacking. The noise rumbled through my head, shook the foundations of Ruby's house.

She will come now, she will come, and I must be ready.

My knees gave way. I sank to the floor beside a small table. A porcelain doll upon it leered at me.

Footsteps in the kitchen. Ruby calling my name.

I grasped for my purse, thrust in a hand, seeking . . . seeking my cell phone and gun. *Must call somebody. Must protect myself.* Fumbling fingers. Wallet and comb and keys. They poked me, cut my skin.

Where's my cell? Where's my gun?

Where's my gun, where's my gun, where's my gun?

Up, up, over the couch, Ruby appeared in the doorway, murderous eyes roaming. One hand carried something. The tip of it stuck out and glinted in the light.

Syringe.

She spotted me. Pulled her head back like a hooded cobra. "Annie." Her voice poured syrup over ice. "Whatever are you doing on the floor?"

The world flattened, time spilling over a distant and unreachable horizon. All I could do was stare at Ruby.

Now I die.

"Are you looking for your gun, dear?" Ruby shook her head at me. "Really, do you think I'd have let you bang around my hallway like that if I'd left it in your purse? I took it as soon as you closed yourself in the bathroom. It's on the kitchen table. With your cell phone."

She smiled a withering smile. Started to move around the couch. She drew closer, telling me it was too late, that my fate rose up to devour me. "But, oh, I have an idea!" She waved a gleeful hand. "While you're on your knees, let me hear you pray. That would be *so* entertaining! I'll even strike you a deal. As long as you pray, I'll let you live."

Oh, God, please . . .

The doll snickered.

"Come on, Annie, you can do it."

A sudden, searing rod jammed through my right arm. My hand flew out. Snatched the doll. Pulled back. Let it fly.

Crack. It hit Ruby in the eye.

"Aaah!" She bent over, fingers pressing over the wound. The syringe fell from her grasp onto the carpet. Rolled under the couch.

I scrabbled away like a crab. Crawled, hitched, rolled, around the sofa and toward the hall. Ruby screamed curses. I heard her knees thump against the carpet. She was looking for the syringe. She would run after me, stick it in my skin—

My legs and arms scurried onto the hardwood floor of the hall . . . the kitchen linoleum. I was an emptied brain riding on top. Somehow I reached the table. The second I did, the frenetic energy in my limbs tightened. Soon they would begin to seize.

Ruby pounded behind me. "How dare you, how *dare* you?"

I raised jerking eyes. Saw my gun. My hand reached up and grabbed it.

"No!"

My body twisted around to face Ruby. I raised the gun.

My hand locked up tight.

Ruby's face shriveled with hatred. "Annie Kingston, your time has come."

She launched toward me, syringe lifted. My hand gnarled and cramped, drawing the gun down . . . down . . .

My finger froze.

Then in a flash the muscles released.

I pulled the trigger.

Bam! The sound of the bullet ricocheted through my brain.

A hole opened in Ruby's thigh, blood leaching onto her skirt. She slapped both hands over it, staggered. Fell.

Air puffed from my lips. I couldn't move, couldn't think, the *clap* of the bullet splintering in my ears. An inner voice screeched at me to *get up, get up, get up!* I shoved to my feet, gun clinched in my fingers, my other hand scraping the table

. . . over wood . . . over my drawing of Stephen's face . . . until it closed around my cell phone. My back muscles shortened. I lurched away from Ruby, who lashed and writhed in pain.

Outside, Annie, outside.

My body pitched into the hall, my lungs closing up. I staggered and swayed and dragged in oxygen, air guttering in a death rattle down my throat. My bare feet jolted against the hardwood. *To the door, get away from her . . .*

I hit the entrance, tried to twist the knob with my left hand, but the cell phone was in the way. And the door was locked. I fumbled for the latch, fingers shortening, turning into claws. I needed both hands empty, but I wouldn't put down the gun and phone.

Behind me, Ruby hissed. "You will not get away from me, Annie Kingston. Your time has come. I will take your life, and then I will take more from you."

Grunts and moans. Ruby struggled to her feet.

The lock gave way and turned with a resounding *click.* My spine arched at the sound, my head snapping back. I shoved my chest forward, dragged open the door, and stumbled outside.

The sun blinded me, beat my head with flaming bricks. I shuffled across Ruby's porch, failed to gauge the one stair, and fell down it onto her front walk. My bones brittled and crushed. My cell phone hit the cement, the sound like a smashing meteorite. *Hot, hot, sizzling hot!* I threw myself in a desperate roll onto the grass. Somehow the gun stayed in my right hand. *My phone.* I dragged an arm over the desert heat of the sidewalk, pulled the phone toward me. Stared at it. *Who do I call?* I couldn't reason. Couldn't think of anyone's number.

In a flash of clarity, I hit the *redial* button.

Thrashing noises came from Ruby's house, her curses streaming to my ears.

Grass prickled and poked. My body went rigid. My arm drew up, automatically bringing the cell phone to my ear.

"Hello." A voice, somebody's voice. A man.

"H–h–hel . . ." My throat froze.

Silence.

"Hello? Who is this?"

The voice, that familiar tone . . . I groaned out air. Pushed my tongue against the roof of my mouth. "D–Da . . ."

"Who is . . . Annie? *Annie?*"

"Ye—." Under the oven sun, my teeth chattered. Every square inch of my skin pebbled cold. My throat relaxed, sagged open. "D–Daave. It's Ruuuby. Killller. I'm at her h–house. She gave me poi . . . p–poi . . ."

My left elbow unhinged. The phone flew away from my ear, landed with a *thunk* in the grass.

I struggled to move, but every muscle flowed into water.

Ruby panted from her doorway. "Is it . . . hot out . . . there, Annie?"

Air pooled in my lungs. My jellied head turned toward her. She slumped against the frame, weight on her one good leg. "How long since you had a spasm? You'll bake in this heat, you know, until the next one." Her face screwed up in pain, sweat trickling down one temple. And in her hand, the syringe.

I raised my head an inch off the grass, then fell back. I was utterly, hopelessly spent. My eyes slipped shut.

You win, Ruby. Come on, then. I can't fight you anymore.

My ears raked in ferocious noises as Ruby hitched herself across the porch, fumble-tumbling down the step. She landed feet away, moaning and sputtering that she couldn't wait to watch me die. Scraping sounds then, the grate of cloth and skin as she dragged herself over sizzling cement, ignoring its singe.

A rattle in her throat. It flattened into a syncopated, satisfied hum. "This would be . . . the time for you . . . to pray, Annie. Come on, say . . . a prayer. Just for . . . me."

With a groan, she lugged to my side. I couldn't move, even as I felt the blast of her breath on my neck.

Oh, Jesus. Jesus, Jesus, Jesus.

"Pray for me, Annie, now won't you? Just a sentence or two."

Her fingers were lead weights on my elbow. My eyes opened to see the syringe, filled with a milky white substance, drawing closer. Aiming for me. I flew up and out of my body, hovering, a homeless soul in the fetid, blazing air. Looking down to watch her movements with blessed detachment.

A prick. A deep stab of the needle.

Ruby plunged the syringe's contents into my arm.

Chapter 48

The world crumbles.

Falls away . . .

I hover in the air, flitting, fluttering. Feeling nothing. Then plummet with savagery back into my body, pain wracking, cramps torquing every piece of me. Spasm and seizure. My muscles snap and grind. My face cinches, lips warped and pulling. The sun torches my skin.

When my limbs have pity on me and relax, Ruby puts her mouth to my ear and screams. The sound slashes my sinuses, my head. And my body writhes once more.

Desperately, I fight to suck in air.

Ruby warbles in delight, forgetting her own pain.

Nothing matters but my tormented body. Nothing but the seizures . . .

Relax.

Ruby's scream.

Seizure . . .

Relax.

And then . . .

Something.

As my body hitches and cramps, noises . . . coming, coming. Tires on pavement, engines, screeching rubber. Slamming doors and voices and shuffling, and Ruby's laments and curses lifting my body up, up, arching my back. My muscles spit nails. Someone shouts, "She has a gun!" and far, far away my mind wonders where my weapon has gone and if she will shoot me now.

Shoot me, Ruby, just end this. Please . . .

Tumblings and scuffles, a boiling cauldron of shouts and commands, a woman shrieking. Then someone hoarses my name. "Annie, Annie!" And I know. It's Chetterling, but I can't talk, can't breathe, my ligaments clawing and squeezing, flinging me against the grass . . .

Upward.

Against the grass.

Upward.

My body melts.

I flow upon the lawn, spilling through grass blades and into earth, droplets of me scattering, scattering . . .

My name spoken, whispered commands. "Quiet, keep her stimulation down."

People moving me, someone carefully pressing my hand, another prick in my arm.

I try to struggle, open my eyes. *No, no, it's Ruby, with more poison, another needle.*

"Annie, be still now." Chetterling . . . is that Chetterling? "They're giving you drugs to keep down the seizures."

"Will she make it?" someone asks.

"Maybe." A third voice. "She gets through twelve hours, she'll be all right."

I am lifted, slid into something. A tomb. Out of the sun. Cooler. Bodies follow me, floating voices and clatters and closing doors. I am moving, moving. Where is Ruby? She will come to me still, she will find me no matter where I go, syringe in hand. To the ends of the earth she will follow. Help me, help me, save me from her.

Oh, God. Jesus, Jesus, Jesus . . .

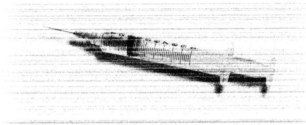

Monday, June 27

Chapter 49

Annie."

A whisper cracked open the door to my dark, cool chamber of sleep.

"Annie."

"Mmm." Vibration of sound snagged in my throat. Like gauze over splintered wood, pulling, pulling. "Mmmmm."

My eyelids fluttered. The chamber door opened a little wider. Light waved and smattered.

"She's coming around." A woman's voice.

"Yes, thank You, God!" A man's.

"Annie? Can you say something?"

No, go away. Let me sleep . . .

"Annie." Sharper now. "Wake up. And that's an order."

Jenna.

My eyes opened.

Her face hung over me, blurred . . . wavering . . . then focused.

"Hi." Her mouth split into a smile.

"Hi."

"Hey, see there. You *can* talk."

My eyes closed. *Go away, Jenna.*

Someone took my hand. "Annie. It's Dave."

Dave. Dave. I forced my eyelids up. Felt my lips curve.

"Oh, great, smile at *him*, Annie, and not at your own sister."

"Mm-hm."

Jenna huffed.

The chamber door creaked on its hinges. Shutting. Everything darkened.

I slept . . .

# # # #

I awoke again, slowly. Dave was sitting by my bed. In a private hospital room. I smiled at him, and he took my hand, then bent to kiss my forehead.

It was Monday evening, he told me. Jenna had been there for hours but had just stepped out to take the kids to dinner.

My mind felt woozy. I tried to grasp the meaning of his words. *Monday.* What happened to the rest of Saturday? What happened to Sunday?

"Am I going to live?" I asked.

Strange, how he choked up. In time, he nodded. "We didn't know at first. I can't tell you how many people were praying for you, all through that first night. The doctors gave you lots of drugs. And pumped your stomach. Kept your room dark and quiet. Jenna and I—we tiptoed. The nurses wouldn't let the kids in. They'll really want to see you now."

He left me long enough to fetch a nurse, who cooed and fussed over me, shaking her head of blonde hair.

I envisioned the locks of hair on Ruby's dresser and shivered.

"You cold?" The nurse reached to unfold a blanket at my feet. Laid it over me. Dave helped smooth it down.

"No, I'm fine. I just . . ."

The woman eased away, saying she would inform the doctor on duty that I had awakened.

Dave held my hand again. My thought processes hummed and warmed. Questions began to thrum in my mind. "The kids and Jenna, are they okay?"

The kids were fine, Dave said. Scared out of their wits for me at first, and this afternoon had been tough, with them all attending Karen Fogerty's funeral. But Erin and Kelly and Stephen were so happy to know I was better, that God had taken care of me. As for Jenna . . . well, Jenna always seemed to hold her own.

I nodded, wincing. Karen's funeral. I should have been there.

But how could I ever look her parents in the eye? I couldn't begin to understand the *unfairness*. Why had God chosen to save me and not their daughter? *Why?*

I swallowed hard. "Dave, is Ruby . . . ?"

He squeezed my hand. "She's not going to hurt you or anyone else ever again."

Ruby had been arrested on Saturday, and her bullet wound treated. Just this morning her arraignment had been held. She was charged with eight counts of murder and one count of attempted murder. She'd pleaded not guilty, still defiant. Hadn't spoken a word of admission or explanation.

Dave shook his head. "A lot of things—the whys, the hows—we still don't know."

In Ruby's dresser drawer detectives had discovered a yearbook for Foothill High School, with the page containing Stephen's picture paper-clipped, his photo circled in red. And on her kitchen table lay a drawing pad with a sketch of Stephen's face. Reporters had been going wild with speculation about these items. They did hope I would explain all that had happened in Ruby's house.

"Oh, Dave," I sighed, "don't tell them I'm awake. They'll bust down my door."

He smiled. "Not on your life."

I closed my eyes, rested for a minute.

Stephen.

"What about Blake Dalveeno?"

"He's in jail. The search warrant worked. They found drugs, all sorts of paraphernalia, and even accounting ledgers of his dealings. He'd hid the stuff well, but I guess determined detectives can find about anything. Jenna's been talking to your friend, Ralph Chetterling. The detective still promises that Stephen won't be charged with anything in exchange for his testimony against Dalveeno."

Oh, God. Thank You, thank You.

I asked for some water. Dave brought a glass with a straw to my lips. The water tasted so good.

"Do you want to sit up?" he asked.

"Yes, thanks."

He worked the controls to raise the bed, then helped me adjust my pillows.

A distant memory surfaced. "Jenna was supposed to take the kids to Disneyland."

Dave tilted his head. "That's true. But we've been discussing a change in plans. For when you're up to it, of course. We're all going back to Hawaii, just like last year."

Hawaii. Beaches and sand. Swaying palm trees. And Dave. Oh, yes, I could do Hawaii.

A light knock on the door. Chetterling entered, face creased with anticipation, carrying a vase full of red roses in his huge left hand. Dave straightened, eased his fingers away from mine. Chetterling spotted him, the movement of our hands, and drew up short. An unreadable expression flicked across his face.

"Ralph, hi." I raised an arm toward him.

He hesitated. "Hi, there, Annie. Hello, Dave. It's been awhile."

Yes, over a year. The last time the two men had talked to each other would have been the Bill Bland case. I'd been in trouble then too.

"Yes, it has." Dave held out his hand, and Chetterling shook it briefly.

Ralph turned toward the bed and gazed down at me with an adoration that could not be masked. "The nurse was under strict instructions to call me when you woke up. You have no idea how glad I am to see you're okay."

"I'm glad to see you, too, Ralph."

We smiled at each other.

He glanced at Dave, then at the flowers in his hand. "Oh. These are for you. From . . . from everybody at the office." He set them on the table by the bed, busying himself with moving aside my water glass, the telephone.

"Thank you. They're absolutely beautiful."

"Not half as beautiful as you are." The words blurted from his mouth, followed by an embarrassed shrug. "I mean, you sure look a whole lot better than a couple days ago."

I managed a laugh. "That's not saying much."

He turned to me, grimness washing over his face. "Annie." He stopped, swallowed hard. "I'm sorry."

I frowned at him. "Huh?"

He ran a hand over his face. "I sent you out there. I should have *known*. When I found out, you don't know how I . . . If you hadn't come through this, I'd never have forgiven myself."

Stunned, I looked into his face, saw the pain in his eyes. "Ralph, come on, this wasn't your fault. How *could* you have known? I didn't know myself."

"But *I'm* the detective. I was too focused on Dalveeno, not taking time to think—"

"Stop it." The words shot from me. "Stop it right now. This *wasn't* your fault. I don't *ever* want to hear you say that again."

He opened his mouth, then closed it. Blinked a few times. Then nodded.

No one spoke for a moment.

Chetterling's eyes drifted to Dave, then back to me. He drew a long breath. "Someone wants to talk to you. Ryan Burns. Remember he put up that $50,000 reward? It's yours."

A reward. I almost laughed. Money was the last thing on my mind. "I don't want any reward."

"It's yours, Annie. You earned it. He's ready to write you the check. Want me to call him for you?"

I looked to Dave, uncertainty in my eyes. He gave a little shrug. Chetterling waited, and I could feel the lingering guilt wafting from him. That, I could not stand. Not at all.

Suddenly, I knew what to do.

"Ralph, leave me the number, and I'll call Ryan later. I'm going to tell him to give the money to the Sheriff's Department. *You* all are the ones who earned it. And if you hadn't come for me, I'd be dead right now."

Of course, he protested. But I would not hear it; my decision was made. "Shame on you, Chetterling," I gave him a look, "arguing with a weak woman like me."

That shut him up. He turned to go, but I wanted him to stay, begging to hear details of all I did not know. What did Ruby do when she was arrested? What about Dalveeno; when would Stephen have to testify against him?

Chetterling shook his head. "Annie. We got her. We got him. Let the other stuff rest for now."

A sigh escaped me. "Okay. But you have to tell me one thing now. How did Dalveeno know about Karen Fogerty's finger?"

The detective put his hands on his hips. "Come on, Annie, this can wait."

"No, it can't. I want to hear *now*." Good grief, I sounded like a kid.

So what? I deserved to know.

"Okay, okay." Chetterling shifted his weight. "It came from Stephen."

I blinked at him. "*Stephen?* How?"

He shrugged. "You know how kids are. After you opened that package at your house, he just had to tell someone. He called a friend . . . who called another friend . . . And eventually word got to Dalveeno."

Oh.

I closed my eyes, suddenly exhausted.

"Well." Chetterling cleared his throat. "I should leave you two alone."

"No, Ralph, stay. I just . . . Thank you for answering my question. It's just hard to hear that it was Stephen's doing. Again. I'm sorry."

"Don't be. It's over and done with now."

I managed a smile. "I sure hope so."

Chetterling's gaze wandered to Dave.

"So, Ralph," I prodded, "pull up a chair and talk to us for a while."

He lifted a shoulder. "Probably shouldn't. I have a lot to do at work."

Work. Did the man *ever* take time off? "Then come see me tomorrow, okay?"

He promised he would, then turned to Dave. Ralph raised his arm, and again they shook hands. Chetterling held on for a second too long, peering at Dave with sudden intensity. Dave looked back with a slight frown, assessing . . . absorbing . . .

Chetterling's mouth pinched. He gave a small nod, almost, I would swear, as if acknowledging a victor. Then released Dave's hand.

With a sad smile, he looked back to me. "Bye, Annie." His voice sounded gruff.

He walked out the door and closed it softly behind him.

Dave stared after him, as if the ghost of Chetterling still lingered. Then he drew a breath and sat down in his chair. Laced his fingers through mine. We gazed at each other, our expressions saying all that needed to be said. Slowly, Dave leaned over and pressed his lips to mine.

The tingling that ran down my nerves had nothing to do with fear or worry. Or poison.

Soon, tiredness washed over me. I could have fallen asleep, comforted and secure in Dave's presence. But not ten minutes after Chetterling disappeared, Jenna and the three kids piled into the room, with kisses and hugs and presents and doting. Including Stephen, who'd brought me a piece of chocolate cake from the restaurant. I couldn't hold Kelly and Erin tightly enough, couldn't look into my son's fading-bruised face long enough.

Stephen sat on the bed and leaned down to whisper in my ear. "Mom, once we get home, we'll talk more, okay? But I want you to know I'm really sorry. For everything. And I'm not gonna do that stuff anymore. I just . . . I'm tired of being like that."

He pulled back to gauge my reaction. In his expression I saw traces of fear for my life, and the vast relief that he hadn't lost me before he could tear down the wall he'd erected between us. Tears bit my eyes. Then a stunning thought struck me. Had God allowed me to go through what I did in order to finally bring my son to his knees?

I put my hand over Stephen's and squeezed, too full of emotion to say anything. When we did talk, I would tell him all I could not say now—and wouldn't say until we were alone. That if he really wanted to change, he would need to turn to God for help. That God's power would enable him to remain strong and withstand the temptations that were sure to come his way.

That—always—I would love him. And pray for him.

When Stephen eased away, Jenna replaced him, looking more worn than I'd ever seen her. She sank down beside me—and started to cry. My own tears spilled then, down both cheeks and onto my neck. All we could do, my sister and I, was hold on to each other and blubber.

Oh, Jesus, hear my prayers for Jenna too. She needs You in her life.

Some time passed before we cried ourselves out. Kelly pressed tissues into our hands.

Jenna sat back and surveyed me, her mush-mouth slowly firming. I could practically see the switch of gears in her head.

Uh-oh.

A gleam entered my sister's eyes, and she lifted her chin. "So, Annie," she sniffed. "Guess what."

Oh, boy. "No telling."

"You have no excuse now." She raised an eyebrow, a smug expression creeping over her face. "You *have* to let me go out with Eric."

Afterword to My Readers

Intense prayer, as experienced by Annie in this story, is real. In times of crisis, I've experienced it myself. On a day-to-day basis prayer can seem far more routine. It can be whispered, sung, shouted, even cried. But no matter its form, it changes things. As Pastor Paul Sheppard said in his PUSH sermon, prayer is never wasted, but is "a meaningful relationship between an all-powerful God and powerless people."

My intent in writing *Dead of Night* was to deepen your trust in the power of prayer. The roller-coaster ride of this story has taken you through darkness and now brings you to victory. That victory is the unfailing effectiveness of prayer to unleash God's power in any situation, no matter how bleak it may seem. May you discover this truth and make it the foundation of your life.

Brandilyn Collins

We want to hear from you. Please send your comments about this book to us in care of zreview@zondervan.com. Thank you.

GRAND RAPIDS, MICHIGAN 49530 USA

W W W . Z O N D E R V A N . C O M